HOUSE OF HORROR
PRESENTS

Best of
House of Horror
2010

Published by House of Horror
www.houseofhorror.org.uk

ISBN: 978-4461-1016-4

CONTENTS

Fiction

Poetry

Artwork

Articles

Interviews

Book Reviews

THE ROCK GARDEN

By Stacey Boli

I became aware of my power when I entered puberty, before puberty I was miserable. I had a patch of fiery red hair on my head that I texturally compared to cotton candy; then I discovered how sweet and irresistible cotton candy could be. In high school I learned to sway my hips just so when I walked and it would make the anxious, little boys drool with desire. My flowing sexuality graced me with a perfect GPA and supreme popularity; even the girls respected my presence. I was idolized. I graduated from a top university and my charm and charisma earned me a position with a lucrative advertising agency. I was on my way, but I was not sure where.

I began to become dissatisfied with my sex life in my mid-twenties. I had tried everything to make it more gratifying. I painted my room black and adorned all my furniture with pieces of red silk and roses; I felt it would give the room an air of erotic mystery. I desperately longed to reach that fabled, feminine peak and to cry those tears of victory as orgasm wracked my body. No man has ever been able to lead me up that victorious peak. After sex I was often left broken; I would sit upon my pretty silk bed and my thatch of fiery red hair between my legs limp with hunger. At times they seemed to squirm and cry out with a life of their own and I began to refer to them affectionately as "My Girls". Some lonely nights I would feel them tickle the sides of my thighs and top of my belly as if they were searching for something. When their agitation seemed to reach a crescendo I would reach into my panties to pacify them with soft strokes and sweet lullabies. This would soothe us all into a relieving and empty slumber.

One brisk October day I arrived to work early. I was carrying my coffee across the hall when I noticed a new addition being given a tour of our office by the senior supervisor, Dave. Our new addition was electrifying and I had to know this man! The girls down below felt that tingle of electricity and began to wriggle out of control. I sauntered up to them and gave both my boss and the new recruit a sweet smile. I introduced myself and held out my hand in an offer of welcome. The man graciously took my hand into his and I could feel a deep warm jolt slither up my arm into my chest, sending my heart into a flutter.

"Hello Roni, pleasure to meet you, my name is Benjamin," his

9

chiseled features received my welcome with a genuine smile.

"Stay away from Roni," Dave warned with a joking tone to his voice, "She has a voracious appetite, but she is also my most esteemed employee. Heed the warning and interpret it for what you will," Dave raised his eyebrows to me and gave me a twisted smirk. It was not secret of Dave's sexual preference and this was his way of telling me to withdraw my claws.

"Don't let Dave here frighten you from speaking to me again in the future. I would be happy to show you the ropes and some hot spots around town if you are a newcomer." I smiled and added, "Don't be a stranger, Benjamin."

"I won't be and please call me Ben."

I nodded to Ben with a coy smile, walked to my office and closed my door. Behind closed doors the girls began to excitedly chatter among themselves.

"Shh, I will get him for us, I promise you that," I gave them a little pat to calm them down.

Later that afternoon, Ben approached me and we decided to have lunch together at a new Bistro down the block. Our conversation was smooth and never once was there one of those awkward moments of silence. I filled him in on the office gossip and all the rumors connected with each of our co-workers. He especially seemed shocked when he learned that Dave was gay.

"Well don't worry, I do not play on that side of the fence," Ben assured me with a flirtatious smile. "I did move here from Chicago and would love to see some of the nightlife here in Miami. You did offer to show me around."

"I did offer and that offer still stands. I would be delighted."

"Well then how about Saturday?"

"It's a date," the girls did a rhythmic dance inside my pink silk panties and I swatted them from under the table.
Work finished up very slowly that week and word got around to Dave of our plans.

"Bitch," Dave whispered teasingly when we passed each other in the hall and gave me a tight smirk. "I will win the next one."

"We will see," I laughed and almost skipped in victory back to my office.

Saturday came and plans were made to meet at his apartment since my house was well over 30 miles past the outskirts of town. I loved to live my life in isolation and work on my private rock garden in the nude without

10

the fear of being noticed. I loved to collect geodes and odd colored river rocks, always on the prowl for new candidates. The entire right side of my house was devoted to this rectangular garden of unpolished, uncut gems and pieces of winding, convoluted driftwood. All the gems I had gathered myself when vacationing in various spots around the country. Geology was my passion, along with my girls. I credited them with my success in life.

Before the date, I spent time carefully prepping and adding careful details to my bedroom and primping myself for the evening ahead. If all went well, I planned to be back here with Ben after dinner.

I slipped into my favorite little black dress that hugged my curves closely and showed the perfect amount of skin. I made sure my red hair was pulled back tightly from my face; I wanted accentuate my high cheek bones and wide set brown eyes. Satisfied with my appearance, I filled a spritzer with baby oil and placed it beside my bed. Baby oil can be quite an entertaining accessory if used correctly.

The date commenced smoothly and the food was delicious. There was a definite connection between us and often our gazes locked for minutes at a time. We started to play footsie under the table and my toes inched between his legs; I found him becoming aroused. Ben's breaths became deeper and he bent forward to take my hands within his.

"Let's leave," Ben whispered. He pulled my hands up to his thick lips and kissed them lightly.

I just nodded back to him, a little breathless myself. We climbed into my silver car and I drove quickly in the direction of my house.

"How far out in the sticks do you live?" Ben asked in amazement after twenty minutes on the road.

I laughed and told him it was only fifteen more minutes away. I reached over to him and rubbed between his legs. To my delight I found him still aroused. I laughed and teased him with my tongue, flicking it back and forth between my teeth with the speed and precision of a viper.

"OK girl, you better stop or we will never make it to your house! I am almost tempted to make you pull over here and we can hump like bears in the woods."

"No, we have to get back to my house; you will enjoy it. I worked very hard in perfecting the details for tonight."

"Oh, what makes you so confident I would have fallen for you; are you that sure of yourself?" Ben mocked me affectionately.

"Who can say no to me? I am the most unique woman you will ever meet and I can promise you the most intense and sensual night of your life."

Ben did not answer me, just clutched the hand rest a little tighter. I could see his knuckles turning white with the added tension and I depressed the gas peddle a little harder and we sped into the night.

When we finally pulled up my gravel driveway, Ben stepped out of the car and gaped at my rock garden.

"What fantastic and unusual rocks! Where did you find them all?"

I shrugged, "Here and there, vacationing around the country and some of this drift wood washed up along the banks of the river that runs in back of my house. Enough small talk," I smiled to him coyly.

I grabbed both of his sweaty hands and guided him into my house like a Black Widow Spider pulling her prey deep into her web. As we walked hand in hand, I felt the girls begin to vibrate between my legs. They knew their time to come out and play was drawing near.

I led Ben through my cold, white living room and directly into my bedroom. I closed the door behind me, isolating us together into my playful and erotic set of seduction. I went around the room and lit the small tea candles strewn about the tops of my furniture. After the small flames filled my bedroom with their warm glow, I turned the overhead light, immersing us in Nature's light.

"This room is amazing, just like the woman who sleeps and dreams here," he whispered in awe after taking it all in.

I put my finger to my lips to silence Ben's chatter and began to pull forcefully at his clothes. I needed to expose that rock hard chest of his, my tongue wanted to cavort along his sculpted abdomen. After I unsheathed his body, I let his clothes fall to the floor and I kicked them under the bed. I placed my hands on both his shoulders and roughly pushed him backwards into my waiting silk sheets. Ben laughed a little nervously and leaned forward in an awkward attempt to kiss me.

"Not yet," I whispered and put my fingers to his lips and pushed his head back into the pillow.

Ben let out a small groan in frustration but remained recumbent in my silky nest.

I leaned over and opened my nightstand beside my bed. I took out several red, silk scarves and scattered them around Ben's perfect, Adonis body. I dropped a scarf over his penis and let gravity arrange it around his obvious eager state. I used several of the remaining scarves to secure his arms and legs tightly to my wrought iron bed frames. Ben just laid in silent anticipation, looking at me like a hungry puppy. I heard my girls begin to

12

whisper and giggle.

"What is that?" Ben inquired with a smile. "Is this some kind of weird music?"

"No, you will find out soon enough," I promised.

I stood up and sauntered to the foot of my bed and began to pull down the straps of my little black dress. Ben's eyes widened as my little strip tease show commenced. I let the little black dress slip easily down my slender form and fall to the floor around my feet. I sashayed and twirled in circles to the side of the bed so Ben could get the whole effect of my nude body. I put in a lot of effort to my physique and I prided myself on my firm bottom and perky little breasts. I reached into my nightstand and pulled out my trusty baby oil spritzer. I looked down to Ben laying upon my bed, so helpless and at my mercy. I turned my back to him, faced the wall and spayed the oil between my legs. The girls seemed to jump and catch the oil droplets in mid-air. They became gravid with the oil and glistened like spun gold. I smiled, pleased with myself, and turned around.

Ben's eyes grew even wider. "I see you are a natural red head! That bush is as breathtaking as your rock garden." He squirmed reverently with even more impatience. I again placed my finger to my lips imploring for silence.

I walked back to the foot of my bed and slowly crawled up on Ben's muscular legs, massaging the oil up his midsection with my torso. Ben let his head fall to the pillow and let out a small little whimper of defeat. I rested my body on top of his and let the oil glide me around as if I were a hungry eel. Ben slowly opened his heavy eyes and looked to my face. I watched his gaze fall to my breasts and I slid down his body and sat up, straddling his legs so he could get a full view. His eyes finally reached to my girls down below. They were dancing in unison, eager and starving with anticipation. Ben's heavy eyes suddenly bulged in shock and his mouth worked silently for words. The bound Ben could do nothing but work his pitiful, useless lips and search for a scream his frozen lungs couldn't muster at that crucial moment. I smiled patiently at the silent creature, waiting for a sign of intelligence.

"What the hell is this, some kind of crazy STD?" Ben whispered hoarsely when he finally found his voice. He then began to frantically twist his body back and forth in a futile attempt for freedom.

"Ben, be still, it will make it all move forward much easier."

I bent over him and tied a red scarf around his eyes. As I was tying Ben strained to bite my hands in a weak attempt at self defense. Finding he could not quite reach my flesh, Ben then began to scream for help, begging me for mercy.

I shook my head at him, as if scolding a small child for being disobedient.

"No one can hear you. We are miles from no where, Ben. You know that."

Then Ben began to cry. I could see the tears gather below the red silk scarf tied around his eyes. This human and submissive act empowered me. I felt a deep arousal I had never felt before and I quickly mounted Ben. I took his flaccid penis within me and ground him deeply forward, it was an incredible moment. Despite his terror, I felt Ben grow within me. I worked my hips frantically and I finally climbed to the top of that mysterious peak. The climax was just as sweet and victorious as I anticipated. I quickly withdrew, my muscles spent and exhausted. Ben remained erect and silent. Drool had gathered on the corners of his lips and trickled around his ears. I reached down and began to massage him. Men were such funny creatures, so easily aroused even in the face of death. I empathized with the betrayal he must be experiencing, betrayed by his own body.

I then felt a tugging and a sudden cold draft between my legs. I quickly spread my thighs and to my shock and horror "My Girls" jumped from my body. I watched in fascination as they inched their way up Ben's legs, like slender black worms and weave around his penis. They began to dance and circle his penis; the sight reminded me of children dancing around a may pole. Then Ben came, it showered all around the girls. They screeched and jumped to catch the spray but this did not satisfy them. They wriggled about in a fevered pitch and again Ben began to cry. They inched up to the tip of his penis and began to slip down his urethra. Ben began to scream frantically and writhe back and forth.

"Please, Roni make them stop. Pull them back, it is beginning to burn!" he begged me pathetically.

"I can't, they have chosen you. I cannot stop them now. I am sorry..." I moved down to the floor, a little afraid of what was going to happen next.

Close your eyes, Roni. You do not want to see this; the words collectively reverberated in my head.

Sitting on my floor: I scuttled backwards until my back hit the wall. I closed my eyes and put my hands over my ears trying to muffle Ben's heart breaking screams.

I must of fallen asleep because when I awoke the girls were back in place, a little fatter for the wear, but in their proper place. I stood up and looked at the bed. I gasped and covered my mouth. Ben's body was totally drained of any fluid. His body resembled a burnt potato chip you sometimes found in the bag while snacking. I walked over and poked him with my toe. His body lifted and fluttered back to the bed with the ease of a feather.

I got dressed and gathered the silk scarves from around my bed. I was able to roll Ben up into a little cylindrical tube on top of my bed. I gathered my red scarves and wrapped his dehydrated carcass up into a little red cocoon. I dropped the morbid cocoon into a plastic grocery bag and stepped outside my house. I picked up a few rocks from my garden and dropped them into the bag with Ben's cocoon. I tied the handles and walked quickly to the river. When I reached the banks I flung the bag over my head. It sailed towards the middle of the murky river and I watched it smack the smooth surface. The air billowed out of the top of the bag as the rocks pulled it deep below the surface of the icy dark water. Ben was gone.

I turned my back to the river and started back to the house. I felt my footing slip and I caught myself before I fell to the ground. I stood up and looked down to the culprit. It was a large smooth rock and I bent down and to pick it up. When I inspected it I could see small red crystals embedded into the grain, what a find! I slipped it into my pocket and continued home.

When I got inside the house I wrote Benjamin 2009 on the rock and went outside to place the small memorial in my fabulous rock garden

BLIND DATE
By John F. Taylor

Alex had always been OK with dating but he had never been a ladies man. He'd never been any good sustaining a lasting relationship. There were flaws in the women and he focused on them. It could be anything from the way she laced her shoes to the way she chewed her food. Friends accused him of being a misogynist, which he usually laughed off.

Jake a friend from high school and now business partner had set-up this date. He wagered that Alex couldn't find fault in this woman no matter how hard he tried. Alex felt a slight pang of guilt, not because of the girl or her feelings but for taking his friends money. Alex shifted in his seat looking around the crowded coffee house.

He scanned all the faces looking for one, which matched his own, somewhat lost trying in vane not look desperate. He looked down at his watch checking the time.

"You must be Alex. You also thought I would be late. I'm not sure if I'm insulted yet so you'd best come with you're A game sir."

Alex stood as smooth as that voice that had just slid through the marrow of his bones.

"I presume that you'd be none other than Lisa?" Extending his hand.

The woman before him was five feet eight inches with dirty blonde hair. She worked out by the look of her body, taught in all the right places. She had ample breasts, flat midriff, which lay exposed by the large hole in the black one-piece dress she wore tonight. A bright silver hoop dangled from her navel. Long legs extended from the high cut dress into stark stiletto heels that were no less than three or four inches high. She took Alex's hand into hers with her wrist bent downwards leaving the top of her hand exposed in lady like position. Alex taking his cue and appreciating the manoeuvre raised her hand to his lips giving it a quick peck. He made sure to keep his eyes locked on hers as he performed to catch her reaction.

Her face gave nothing away. A bright white smile and deep blue eyes clear and alive. Her hand was cold Alex made a mental note. This fact could be used later to his advantage. Her white skin was clear, unmarred by acne or freckles.

16

"So Alex, What will be on the agenda for this evening?"

"Well, being a distinguished woman as you obviously are, I thought…"

"I have a better idea why don't you just show me."

"OK." Alex cocked his arm to escort Lisa to his car. He'd already planned a drive to the beach with the restaurant on the board-walk.

Throughout dinner, Alex and Lisa exchanged small talk. He watched for flaws, which he could find use to end the date with some civility. He'd have to sleep with her first, he did pay for dinner after all. But He could find nothing. She was perfect in every way. After dinner, they went to a local club and danced until the small hours of the evening.

Lisa admitted. "I have had a really nice time but I must say I am really tired. So what do you say we go back to your place for a night cap and then you can drop me off afterwards?"

"Fair enough."

As they left, Alex being the gentleman he was helped Lisa put on her coat. They drove to Alex's house with the radio on so they didn't converse at all. Alex made a mental note.

She is all right with not talking.

Most women it seemed couldn't go more than a few hours without some type conversation. Lisa was obviously not one of the typical females. She was content it seemed just being in the presence of Alex.

They arrived at his place; she offered to make the drinks while he hung up the coats. Alex agreed and pointed her to the bar in the kitchen. He watched her walk away enjoying the swing of her hips. He allowed himself to imagine of what it would be like fuck Lisa. As if on cue, she turned and caught him staring.

"Do you have any of those green olives with the pimento? I simply love to work my tongue around inside to dig out the pimento."

"Uh, yeah you'll find them in the door of the refrigerator."

He turned his attention back to hanging the coats up. He met her in the kitchen she was finishing the drinks.

"So, you ready to go and grab a seat out on the deck?"

"I didn't know you had one. It's a little chilly outside though, so why don't keep it inside tonight?"

"As you wish, follow me we can head to the living room where I can turn on some music and we can relax."

"Sounds nice." Lisa said handing Alex his drink and following him to the living room.

17

Lisa let her eyes wander around the expansive living room as she sat down on a long white leather couch. The entire room seemed like a sanitarium, completely white even the electronic devices. Alex pushed a few buttons on a remote, a large screen dropped slowly from the ceiling, and music arose seemingly from all around them.

"Hidden acoustically designed speakers. Very impressive."

"I'm impressed that you are so acutely aware of them not to mention the fact that you pronounced the term acoustically correctly."

Lisa turned her head to act as if she was shy then turned back to Alex staring into his eyes.

"So Alex, tell me something. Old or new money?"

"A little forward aren't we?"

"A woman can not waste her time these days, you know."

Alex was having trouble focusing on Lisa's face or anything at all for that matter.

"So, where were we again? Oh yes, old or new money. It's all new money."

"What's wrong Alex?"

"Well, either these are really strong drinks or you slipped me a rufie."

"Huh, I don't know if I should be insulted or flattered. But we'll get to that later. For right now let's just say that the eyes have it, shall we."

Alex awoke with a migraine headache and discovered that he was still having trouble seeing all he could see was blackness. He reached up to touch his eyes and he heard Lisa's voice she was in the room but not close.

"Oh just an F-Y-I kind of thing for you Alex, there is another colloquialism that maybe you should pay better attention to. It says, "Beauty is in the eye of the beholder." I have taken your eyes because you brought my sister home fucked her and then in the morning told her she was ugly. She went home and committed suicide the very same day."

Alex's fingers touched his face ever so gently and his finger slipped into a wet hole where he once had an eye. He never bothered to check the other one.

MY SWEET PRINCE
By Nandy Ekle

The sun blared louder than any alarm clock could ever scream. My eyes popped open and looked at the hateful light coming in through the window. I would have to get out of bed, but my body ached. I had a few new bruises, some on my skin, some down deep. I winced as my abs contracted sending a message to my brain, also crying in protest. I must have been completely loaded last night. My head sent messages to my stomach to empty out if I made one quick move.

Rolling slowly over to the edge of the bed, I was careful not to wake Mark. It had been a horrible fight – something to do with my books and book marker. My memory was fuzzy as the pain in my head threatened to unlock all kinds of doors I did not want opened.

I pulled on my t-shirt. I didn't remember going to bed naked, but I certainly woke up that way. Looking down at my legs, I noticed the giant bruise on my left thigh opening up like a flower. Yeah, once my head cleared, that spot was really going to hurt. My stiff hands closed in fists and a sharp dry pain raced up to the crevice of fire in my head. A cut – there was a deep gash in the palm of my hand. What the hell happened there? Maybe it would come back to me after my shower.

I did not want to wake Mark, so I slid out of bed as gently as I could. If we were as drunk as I thought and had the fight my body told me we'd had, he probably would sleep a little while longer, but I didn't want to take any chances. I deserved the peace and quiet to read my new book.

I loved to read! I loved opening a book and getting lost in someone else's life, their surroundings, their problems, and forgetting mine. I used to tell Mark that I wasn't only reading a book, I was visiting another world for a little while. He never understood that. He could not open a book and decipher letters and words into a story that filled his soul with feeling and emotion. He just didn't get it. I always wondered if that's why he got so furious with me so easily, because I had relationships with the people in my books.

After a quiet tiptoe to the bathroom, I peed and started the shower running. I still had no idea what time of day it was, but I couldn't stand staying in that bed a minute longer.

In the mirror, I looked at the new bruise covering my eye. No way to hide that, or the one that decorated my jaw. I decided to stay home from work because I didn't want to come up with another explanation about them. The people who came into the Quick Stop convenience store stared at me every time I came to work with a new bruise. I knew what they thought; I could see it in their eyes. "He must beat her. She must be a retard for not leaving him. Why does a girl stay around and take that kind of abuse?" I wondered that myself every morning when I woke up feeling like I had been through a meat grinder.

As I stood in front of the mirror I took off the t-shirt and looked at my belly. There was no mark, but that didn't mean I didn't feel the soft and gushy spot where his fist had tried to punch a hole. No, that was definitely sore. My boobs had marks where he had grabbed them when he wanted to have sex with me after punching me in the eye and then the stomach. By that time I was tired and hurting and let him do whatever he wanted just so he would pass out. God, I must be the dumbest girl in the world.

The air in the bathroom turned warm and humid as the water heated up in the tub, but I continued to look in the mirror. My scalp ached in a patch on the side of my head and I discovered a lump that grew there from the bottle that had crashed on my skull. I also realized that my hair was a little damp but not bloody. Well maybe I took a shower last night after he passed out.

I stepped under the water of the shower and felt it sting my skin like millions of tiny needles trying to perform acupuncture on my arms and legs, belly and face. Ah, the energizing feeling of steaming hot water piercing through me. It might not wash the bruises away very fast, but it certainly washed away some of the fuzz in my head. I had until noon to call Lance at the store, so I intended to take my time and just feel the water blister me.

I stood there in the shower and thought about what had attracted me to Mark in the first place. He wasn't like my fairy tale at all, like I'd always dreamed of. In my fantasy I travel somewhere – anywhere – and a tall beefy man with a very broad chest, dark hair and dark eyes, and sexy accent comes up to me and introduces himself as a Prince. His scent excites my awareness and I feel my face grow warm. He looks at me and takes my hand, tells me he has been looking for me all his life and then sweetly and gently kisses my hand sending thrills through me like shimmers that play havoc with my senses. He calls me and we go out for dinner and dancing a few times, then he gets down on one knee and proposes to me right out in

20

public - just like in the storybooks. My heart trembles and my breath speeds up just thinking about it.

The way I met Mark didn't even come close to that. I had gone to the Empty Stable Bar with Susan. We were drinking beers and laughing, cutting up, and Mark danced up with his bowlegged swagger, very cute but tough, so self-confident. He wore his jeans, tight in the right places, just enough to look interesting. The top two buttons of his shirt hung opened and a little of that beautiful curly hair popped out and waved at me. He even wore those fabulous pointy-toed boots. I remembered thinking that just looking at him coming up to me made me shiver with excitement – of course, I had had several beers.

He had step ball changed right up to me and smiled that lopsided smile, very square jawed, and politely asked if he could buy me a drink. We danced some, partied until the bar closed, then he came home with me. We made love in a drunken stupor and slept like rocks all night.

And we'd been together ever since. During that time, I think it'd been almost a year, we'd had more fights than I could count, but making up was filled with story-book passion. I wonder if that's why I stayed with him, just waiting for him to apologize, bring me flowers and little gifts, kiss me like he thought I was a princess. I think I loved that about him more than anything – making up.

I came out of the shower, wrapped a towel around my head and dried off. The headache was dulling down a little, no longer threatening to turn my stomach inside out, and some of the achiness was easing up. I put my t-shirt back on and tiptoed back into the bedroom to find a pair of sweatpants and socks from the cleanest pile of clothes lying on the floor. Mark had not budged an inch on the bed so I quickly left and headed into the kitchen.

The cabinet where I keep my meds and Band-aids, stuff like that, gaped open because we never close the cabinet doors when we get something - just open the door, find what we need and walk off. Sometimes I get fed up with it and close them all, but then the house looks weird with all the cabinet doors closed and drawers pushed in - it's not normal.

Finding the pills I wanted, I took what the label suggested as a good dose and swallowed them; I didn't even need water. In fact, I nearly crushed them with my teeth just to see if I could taste the bitterness, but decided to swallow them with what little spit I could work up.

I looked at the dishes piled in the sink and then remembered that's partly what the fight was about. He was tired of living in a mess. I told him

21

he could leave, that this mess, this old trailer house, no matter how broken down it was, how full of junk, was mine – my only possession – left to me by my grandfather when he passed from this world to the next. I think that's when he grabbed my hair.

I didn't have anything much to eat in the pantry besides a half a loaf of bread, so I took a piece of that, then checked to see what was in the refrigerator. All I found were some beers and something green and fuzzy in a bowl with no lid. So I took a beer. The clock on the wall said 10:17. Good, I had a few minutes to read my book.

I sat on the couch with my book. My favorite reads were romances. I loved love. I loved reading about the way a woman and a man meet and the chemistry immediately splatters across the pages. I could tell who would wind up with whom before page ten and it thrilled me to find out I was right. The men were so strong and sexy and the women were smart and beautiful. They had their arguments, but they always found their love by the end, sometimes sooner. And those erotic sex scenes could nearly bring me to climax from just reading them. Beautiful places, beautiful people, beautiful fairy tale endings – my heart always felt full after reading a delicious love story.

About 30 minutes went by and Mark was still not out of bed. By this time, my sore spots had started to settle back into stiffness, enjoying the idleness of sitting still and reading my book. But I needed to call my boss and tell him I was staying home. The clock said 10:47 and that would give him plenty of time to call someone to take my place with the cash register. I took the phone from my purse, still in its sprawled position on the kitchen table next to some fried chicken and potato salad we had not eaten. Mark tossed my bag there when he yanked it off my shoulder. I had walked in the back door with my new book in my hand. He wanted me to wash the dishes so I could cook dinner in clean dishes. I remember looking at him, the beers I had been drinking all day bathing my brain and making my tongue say stupid things, "You wash the dishes, you dumb cowboy." Some day I would learn either to say nothing or to leave, which is what I should have done a long time ago.

Walking out of the door onto the back porch, I dialed the number to the Quick Stop and got Lance's voice.

"Hey, Lance, this is Tish. I don't think I can come to work tonight. I'm pretty sick."

"Well this is the second time this week. Have you been to a doctor?"

"No, it's just a virus bug going around. I'll be in to work tomorrow."

"I hope so. I would hate to have to replace you."

"No, you won't. It's just a touch of flu. Twenty-four hours. I'll be back tomorrow."

"Okay. Take care of yourself." Did I hear pity in his voice? Did he know? Did he know that Mark had beaten me stupid again? Did he know that I really hated that job anyway? I hate the way the people come in there and stare at me like I'm a moron or a freak for staying with a guy who shows his love with his fists. I hated the ones who looked at me as if I didn't have any brains in my head. I hated the ones who sniffed at me like I had the plague. And then there were the truck drivers who came in and acted like they could smell danger and violence on me. They had such stupid little things to say, then laugh as they left the store like they were the cleverest men in the world.

What I didn't tell Lance was that I wanted to take the shot gun from under the cash register and blow all his customers to bits. It would have made me laugh to see trucker guts and holier-than-thou guts and smarter-than-the-world guts drip from the walls of his stupid little store.

I walked back in the house, put my phone on the table next to my end of the couch and curled back into the seat. There was still no sign of life from the bedroom so I opened my book to the page held by a toothpick. I loved those colorful bookmarkers you could buy at the bookstore, the ones with clever little sayings about time spent in a book or the benefits of reading. I had bought one like that, but Mark tore it up. He said all I needed was a scrap of paper or a paperclip or a rubber band – just something to stick between the pages so I would remember where I left off reading. He said I could just fold the corner down for all he cared. He didn't understand that folding the corner down was cruel punishment to the book.

Another 20 minutes went by. The story was lovely. Combustible Chemistry, it was about a young woman desperately in love with a brilliant scientist, who also happened to be very handsome, but their love was stalemated because he was desperately tied to his job. She needed to find a way to get his attention back on her, but his research kept pulling him back to the lab.

I put my toothpick back in the spot and went to the bedroom door to look in on Mark. He still had not moved. He must have been pretty tired after the beating, even for him. I had never seen him sleep so soundly before.

Mark was the kind of man that could change gears instantly. One minute he's buying me drinks, slapping my ass and laughing with lust in his voice, the next minute he's ripping my hair out of my scalp and slapping my face, ramming the pointed toe of his boot into my ribs; and then he's kissing me and telling me how sorry he is and that I'm the best thing he's ever had and he'll never hurt me again. He's just so physical! And I think this is what normally makes him such a light sleeper. Usually he's the one that wakes me up. He jumps out of bed and the covers go with him. Sometimes he even yells, "Tisha, get up! Let's find some food! Good God, girl, the day is nearly gone!" And I get up when he does that and go into the kitchen to look for cereal and milk and a clean bowl to feed my man.

But he must have completely crashed last night. I didn't remember anything after he rolled off me already asleep. I must have passed out just as soundly.

I stood at the door and watched him for a minute, emotion flooding my brain. He lay on his stomach, the covers across his butt, his bare back facing the ceiling. I could see his dark hair all tousled, like one of the characters in my book and a prickle started in the middle of my chest. His right arm was off the bed, fingers almost touching the floor, a dark smear running down his hand to the tip of his finger.

I looked at him curiously while he slept. He really was a good-looking man. So what if our relationship didn't come out of a love story book; we had fun. I stayed with Mark because I didn't want to be alone, I really needed someone to take care of me.

Walking over to the bed, I caught the whiff of a strange smell, something metallic, something not quite right. Now I was a little nervous of what I would find. I couldn't put my finger on the fear I suddenly felt, but the headache and the fluttering in my heart came back.

"Mark?" He didn't answer. My eyes locked on the dark smear on his hand, the hand hanging unmoving over the edge of the bed. "Mark?" I was close enough now to see some of the covers around him. My sheets are black, but the black looked even darker. I felt the bread in my stomach try to crawl back out. "Mark? Are you okay? Mark, wake up!" I had a little hiccup in my voice, but I couldn't help it.

The closer to the bed I got, the worse it looked and smelled. The dark on the sheets looked like blood. I touched his shoulder and it was colder than the ice in my freezer.

"Mark! Mark! Wake up!" I rolled him over and saw the blood covering his belly and the holes in his chest.

24

The last of the fog evaporated from my head and I saw the events that had happened the night before.

Yesterday was pay-day and I cashed my check, which was shorter than normal because I had been off work for a day or two after a previous fight with Mark. I went to the store to get fried chicken for supper and potato salad. I made the mistake of walking by the book section and, of course, I had to stop. I felt the old tug, the need for a new world, a new set of friends and sighs. I was two chapters away from finishing Farewell To Ice and I didn't have anything new waiting for me. I do reread my books when I have to, but sometimes something new is the best prescription ever. I walked along the shelves, touching as many book friends as I could and waiting for a response. Finally Combustible Chemistry sent me the message – that was the one. So I dropped it in the back of my cart and headed toward check out counter.

But there at the end of the aisle was an entire carousel covered with the sparkly shiny book markers. They were only strips of cardboard with cords tied through the tops, but they had been colored and printed with pretty pictures and nice little sayings about reading books and where stories can take a person. They were so nice and I had never had one before, only a dollar, so I grabbed the shiniest one to go with my new friend.

When I walked in the back door, Mark met me with a terrible frown on his face.

"Where you been, Tish?" I knew the tone. I knew what was in store for the night.

"I went to the store for some food."

"Oh good! I'm starving! What'd ya' get?"

"Fried chicken and potato salad." Then he saw my book.

"What's that? Another book? Damn, girl! You think money grows on trees? You got more books than you got roaches here! In fact, there ain't no place to even sit in this piece of crap house for all your dumb books!"

"Don't you bother my books, Mark. Leave 'em alone! Here. Eat some chicken. I'll pick up the house tomorrow." I pulled some paper towels off the roll to make a pretend plate and opened the paper sack containing dinner.

"Give me that!" He snatched the book and the marker from my hand. "'Ten Reasons To Read,'" he read from the book marker. "Number one," his eyes looked directly into mine and his gorgeous smile turned into a mockery of a true book lover. "Gives me a reason to sit on my fat ass all day and not clean the house!"

"Mark, give it to me." I reached my hand out to take the colorful piece of cardboard back from him.

"No. I didn't say you could buy that, or the book either." He bent the book marker in half, then bent it the other way, back and forth until it broke. Then he turned the flame on a burner of the stove and dropped my sparkly book marker into it.

I screamed. He ran into the living room and picked up a stack of my beloved books and dropped them in a heap on the floor. Then he reached down and picked up the first one he touched, opened it up and ripped it right in half. I felt my heart rip. "You bastard! You leave my books alone!" He tore another book in half and I launched myself from the kitchen right into him. That was the start of the fight. He slapped my jaw, he punched my eye. I think I landed a few punches, and then he grabbed an empty beer bottle in one hand and the other hand held a handful of my hair. The bottle crashed into my head and I felt the stars explode out of my head.

"Always got your damn nose in a book and you never do a damn thing around here! No more books! Do you hear me! No more books!"

"Mark, let me go! Get out of my house!" And that's when his fist plowed into my stomach.

The rest of the night was filled with pain and ended with him pinning me to the bed and raping me. Then he rolled over, asleep before he even stopped rolling.

I remember shaking. Every part of me ached and I cried the same tears I cried a few nights earlier. I walked into the living room and saw the destruction of my books, smelled the ashes of my real bookmarker. I thought about the looks from the customers that would come in the store when they saw my new bruises. I thought about the pity in Lance's eyes. I couldn't stand this life anymore. I cried for my prince to show up and rescue me.

I sat on the couch while Mark snored like a well-fed animal in my bed and thought about the prince that continued to hide. What could be keeping him? Had I not suffered enough for him to show up? How many more beatings did I have to take before he heard me? Could it be that Mark kept him away? Maybe if he was out of the picture my prince would then be free to pull me up on his horse and carry me away to abounding love and riches.

I sobbed loudly. Let Mark wake up! I didn't give a damn. He could wake up and start beating me again – maybe that would be the one time too many that would bring my dark sexy love to me.

I went in the kitchen, straight to the sink and shoved my hand down in the sink full of dishes. I knew it was in there. When it sliced through the meaty part of my hand, I smiled. Yes, that was exactly what I wanted. I pulled the carving knife out of the bottom of the sink and walked back into the bedroom. Mark still lay on his back snoring, without any knowledge or care of what I had in mind.

I stared at his face. I remembered wondering one time if he was my prince in disguise, but now I knew he would never be anything more than a dumb stupid cowboy bully. I raised the knife and plunged it down in his chest over and over in my own version of rape. He moaned and his eyes opened, but at that point, he was too weakened to stop me. I kept stabbing him. He turned to his belly and I stopped, dropping the knife. He didn't move and I suddenly felt tired. The spell was broken and now my true love could come to me.

I then had showered to wash his blood and smell off me, and the memory of my revenge went down the drain with his blood.

Now looking at the room in the afternoon daylight, I sniffed and lifted my hand in the air in a disregarding gesture. My books were calling me.

ROPE

By Gayle Arrowood

Jennifer liked talking to her oldest sister, but tonight Amanda irritated her. Jennifer wanted to listen to the near silence of the night. The oldest sister described her new dress for the Valentine's Party tomorrow night. She was going with Richard.

He is perfect for her. Amanda talks and he listens. Why does she have to be on one of her rampage tonight? She hasn't taken a breath.

"It's almost midnight, let's go in the house," said Amanda.

Finally! "I want to stay on the porch a while, enjoy the night air," said Jennifer. "We're in the middle of winter, and it was in the eighties today. The climate changes with the day. Tomorrow, it's supposed to be fifty. But the weather is perfect right now."

"That's the desert for you. OK, but remember tomorrow's Valentine's Day. Ned will be over first thing in the morning."

"I'll come in at midnight. I want to be alone for a few minutes," Jennifer said.

Amanda took one last glance at the quarter moon and hurried into the house.

The crisp breeze tossed Jennifer's long hair while she sat on the porch. The moon graced the black sky. She gazed at the big dipper and checked her watch. Not quite midnight. A few more minutes won't matter. Eight o'clock will come fast. I have to be peppy for Ned. He's the best boyfriend I've ever had. But I love to feel a part of nature, at peace with the universe. Whether skiing in the winter and shooting the rapids in the summer, or sitting quietly.

The warm breeze blew a wisp of hair over her nose. She closed her eyes and the night poured around her, through her body, and out her pores. I could stay like this forever. I love the night sky. Everything's so peaceful. Nature is good, the night is great. Finally, she opened her eyes and checked her watch. A quarter after twelve. She stood up and headed for the door.

From behind, a gray and grisly arm grabbed her around the neck and yanked her down the porch steps. She screamed. He tightened his grip on her throat and stopped her shriek. I can't breathe. She tried to cough. It stuck in her throat. Let me go. Let me go.

28

But no one could hear.

Amanda came to the door, opened the screen, and almost yanked her sister's arm. But she missed.

Mom grabbed Amanda's shoulder and hauled her into the house. "I don't want both of you killed."

"Mom, it's a werewolf," Amanda screamed.

"It's a man dressed like a werewolf." Mom insisted. I love the sound of their voices. I have to do something. Although she didn't know Karate, she tried to flip him over her head. She almost made it.

He landed on one of his ankles. "Ouch!" Yelled the werewolf. He steadied his legs.

His grip on her neck was loose now. Jennifer took a deep breath and ripped out of his grasp.

"You little bitch!" He grabbed her again and tightened his arm around her waist.

She kicked him in the leg. "Damn you!"

She pulled on the fur. He screamed louder than she did. Nearly losing his grip on her, he grabbed her around the waist, arms pinned against her.

I have to get away. This can't be happening. I don't believe in werewolves. But what else could he be. The fur's real. She struggled, kicking and screaming, even pulling the hair on his legs. He's naked. Shit I have to get away. She tried to pull her arms up, but she couldn't get out of his grasp. She still kicked, but it didn't seem to hurt him.

"You're not going anywhere." The werewolf laughed. "I'll put you where I want you."

"No, you won't." Jennifer fought even more. She kept kicking his shins all the way to the street.

They reached his black van. Big white letters on the side of it said, "City Morgue." The hatch was already open. He threw her into the darkness. The werewolf grabbed a rope and struggled to tie her up. First her hands. She kept them apart, and hit him any place she could. Jennifer grabbed his nose and twisted it. He caught that hand. Like lightning, she smashed him on the head. When she rammed her fist between his eyes, he fell back.

She tried to push past him, but he recovered, grabbed one hand, then the other, put one huge hand around both of her wrists and used the other one and his teeth to tie her hands. "They'll have to go in front for now." He held her knees against the van, so she couldn't kick him again.

"Finally," he said, "Half down, half to go."

"Help me," she screamed. "Help me." She starting sobbing and she seldom cried. Her tears turned into another shriek. Her whole body went tense. She shrieked again. The night held a terror she had never seen before.

A siren in the distance. She quieted down. I'll be rescued. She sighed and her body relaxed.

"Shit! This better not be a sign of the way things are going to go tonight." Without bothering with her legs anymore, he closed the door and locked it with a key. She barely got her legs back into the van. He hurried to the driver's seat, started the ignition, and drove out of the area before the cops arrived.

Jennifer screamed continually. "Help me! Somebody, please help me. I have to escape."

"Shut up!" He raced the car down the road, turning wide at corners. Horns blared.

She pressed the window button down. Nothing! Jennifer smashed her face right up to the closed window and shouted to get someone's attention.

He yelled. "They're locked from up here. The DOOR and windows. Hee, Hee!"

She burst into tears again and pounded her tied hands against the window. If someone noticed, they ignored it. Then she rolled back and slammed her feet against the glass. Not even a crack.

He laughed as he drove fast into the night. "Yep, lady, you've been caught by the Holiday Grabber. At least that's what the papers call me. You must have forgotten this is Valentine's Day. I love to see holidays come. Just love it."

Again, she smashed her feet against a window, but it still didn't break. She kept hitting it. The glass made a sound, like it was breaking, but there wasn't even a crack. She sobbed. Her mascara ran over her cheeks and slid off her chin. She had to blow her nose, but her hands were tied. She glanced around. Nothing but her in the back of the van. She kept sniffing.

Not too long down the highway, he turned onto a wide dirt path. The van hit potholes. Jennifer bounced up and hit her head on the ceiling.

"Don't go so fast." She rubbed her head and then kept her hands against the roof of the van. Soon they were in a forest.

After some long agonizing minutes, Amanda again kicked the

window, hoping it would break.

He laughed as he stopped the car. She stared through the front windshield. The woods were up to the front of the car. The wide path had come to a dead end. He left the lights on, but cut the engine.

Once he was out of the van, he hurried to the hatch and unlocked it. Jennifer was ready. He leaned in and said, "Let me tie your feet up." She raised her legs and rammed his face. He fell back and landed on his butt and elbows.

"You...You bitch..." He was up in a second and reached for the rope. The werewolf put an arm up to block her feet. Finally, he grabbed her legs. When his head was down, she smashed her balled fists into the back of his skull. He fell forward and conked his head on the floor of the van.

Jennifer slid around him and jumped out. She almost fell forward, but at the last minute regained her balance. She ran down the wide path toward the highway. She was part of the high school's La Cross team. "Why am I going so slow? Maybe I'm going as fast as I ever have in my life. Where can I hide? I have to hide." She spoke to no one except herself.

"Get back here." His breathing was hard and heavy. He gained on her every minute. Because her hair flew out behind her, the werewolf was able to yank it, almost pulling it out. He grabbed her shoulders, then swung her around to face him. The werewolf backhanded her across the nose. Like him, her face was now bleeding.

He let go of her shoulder. "You have to let me tie up your legs. I tied all the women up. You can't be any different. Do you understand me?" He tried to knock her down, but she rammed her fists into his chest. He seemed to stop breathing even though he was standing.

She ran toward the main highway again. Where is he? I can't hear him behind me. Maybe I can shake him. She turned a bend, the back lights of his van faded into the darkness. No! Wait a minute. I'm going to hide in the woods. There are plenty of bushes. He'll be looking on the path all night, I hope.

Her eyes had become accustomed to the dark. She gazed into the forest. No sound of his footsteps, but Jennifer was still cautious and slow. She tiptoed around the trees, hoping she didn't run into a snake. The werewolf snake was enough for her. She could only see three feet in front of her.

In one tree, she saw an owl, who seemed to stare at her. Are owls safe? Don't know. No other birds. They must be sleeping. She saw one bush, then another. None big enough to hide behind. He might have snake eyes. She didn't know if he could sniff her out or not. I have no idea how werewolves act. I've never read a story about one. From what little I've heard and what little he said, this thing isn't typical.

A long way into the forest, she found six bushes grouped together. And a small place in the middle. After checking each bush to make sure there weren't any thorns, she scooted on her stomach into the middle of the bushes. Thank goodness, he tied my hands in front of me. I must have fought too much for him to tie them behind me. Jennifer sat in the mud. She trembled. Both eyes twitched in an alternate fashion. My camping experience is a god-send now.

"Where are you, you bitch." He ran down the dirt road toward Jennifer. "Why can't I catch up with her?" He raced past the point where she had entered the forest.

The werewolf called to her. "You're destroying me. You can't be different. I always tie them up, but the cops were coming tonight. Do you hear me, you bitch."

I hope he doesn't search the bushes. If he can wait till dawn, he'll see me.

"I have to tie you up and throw you in quick sand with the others. Every holiday, there's a party down there to celebrate the new arrival. We can't disappoint them. WHERE ARE YOU?" Soon he stumbled through the woods and beat every bush. It was a long time before he was near Jennifer's hiding place. How long she didn't know. Her watch had been ripped off in the struggle. Besides, it was too dark to see it anyway.

The closer he got to the bushes where she hid, the more she held her breath. Jennifer let out only enough air to keep herself conscious. A couple times, he hit her back with his stick, but she held her mouth shut with her hand and made no movement or sound, even when it felt like she was bruised. Tears formed, but she held her mouth shut, so she was quiet. What next? If I pinch myself, will I wake up? She couldn't do it because her arms were frozen. Screams, tears, and dirt were frozen in her throat.

Then he moved on.

How could he not know he hit me? Surely I don't feel like branches. Can't he smell my perfume? She sniffed. Oh, do I stink. Maybe he's just letting me think he can't find me.

Her legs fell asleep and needle-like pricks were poking her limbs inside and out. She nearly screamed. They hurt so much. When he was deeper into the woods, she changed positions and stuck her legs under the bushes in front of her. Now she could rub out the cramping and needles. Her hands were still tied, but she did the best she could. When she heard him coming again, she pulled her knees to her chest and rested her forehead on them.

The night wore on. He beat bushes and stopped again to beat the ones she was in. He spread branches apart. And he carried his rope. "WHERE ARE YOU?" The sound of the rope flying through the air echoed through the forest.

He plopped down on the mud near Jennifer and put his face in his hands. "She's destroyed me. I need a victim to keep from dying. Every holiday, I have to make sacrifices to the god of money. SHIT!"

Thank goodness, my hair and clothes are dark. I blend right into the forest, even my stench.

"Dawn's almost here. She's killing me. I need to throw her into the quicksand, like I did the others. And I have to do it by dawn. Why couldn't those cops have stayed away for five more minutes?" He cracked the rope on other bushes before reaching hers again.

She nearly shrieked when the rope hit her back. I can barely stand this. Mommy, help me. Don't let the bad man hurt me.

"I could have tied her legs and dragged her to the quicksand. Then she wouldn't have been different. She wouldn't have beaten me." Moving away from her, he searched further into the woods. He looked to the east. The first ray of dawn struck his eyes. Someone shrieked and a thump echoed through the forest.

Jennifer trembled in the bushes till the sun was straight above her. She hadn't heard him since the thud at dawn. Still, she was cautious. He might be sleeping somewhere. Finally, she could think again. I'll go to the main road and find someone to help me. She barely had enough strength to push the bushes apart and peek around them. Is that a man lying on the ground way back there? He must have fallen asleep. Still, it doesn't look like a werewolf.

She scooted out from between the bushes, crawled from one to the other until she could make out who it was. I have to be cautious. This is a survival game. One I plan on winning. At least I'll give it my best shot.

He's no werewolf. That's the Senator for our state. Was he the werewolf? Can't be. He has to be dead. His face is turning blue. Did the monster kill him? And he's naked, like the grisly one. She dropped to the ground for several minutes. I don't believe it. Can this be over? Might not. Still Valentine's Day. Don't mess up now. Mommy, help me. Where'd you go?

33

She kept saying these words until they were driving her bananas. She pushed her hands into the ground, so she could stand up. Jennifer stared around her and listened for him. Can I walk back to the dirt road? Do I dare take the path to the highway? I have to get out of here alive. I just have to. Someone has to come by and help me. Mommy? She stopped a minute. What am I thinking? Mommy? I've gone crazy. But I will get out of here.

She crawled through the woods because she couldn't walk very well. Jennifer made it to the dirt road. She kept muffling a shriek trapped in her throat, like a chicken bone. She didn't want to yell just in case the senator wasn't the werewolf. Every few feet, she had to stop to regain her breath and rest her knees. Her blue jeans had worn all the way through to her raw knees. A couple times, her arms or knees gave out and she fell forward. Each time, she stayed down to gather her wits about her. She was beyond thought.

Finally, Jennifer saw the main road. If she'd had the energy, she would have shouted her joy. But her scream captured deep in her throat would have to come out first. Nothing came out. She stood up and tried to walk. Her steps quickened. She didn't rest now. A few feet from the main road, she stumbled on a pothole, fell, and fainted.

Through the veil separating her and the world, she thought she heard a car coming. It turned down the wide path and stopped beside her. Their words were mumble-jumble to her, although they were loud. The veil garbled words, but not pictures. One man brought a blanket and carefully rolled her onto it.

Her scream finally dislodged from her throat.

"I thought you were in a coma."

"The pain must have brought her out of it," said the other man.

"Get me off my back. It hurts too much." Jennifer arched her back, but it didn't help.

The men carefully lifted her and laid her on her stomach. "We've called 911. You're Jennifer, aren't you? You're all over the news. Everybody's out looking for you. We were too," said one of the men.

The other one said, "We won't hurt you. We need to cut the rope off your wrists. It's digging into your skin. So don't be afraid."

She heard sirens. I'm being rescued. Finally! She closed her eyes and passed out again.

LUNCH DATE

By R.A. Hunter

"Come on, baby, it'll be great," Scott said, running his hand down Michelle's back and trying to pull off her sweater.

"No, I really don't want to," she said, pulling away from him and straightening her clothes.

She pushed away from the table and walked over to the window, staring out at the squirrels chasing each other up and down a tree.

Scott leaned back in his chair and moaned his frustration to the ceiling. He glanced at his watch and saw that it was ten minutes past noon. He only had an hour for lunch and he could not push back his meeting with Peterson. He was going to have to push it up a notch or he was going to be going back to work unfulfilled.

"Don't you want to be close to me?" he asked, cocking his eyebrows at her in that way that he knew made her melt.

Michelle's eyes didn't leave the squirrels, she knew he'd be doing the eyebrow thing and she didn't want to see it. "Of course I want to be close to you," she said, fogging the window with her sigh, "but not that way."

"It's the only way to truly be a part of each other, you know that."

"No, it isn't," she said, turning to face him. "People don't have to do that to be a part of each other. At least, they didn't used to. I mean, when I hear about what my parents did, what their entire generation did, that was not a part of the picture. They wouldn't even have dreamt of it."

Scott looked at his watch again, in forty five minutes he was going to be staring across the desk at a fat bald man wearing a suit that would cost Scott two years salary. He wasn't going to be able to face him with a smile if he didn't release some of this tension. "Our parents lived in a different time. Hell, they were practically puritans."

"Maybe that isn't a bad thing!" Michelle said, the tears threatening to break. Scott could see them gleaming in the corners of her eyes and wondered, not for the first time if the gays didn't have something going for them. Men never seemed to have a problem with the intimacy; hell the physical aspect was practically aerobic. To have someone you cared for match you in strength, to roll with them, almost fighting them for

35

dominance, to come out on top, no pun intended. It certainly held its own charm. But the act itself, Scott knew that he could never follow through. There were just some things that just did not belong in his mouth.

"It sounds so beautiful," Michelle said, leaning into the counter, tears flowing freely now.

"It is beautiful, Darling, I promise you."

"No, I mean the way our parents did it; the way they courted, so innocent, so sweet. They didn't rush into it. Hell, some of them never did it at all."

Scott laughed in spite of himself. "We all like to think that our parents didn't do it, Honey. But believe me when I say they did. After all, they're human too, they have needs."

"Do you think?"

"I know." Scott glanced at his watch; twenty after. If she didn't give in soon he wouldn't have time. "Sweetie, it's the only way to truly be a part of each other. You know that."

"I do, I know it. It's just... I'm not sure."

"What aren't you sure about? Is it me? You don't want to be a part of me?"

"That's not it. It's not. But, why do we have to do it now?"

"When would you like to do it? Next week? Next month? How about when we're well into our eighties and neither of us can enjoy it? Huh? When I probably can't even do it. Is that what you want?" Scott hadn't meant to get upset. The last thing he wanted was to yell when he was trying to be smooth, but sometimes... sometimes women could just be so impossible.

"No, I don't want that. I just... I can't stop thinking that maybe our parents had a better way of doing things."

"Fine," Scott said, "if I'm not special enough for you do this now, then I'm not special enough to do it ever. Have a nice life."

Scott jumped up from the table and headed for the door. If he hurried he could pick up a pro and be done in time for the meeting, but he was going to have to really huff it.

"Wait," Michelle said.

Scott turned to see her pulling her sweater off over her head, the swell of her breasts heaving from beneath the black lace bra she'd worn to commemorate the occasion.

"I'm sorry," she said, "You're right, it is time." She unhooked her bra revealing her breasts to him. He'd dreamed of seeing them for weeks, since he bumped into her in the produce section. They were white, round and supple. Her nipples, tight in the cool room, were pointing at him, choosing him.

She gingerly folded her bra and placed it lovingly on the table. "I don't know what I was thinking. I'm sorry," she said.

Scott stood in the doorway until Michelle had removed her slacks and panties, the latter she placed folded next to the matching bra. Scott crossed to her and, taking her by the hand, helped her onto the table. Her breath caught for a moment, surprised by the cold tabletop on her naked flesh.

She looked up at Scott, staring deeply into his hazel eyes. "This is what I want," she said, "I love you."

"I love you too," Scott said, picking up the mallet and shattering her skull with one quick blow. Her legs jerked twice and then she was still.

Scott remembered his first time, God that had been awkward. He'd had no idea where to hit or how hard, the tears, and oh God the mess. He'd gotten much better over the years.

He glanced at his watch again, half an hour, no problem. He sat down and picked up his knife and fork. He could finish one breast easily, and then he'd have the rest tonight. He sliced the nipple off and threw it into the trash, he was no savage.

As he began his feast he thought about what Michelle had said about their parents. How they used to sneak away and roll around together, touching each other with "special" parts and then pretending they'd experienced one another. God, they were such children. There were even stories about how just showing these "special" parts on television caused old men and humorless women to form committees discussing the degradation of society.

Scott laughed and wiped his mouth with a corner of the panties. "Thank God we've evolved beyond that."

DARK WATER

By George Wise

I've come to believe that there are places in this world that collect lives. Places like the Brooklyn Bridge where twenty-seven people died during its construction and where countless others have leaped to their death into the river. Like lonely stretches of highway --sometimes stretches that are completely straight, with flat changeless vistas-- where you find memorial crosses have been placed for those whose lives have been stolen in the blink of an eye. And places like the pit.

The pit is an abandoned gravel quarry that was just to the west of my house in Bristol when I was a teenager. They shut it down when a digger hit a spring and it filled with water. The legend goes that the water rushed in so fast they couldn't get the equipment out in time. The old timers swore that the shovel operator who hit the spring was pinned in his excavator. The force of the water pushed it right over and he was trapped there to drown.

As far as I know, that was the first life the pit collected, but there had been many between then and that hot August night when we jumped the fence for a swim and four of my friends lost their lives in those dark waters.

It was the weekend before classes started up again the summer I was seventeen. This is the first time I'm telling the true story of that night. I told another to my parents and the cops when they questioned me, but I figure it's time to tell what really happened.

Plenty of people will call me a coward for not speaking up sooner. Others will say I'm suffering from survivor's guilt, or that I'm simply seeking attention at the end of my life. None of that is true, I assure you. What happened, happened and I can't explain it any more than I can explain how bumble bees fly, or how a statue of the Virgin Mary in Sacramento will cry bloody tears every Good Friday. Some things just can't be explained, but that doesn't mean they don't happen.

I called Billy, after I got up that day around noon, to see what he was up to. He had nothing going on, so he came over with Kurt so we could do nothing together. We spent most of that Saturday sitting in front of the TV at my house watching reruns of the Twilight Zone. My parents went up north for the weekend to our cabin on Spirit Lake with my little sister Beth, so we had the place to ourselves.

That was more than thirty years ago (God, can it really be that long) in the summer of 1976. It was a hot summer, the hottest on record. We'd simmered through two months of that heat and it hit a hundred degrees the day we went to the pit.

We took Kurt's car over to Silver Lake for a swim before my girlfriend Linea and Kurt's girlfriend Kathy got off work at the Dairy Queen. The beach was so crowded we decided to skip swimming and headed over to the DQ to see Linea and Kath.

Dairy Queen was nearly as popular as the beach. We had to wait in line behind a fat lady in a flower print sundress. She shuffled forward like a mountain of quivering, sweating flesh and leaned her bulk on the narrow counter in front of the order window as her two kids circled below, moving in and out of her massive shadow. She got two tiny ice cream cones with sprinkles and handed them down to the kids, then retrieved the biggest slushy I've ever seen. Heading toward her car, she alternately screamed at the kids to behave and sucked on her slushy. It was a pitiful sight.

"Hey Babe," I said when I got to the window.

"Hi Jay. What're you doing here?"

"We were going to the beach, but it's just too crowded."

"Hi Kurt… Kath, Kurt's here too." Linea called her over. "You guys want something?"

After we got our ice cream, Linea and Kathy took a break and met us at the picnic tables beside the building.

"So, what do you want to do tonight?" I asked around a mouthful of ice cream and nuts.

"I don't know. I really wanted to go to the beach. It's so damn hot, I want to just soak in the lake for hours."

"Can't go to the beach, baby." Billy said and I punched him lightly in the shoulder. "It's assholes to elbows over there. No room at the inn, you know what I mean?"

Linea didn't acknowledge Billy. He was my best friend since second grade when his family moved to Bristol, but Linea hated him.

"Yeah, we won't even be able to find a place to put our towels down." I said, stepping in before Billy said any more and pissed her off. "I mean, I'd really like to go swimming, but we can't go there."

"Say, why don't we sneak into the pit." Kurt said as he scraped the last of the ice cream from the paper cup. "Linea, you and Kath come by Jay's house when you're done working. We can grab some beers on the way back, then we can just climb the fence and do a little skinny dipping."

Kurt had been buying beer for us for two years. He had a fake ID in case anyone ever carded him, but they never did.

"I'm not going skinny dipping with you three, that's for sure," she said her face reddening.

"Oh c'mon sweetness," Billy chided. "It'll be dark and nobody will see you."

"Give it a rest Billy," I said. "Maybe she doesn't want to go."

"I wanna go. I just don't know if I wanna go skinny dipping."

"Listen, I don't know if it's such a good idea. If we get caught we could get arrested for trespassing." I said.

"You chicken-shit son-of-a bitch." Kurt said and Billy threw his empty ice cream cup at me. Linea squeezed my arm and whispered in my ear "We won't get caught. Let's just go."

So that's how it happened. It was just so damn hot everyone in the county was at the lake so we went to the flooded gravel pit next to my house.

* * *

The girls showed up at my house right around nine that night. We'd already made it through my entire album collection and a little over a half a case of Old Style before they got there.

"Listen, I don't think we should go to the pit." I said as I grabbed another beer from the case on the floor. "They put up that fence and got No Trespassing signs all over it. Besides, a couple of kids from school drowned there two years ago."

"Yeah, it was Dave Fitzgibeon and Robyn Liddel." Kathy said, looking to Kurt for support. "I was in homeroom with Dave's little sister Karen. They moved away after he died."

"Robyn Liddel, wasn't he from Chicago? Moved up here and was wearing his Latin Kings colors around school, thinking he was some bad ass or something?" Kurt asked.

"Yeah, that's him. He was a real piece of shit. Good riddance, I say." Billy said and took a slug of beer.

"That's a horrible thing to say." Linea said, glaring at Billy.

"Listen, I don't care whether Robyn Liddel and Dave Fitz-whatzis drown in the pit or not, I say we sneak in there and have a little pool party... what do you say?" Kurt asked.

40

I argued against it for a while but ultimately gave in. To this day…
to this very moment, I can't help but curse myself for it.

* * *

Thank God for laptops. Had I been trying to write this long hand --or even
on a typewriter-- from this hospital bed it would have been impossible.

The nurse came in just now, took my vitals and asked if I needed
more pain medication. I told her that I didn't, but in reality, I very much do.
I feel like my bones are burning and the pain in my belly is nearly
unbearable. I need to get to the end of this if for no other reason than to
receive the peaceful oblivion of morphine.

Anyway, where was I? Oh, I remember. I couldn't talk them out
of wanting to go swimming in the pit.

* * *

It wasn't that I was really too worried about getting caught. I just didn't like
the idea of swimming in the pit after dark.

We headed out the back door into the night. The air was thick and
stagnant. The fresh scent of mown lawn still hung in the air. I could see a
flicker of lightning on the horizon to the west, but the sky above was
cloudless. I led them through the hedges at the edge of my back yard and
into the hayfield that separated my yard from the pit.

We skirted around the edge of the field, swatting at mosquitoes as
we walked.

"I shoulda brought a flashlight." I said, squinting through the
darkness. It was moonless. I guided our way through the field by starlight.

We headed into the brush at the edge of the field and came up to
the fence on the backside of the pit. I remember I could smell the water
from there, a fishy dead smell that hung in the still air.

The sounds of frogs and crickets filled the night as we climbed
over the fence and headed into the brush toward the pit. I led them down a
slight incline through the trees to the water. Cold stars reflected off its slate-
like surface. It was an unnatural looking thing. It's flat, changeless surface,
made it look it like was filled with ink. It's straight edges on the north and
west side gave it a surreal quality that sent a shiver down my spine. A four-
foot wide strip of course gravel rimmed the pit and was barely visible in the

41

faint light.

Kurt said, "Let's build a fire," and started gathering up dry grass and dead branches from around the shore.

"No way, man," I said as I put the half case of beer on the shore beside me. "We'll get caught for sure. Just grab a beer and sit down, or go jump in the lake."

"Yeah, jump in the lake, Kurt." Billy said and everyone laughed quietly.

I think that was our last laugh together. It wasn't a roar of laughter. Not really even a very good comeback but we laughed none-the-less. We all felt a little happy right then... A little lighthearted. It would be the last time in their lives. I would have some moments of levity throughout the rest of my life --always tempered from my experience that night-- but they would never laugh again.

I cracked a beer and sat on the shore to take off my shoes, while I watched Linea and Kathy wriggle out of their shirts and cut-offs. My heart raced a little in anticipation before their swimsuits were revealed.

"Whooo Hooo!" Billy whooped at the top of his lungs when he stripped off his clothes and ran to the edge of the water and leaped as far out as he could, his arms and legs splayed wide.

He came down with a splash that got us all wet on the shore. Kurt and Kathy were next and I was surprised to see that they'd doffed their suits too, Kathy demurely turning her back to me as she pulled it off. They jumped in together and bobbed up in unison.

Linea turned to me as she stood on the edge of the lake. "You comin'?" She asked and undid the tie on the top of her suit. She tossed it in my direction and it landed on my head.

"Yeah, I'll be right with you." I said, "Just wanna finish my beer. You go ahead."

I've always had a bit of a phobia about swimming after dark. Not in pools, but in dark water... in lakes. I'd done it in the past and it had always been a challenge. I could just imagine the fish and turtles swimming up between my legs. I could sometimes even feel them. And I always inevitably strayed into weeds slimy with algae, slithering down my bare legs, or standing in gushy mud that squirted between my toes.

So I stalled. I sat on the shore and I stalled, finishing my warm beer. It's haunted me ever since.

"Fine," she said, and I could tell that she was pissed. Kurt and Kathy went into the dark water together and she was expecting me go with her so she wouldn't be alone. She turned away to take off her bikini bottoms then made the perfect dive into blackness. I watched as her pale silhouette disappeared below the surface.

I slugged down the last of my beer and toed off my sneakers. I pulled off my socks and shirt, rolled them in a ball and set them on the ground beside me, then looked into the darkness. I could hardly see them as they gathered together in a tight group about twenty feet offshore. They were giggling and talking softly and then Linea swatted at Billy and shouted, "Keep you hands to yourself."

"It wasn't me," he said, and backstroked away.

That's when I saw them... Pale figures gliding through the water below. They had their own ghostly inner light that made them faintly glow in the depths. I saw as one slithered up under Billy and along his back.

"Hey, what the fuck?" He rolled over and got his legs under him, treading water. "There's something in the water!" He shouted.

"You're so full of shit." Kurt barked, but I could see him looking into the depths at the shapes that swirled around them. They were all looking.

"No! There is something in the water! Get out! Get out quick." I shouted from the shore. They broke up then, everyone shrieking. Kurt and Billy were the strongest swimmers, but the girls rolled onto their bellies and began stroking toward the shore at the same pace.

"Hurry for God's sake! They're right behind you!"

I ran back and fort along the bank as I watched the pale figures grab them and drag them under. I could see in the faint light, gray-green arms reaching around their necks and pulling them down. And faces... I could see retched faces with haunted, empty eyes, starring out at me from the water. Beckoning me to jump in. I could hear whispers in my head, imploring me to... Come into the cool dark water.

It didn't take long. My friends screamed and struggled for only a short while before they put all their effort into fighting for their lives. All I could hear from the shore were splashes and the faint grunts of exertion. That soon faded too, and I was left alone in silence, the surface of the pit calming to its slate-like sheen again.

I've often wondered what those pale silhouettes were. I don't know for sure, but I think they were what remained of the lives the pit had collected over the years.

* * *

As I said before, I've been getting the Bristol Dispatch paper for years and saw several articles about the pit. Over thirty years many people have been claimed. They finally decided to drain it in 1993, but the pumps (no matter how many they used) couldn't keep up with the spring that fed it. No matter how much water they pumped out during the day, overnight it would all be replaced... even when they got smart and left the pumps running.

They finally settled on putting a full time watchman on duty in 1999 and that seemed to work. There were no articles in the paper until last year. That article stated that the watchman on duty during the night shift was missing when his day shift replacement showed up to relieve him. The reporter speculated that he'd silently slipped away during the night to get out from under some $10,000 in credit card debt, but it also reported that he'd left his wife of 11 years and two kids, nine ad six, behind.

I think maybe he didn't leave at all. I think that the pit hadn't been able to collect any lives for so long that those whispered voices got louder and finally got to him and talked him into joining them in the cool, dark water.

Well, I'm finally done and my morphine calls to me. I'll send this off to my sister Beth and hope it doesn't make her think less of me... but it doesn't really matter anymore. It's getting it out before I die that matters. Someone other than me has to know the truth about the pit. I don't expect that to make any difference, because I think more than a few people in Bristol already suspect what I know. Maybe not about the pale silhouettes, but about the heart of the pit itself. The fact that it is a deadly place... an evil place.

I'll call the nurse now for my shot. It'll knock me out for sure and I really need some sleep. I haven't slept well in years... well, since that tragic night in August. It always seems those things I saw swimming in the pit below my friends are nearer in the dark when I sleep. I've noticed that as I get sicker and sicker, they are very near indeed and I wonder if one night when I go to sleep for good I'll find myself in their midst. Just another pale silhouette gliding through the depths of darkness.

ROUTE COBRA
By Jason Duke

Dust kicks up behind the Strykers in a long trail of morbid gray that chokes the desiccated dirt road along Route Cobra.

I stand in one of the air guard hatches looking through the scope of my M4 rifle at the thick tires and how deep they sink into the rutted road. The tires fit perfectly and follow the ruts, like a train fixed to a set of tracks.

Above the acrid dust, the whiff of diesel, permeates the stink of death. There is no escaping it; it's all around, infiltrates everywhere, in everything. I put on my gas mask, and I can still smell it.

Skeletons line the road ahead. Some partial, maybe a ribcage, or a pelvis and a femur, but most remain intact, where the last flesh has decayed from their bones and forced them to permanent rest. Tattered flesh cakes to otherwise bleached bone, blackened and shriveled, tougher than what the scavengers can handle.

The skulls turn and face us.

Their mouths open in silent protest, the empty sockets following the Strykers as we pass. Some have enough rotted flesh that they twitch in excitement, then go limp from the exertion. In the final stage, it's all their trapped souls can will, until eventually their bones turn to dust and rejoin the earth from which they came.

* * *

The Strykers run on fumes; every vehicle does.

The first year, logistics and supplies weren't an issue. We rationed everything, down to the cleaning kits we used to clean our weapons. If the supplies weren't for something deemed mission essential, it was disapproved. Rank still had its privileges, and certain items were reserved for those higher in the chain.

We mostly stayed within the confines of our fortifications around Baghdad International Airport, like Camp Liberty, Camp Victory, and Camp Striker. The airport was already heavily fortified before Judgement Day hit.

But rationing only prolonged the inevitable.

We started foraging for supplies, fuel being near the top of the list.

45

We siphoned fuel from abandoned vehicles. We ran missions along Route Cobra to the Al-Dawrah refinery. We tried fortifying the refinery same as the airport, but enemy resistance was stiff, for they needed the same resources to wage war.

* * *

A cloud of fire and dirt consumes the lead Stryker. The blast lifts the Stryker off the ground like a launched rocket. I feel the heat wave wash over me, the percussion like the hand of God smacking me in the face, and I feel more alive than I've ever felt before. The Stryker crashes back down in a heap of fiery twisted metal. It flips over in mid-air and lands on its side like a thunderous comet impacting the earth. A couple of joes spill from the burning wreckage, lit up like human torches.

I see the trigger man haul ass from behind some bushes. The joes almost make it over to him, then collapse. I listen for their screams, but can't hear any. He runs to a grove of date palms. Small arms fire and rocket propelled grenades pelt the convoy. The other Strykers race to get out of the kill zone, the remote .50 cals unloading on the date palm groves at their attackers, shredding through trees and flesh alike. Another rocket sizzles through the air and strikes the third Stryker, but it weathers the blast and keeps going.

"You think they felt that?" I shout down into the Stryker, and the gunner yells back, "Fire your fucking weapon!"

I answer back with my rifle. I take my time, selecting my shots. I'm not afraid. I clip one in the head. The upper left half above the eye rips away, and he drops to the ground. The sensation of heat and percussion have passed, and I feel numb again. I watch for a second to see if he gets back up. Sometimes it takes them a few seconds to come around.

* * *

I remember before the news channels went static, I had walked into the tactical operations center and caught a glimpse of one of the t.v. screens showing a live CNN news feed. The news camera was angled toward a dark, stormy sky, the black clouds parted, the sky opened up, and the hand of God reached down from the heavens. Then a Sergeant spotted me and shoved me out of the room. But that was how it happened, hard and fast. The hand of God reached down from the heavens and swept it all away.

46

All the units and all the soldiers in Iraq found themselves cut off from home, of ever returning. Same thing for the joes in Afghanistan. In the aftermath, some people lived, some people died. The hand of God decided each person's fate. It marked the start of a new kind of war with a new kind of enemy. The movies had it all wrong. They're the same as living people, only dead, as smart and as cunning. They rot until they can't function any longer; even then, they linger on.

The soul stays trapped, until final Judgement, maybe forever, I don't know. I stopped searching for an explanation and understanding a long time ago and now I just don't give a shit. That's what started the war. All those dead people, thinking, reasoning, talking, walking, yet incapable of feeling pleasure or pain, knowing their souls were trapped in cadavers slowly rotting cell by cell, piece by piece, and damned to stay with the bodies, maybe for all time. So faced with that grim prospect, they decided the rest of the living world should share their fate. They figured fuck it, why not, they would tear down the whole shithouse with them, fuck the world, tear out its eyes, rape it in the ass and everyone in it.

After Judgement Day hit, one of the joes, Private Rodrigues, had pulled me aside one time and said, "It's like a kid who builds a magnificent sandcastle – spends hours, even days, building the goddamned thing – then gets pissed when he can't keep the tide from corroding the sand."

Uh-huh I said and kept walking.

We used to count the days, Judge Day plus one, Judge Day plus six, same as our grandfathers and great grandfathers counted the days following D-Day when they stormed Omaha and Juno and Gold Beach all those decades ago. Then the days bled into weeks, and the weeks into months, the months into years, and we accepted our fate, counting the years instead.

God reached out from heaven, collapsed the castle. Like a test that turned into a cruel joke.

*   *   *

The Strykers reach the gates. Cement watch towers set to each side, connected to a line of giant cement T-walls reinforced with Hesco Barriers that encircle the entire perimeter. Tower guards look down at us from their . 50 cal gun turrets. They wear helmets and their faces are covered with goggles and black face masks. The walls are cracked, pockmarked by shrapnel and gunfire, splashed with blood stains and dried flesh in places.

47

Fully intact skeletons sit upright at points along the wall, and look like they're napping. Some of the heads turn in our direction.

At the base of the left tower sets a pile of discarded bodies nearly rotted down to bare bone. Some of them still have enough meat to twitch a little, but one of them has managed to pull free, and drags itself along the wall.

I wonder what's happened.

The gates open, groaning with age. Rust shakes loose along with dust and grime. I taste it, bitter and gritty, and wonder if it's my imagination. The Strykers pass through, until the last of the convoy is inside. The gates creak closed behind us.

The Strykers stop, lower ramps, and soldiers clamor out. They begin unloading fuel drums. I yell up at the tower. A guard appears from inside, shrugs his shoulders, like saying what the fuck do you want.

"When was the new addition added to the pile?" I shout up.

"Yesterday."

"What happened?"

"Mission ineffective."

Jesus Christ I mutter and shake my head. I keep walking. I wish I had a cigarette. I want to feel the smoke burn my lungs. Or a shot of whiskey, of anything, to feel the liquid burn my tongue and throat as it slides down. I try to remember the last time I tasted a drop of liquor or felt cigarette smoke burn my lungs. It's been a long time.

One of the Sergeants catches me drifting and yells at me to help unload the fuel. I snap to attention, run over, and help. When we're done, I feel more drained than before, like I've lost a little piece of myself in the effort.

By time we finish, the day is nearly over. I sit down, leaning against a fuel drum. I watch the sun sink below the horizon. I stare at the sun – a vibrant orange blob of raw energy, magnificent and potent. The glory of God's handiwork. I bask in its brilliance and I am in awe. I do not blink.

The other soldiers lumber off to their sleeping tents, I don't know why. They leave me to my euphoria. The sun disappears, there is a moment of twilight, and the day is consumed into night.

I remember the last thing I tell my family before I deploy. I had a picture of them once: my beautiful wife, Liz, stands behind my daughters, Jessica and Laura. The light catches Liz's blonde hair just right, forming a soft glow around her head like a halo. Jessica wears her cute Orphan Annie outfit, and Laura, her red hair and freckled face stand out vivid and alive. One day, I was out on a mission along Route Cobra, we came under heavy enemy fire, and a rocket exploded next to me. The force threw me into a palm tree and my uniform caught fire. I rolled around in the sand until the fire smothered, but the picture burned to a crisp. I keep other pictures of my family stored on my laptop, but personal computers aren't considered mission essential, and the laptop battery has long since died. *Daddy loves you, daddy will see you soon.* The last thing I tell them is a lie. God made a liar out of me. Sometimes I blame God the same as the other joes, but each time, in my heart, I know it isn't God's fault.

I hear the howl of the wind, feel the sand blow against my face, and I'm grateful. I stand and try to taste the sand, but I can't. I head toward the tents. I walk past a row of tents and the stench is unbearable. I nearly trip over a body and realize it's Rodrigues sitting upright against a tent. He wears a gas mask and full army issue chemical suit. I forget he's been sitting there for days. Hundreds of flies crawl across the suit, taking up permanent residence.

"Watch where you're going," he says.

I smile.

"You're smelling ripe, señor. You know, you lose a quart or more of water per hour when fully suited. Just so you know."

"You're a genuine fucking comedian. It'll be your time soon enough."

I step over him, inside the tent. My smile fades away. Inside the tent is pitch dark and it reeks of decay. I wish my smell had gone first instead of my taste. Someone coughs. A couple more joes move around on their cots. I lay down on my cot. All we have are our thoughts and memories to pass the night. It's all we have left. My memories of my wife and daughters take me away from here, to another, distant place, moments in time, of the past. They offer me solace. I do not sleep. We lay there, waiting for the dawn, and the next mission along Route Cobra, and the next mission, and the next, and the next...

LEECH

By Travis Gates

Stanley huddled in the dark corner, relying on his coat to keep him warm. Ahead of him, at the mouth of the alleyway, he could see her.

She pranced one way, then shimmied the other. Her short skirt was tight over her fishnets, her red halter barely covering her fake breasts. In contrast to her body, her face was very plain.

Sad.

Hurt.

Abused.

Stanley smiled, revealing the rough gums where his teeth used to be. He'd lost them countless years ago. It had been decades since he'd mourned their passing. It was just the way things went. When your diet consists of only fresh blood, there's bound to be a calcium deficiency and the teeth are always the first to go. His skin, papery, yellow and thin, likewise showed its starvation of vitamins. He no longer had any hair on his body. His fingernails were long, sharp and the color of nicotine. His eyes, milky white now, would soon be flooded with the pink of fresh, hot blood.

Vampire.

He always laughed when he thought of himself that way, but the word was the closest approximation of what he was. Curiously, he didn't think of vampirism as being a new species, rather it was a sickness. The Sickness.

And the Sickness kept him alive.

He'd rejected the moniker when he'd first discovered that the Sickness had taken hold of his body. He craved blood. Sunlight hurt his skin and eyes. He slept during the day and was horribly energetic during the nighttime. After he'd finally accepted what he was, what the Sickness had made him, he'd embraced it.

Now he moved from town to town, feeding on the derelict, the forgotten and the forlorn. He only killed them about half the time. He never transmitted the Sickness, even when he'd tried. As far as he knew, he was alone.

One of a kind.

The hooker continued to move back and forth, vainly trying to keep warm. The snow would fall on her exposed skin, melting and releasing just the tiniest wisp of steam. Stanley smiled as the same icy flakes fell on his skin and stayed there. No steam. No melting.

If he was still long enough, the snow would envelop him and he would just become part of the scenery. The old cardboard boxes to his right wilted and sagged in the thickening snow. Even they, inanimate dead, could feel the chill. But not Stanley. For over a century, he could only find one identifiable feeling inside himself.

Desire.

He stood, shedding the old coat he had covered himself with. A powdery dusting of snow, released from the rotten threads, puffed and roiled and then settled. Stanley was still for a moment, as he always was before the kill. His eyes were upturned to the sky, his long scarred arms outstretched in a vile caricature of the crucifixion.

Gingerly, he ran his jagged nails up and down the exposed skin of his arms. He mused that his story was one of pain, written in rough Braille upon his lifeless flesh. Here, the remnants of barbed wire digging deep into his muscle. It was his only souvenir from the first great war. There the swirled melted memories of a fire in Minsk, the result of a feeding gone horribly wrong. He always healed, no matter how bad the injury, but the scars stayed with him.

Teasing him.

Pointing out snippets of his life best left forgotten.

The round indentation of a bullet, a gift from a policeman in Chicago, 1924. The still pink collar of a Missouri noose around his neck, 1873. The whispers of an arrow across his ribs, Germany so long ago.

Pain was the context in which all was remembered. Stanley felt that he wasn't much different from anyone else in that respect.

If he didn't carry the footprints of these events, he would never think of them again. They were like memories that belonged to someone else. All that mattered to him was now.

Now.

To better hide the misshapen, deformed ears that flanked his face, he pulled the toboggan down further on his bald head. He walked forward, gliding on the snow as if he were skating. Careful not to alarm the girl, he tried to keep his movements slight and silent.

Once outside the alley, Stanley shoved his hands into the pockets of his jeans and began walking East. The whore turned around, seeing him.

"Are you lonely tonight, honey?" she asked as she took a long pull

51

on the incredibly thin cigarette held between her fingers.

Stanley stopped and turned, letting his eyes meet hers. This was the moment where it could all go wrong.

Often, his food looked upon him with disgust. Some fight or flight instinct kicked in, revulsion registered on their faces, and they turned and walked away. But sometimes, thankfully, the victim in question would seem to be mesmerized by his face. Perhaps it was a genetic defect, some evolutionary principle that ensured complacent victims would always be around to feed the Sickness. Some people just came willingly into death's parlor.

Stanley didn't think on it. He'd learned long ago that road was paved with madness. Whatever the reason for it, he could see that this girl was his. He could play with her as he saw fit.

Stanley smiled.

"Actually, I am." He'd never been able to drop his thick Russian accent. On good days, he felt it made him more approachable. "Are you looking for company?"

The girl approached him, accentuating her ample hips by swaying this way and that. If he were a lesser man, Stanley might have been hypnotized.

The Sickness, however, made that a moot point.

"Two hundred for a fuck. One for a suck." Stanley marveled at how she became all business in a snap. He pulled a folded wad of bills from his pocket. He counted out four and handed them to her.

"Four hundred, my dear. Consider it a tip. We do it in the alleyway, yes?" He saw her eyes widen at the sight of the money and smiled to himself. It was almost as if she didn't see the carnivorous face hovering above his collar, ready to suck the life from her warm, fresh heart.

"Deal," she said. Her eyes narrowed. Trying to look sexier, Stanley guessed. It didn't work. There's just nothing sexy about a hamburger.

She grabbed Stanley by the arm, leading him back into the alley, wrapping his hand around her middle. Stanley put his other hand on the small of her back, rubbing her skin through the thin fabric of her second-hand top. He hoped the gesture came across as alluring. Truth be told, he hadn't been inside a woman since before the American Revolution.

Not that he'd chosen it that way. But the Sickness had just rendered all sex irrelevant. No erections. No wet dreams. His cock was used for nothing more than taking a cold bloody piss in the snow. But she

52

wouldn't know that.

Stanley never let it get that far.

She led him to the same corner where he'd watched her, only minutes before. Letting go of his hand, she pulled down her old black thong. She kept her back to him.

We do it from behind. It's easier that way when standing up." She dug in her jacket pocket, pulling out a generic condom and handing it over her shoulder. Stanley took it and let it fall to the snowy pavement.

He reached around, his hand probing for her crotch. He found it through the warmth it radiated. His fingers massaged the mound of coarse hair for a moment before he slipped first one, then two fingers inside. The girl reached back, moaning, and pulled Stanley's head into the back of her neck.

This was it. This is what the Sickness lived for.

"Baby," she cooed. "You know how to get me going."

With his free hand, Stanley grabbed a gentle handful of her strawberry blonde hair and pulled back, exposing the pale pulsing flesh of her neck. His mouth filled with thick saliva. His hand inside her worked even more furiously. The girl bucked and gyrated under his touch.

When he felt her heart racing even faster, he licked his lips and opened his toothless mouth.

"Now, baby," the whore panted. "I want you inside me."

Stanley planted his lips onto the side of her neck and let the wetness from his mouth do its work. He'd never figured out just how it functioned, but something in his saliva both corroded the skin of the victim and kept them in a drugged state. Again, he guessed that it was just evolution working its magic.

Once the round patch of skin was thin enough, he felt her blood pulsing through the tiny fissures into his mouth. He sucked harder, feeling alive for the first time since his last feeding. The warmth washed over him, even as her thick secretions dripped onto his penetrating fingers. He rubbed her clitoris between his thumb and forefinger, and the flow of blood quickened. It filled his mouth and flowed freely down his throat.

Her orgasm continued, helping her heart pump her life into him. His vision clouded, going from a bleached, milky scene into a sharp, contrasted red.

The girl's limbs sagged, her knees quivering and Stanley laid her gently in the soft snow. He felt stronger than before, his belly sluggish with her already clotting blood.

Stanley licked her feminine taste from his fingers and retrieved his coat. As he slipped into the thick soggy jacket, he looked once more at the girl.

Now, as always, he went off in search of a safe place to sleep. He didn't dream when he rested.

The Sickness had taken that from him long, long ago.

THE VICTIM

By Jason D. Brawn

Lucinda stared, shocked, into a crowd of rockers, Goths, emos, metalheads, rock chicks and poseurs inside a dingy London nightspot called 'Pandemonium'.

The revellers were rocking their heads and dancing crazily to the screaming guitar riffs and yells of doom metal band 'The Fallen'. Many kept crashing themselves against the barricades, before the stage, known as the mosh pit.

But not Lucinda. A twenty-something goth, with dark hair and pale skin, she could clearly see what was scaring her to death. Her stalker!

The dark, shadowy figure stood across the dance-floor, standing close to the large booming speakers. The clubbers failed to notice his Victorian appearance, a long black cape, suited for his tall frame and a matching top hat.

Lucinda knew very well he had come for her. Now that he had found her, there was no turning back.

Then as a few clubbers danced past the figure, he was gone.

Instead of collecting empty glasses, she immediately rammed herself through the crowd, in search of her bogeyman, as various faces met hers. Some frantic. Some happy. And some scary. But she became more and more determined to find him, as he was nowhere to be seen. Fed up of running and hiding, she felt ready to confront her personal demon.

Her eyes darted everywhere in desperation, but it was no use.

The crowds got more merry and excited when another band stepped on.

"We need some help over here!" yelled fellow bar-worker, Dave, who was fighting to serve a crowd of thirsty punters.

Lucinda spun around and around, more eager to find him, then:

A gloved hand fell on her shoulder, causing her to flinch strongly. She straight away fisted the face of a concerned bouncer. The impact cracked open the bridge of his nose, letting out masses of blood. Her victim screamed in pain, wincing and squeezing his wound.

Stunned witnesses encircled Lucinda, staring into her eyes like she was some kind of a psycho. Then she became more and more hysterical, yelling:

"Where the fuck are you?"

That was when she lost consciousness.

An hour had passed since the incident. Lucinda was in the manager's grotty office, adorned by second-hand office furniture and framed photographs of her boss, posing happily with metal acts. She sat on a torn brown leather sofa, gripping a cup of cold coffee. She was still nervous, now that she had brought some attention to herself. Her eyes were narrowed to a sole painting of Fuseli's 'The Nightmare'. The image had always caught her eye on every visit. More alternative music echoed outside.

The door flew open. Lucinda's head jerked fearfully, seeing her boss' entry. Quarry was his name. A flash-looking man in his late forties, young-looking and always looking slick in his black suit. He violently slammed the door and paced to his desk. There she watched him pull open the desk drawer and take out a cigar box. He lit a cigar and began to inhale hard, while leaning in front of his desk, looking slyly at her.

"Are you ready to talk now?" His voice was soft and seductive.

Lucinda didn't respond. That was her answer.

"You don't just scream out in the middle of the night for no reason." He was still looking for a rational explanation. "Was it boyfriend trouble?"

Lucinda's eyes were still on the painting.

"Talk to me!" demanded Quarry, as he slammed the desk.

"There's nothing you or anyone can do about this!" she shouted back, insisting he leaves her alone.

Quarry sniggered at her comment and rushed to her to lift her chin, ready to slap her. "Look here, you little bitch." Lucinda glared into his eyes. "You better tell us what's going on, or else!" he warned her.

"Or else what?" she dared him.

From that moment, he knew very well she wouldn't tell him. Suddenly, he released her chin and stormed about the room, inhaling more of his cigar.

"Why can't you tell me? You know I don't like employees bringing in their outside problems in here. Besides, I thought you were happy here."

"I didn't want this to happen, but it found me tonight." She realised what she had just said and said no more.

"You say it's an it?" enquired Quarry, who cast a puzzled look at her.

56

Lucinda refused to say more.

Quarry stood and together their eyes were locked, until:

The door opened abruptly, startling Lucinda. A bouncer stormed in, with an urgent look.

"How many times have I told you not to barge in!" shouted Quarry.

"Sorry, boss. The police are here."

Now it was Quarry's turn to be worried. He glanced at her and said, "I'll be back," before joining him. The moment the door closed, she listened further until she could no longer hear their retreating footsteps. Then she ran to the phone, on the desk, and quickly dialled an urgent number. The line kept ringing.

"Come on, answer it." She was already impatient. Then she got a message containing a female voice. Lucinda waited for the message tone, after which she said hurriedly: "Darling, it's me. Listen to what I have to say." She had no time to pause. "It's found us and we got to leave London tonight. If you get this, please meet me at the coach stop for," she scanned her watch, "half-one. Any problems, give me a shout. Love you." She slammed the phone down.

Lucinda removed the painting that revealed a safe. Then her fingers quickly rotated the combination lock, until she heard a loud click. Inside the safe were wads of cash, amounting to 10 grand, a handgun and 8 kilos of cocaine. Her hands snatched the money and gun, and threw them in a plastic carrier bag.

But there was one obstacle that stood before her - the door. Lucinda walked slowly towards the door, feeling nervous, with this dreaded feeling that the door could be locked. Once her hand twisted the doorknob, it opened.

Immediately, she raced out along the passageway, legs leaping and arms reaching for the fire exit.

The fire exit door smacked open. Lucinda charged out and continued sprinting along a deserted rear road, full of wheelie bins and black bags. Then she stopped running and paused to catch her breath. Now she was too tired to move, as she leaned against a wall.

She did this for a minute, when a crashing bang alerted her. She looked ahead, expecting the worse.

An accosting black cat arrived, calling for her.

Lucinda smirked and squatted. "Hello gorgeous," she spoke softly. The friendly cat met her, as she lifted it off the ground and tickled its belly. The lonely cat was enjoying it. This went on for a little while. By now,

Lucinda's idea of fleeing her bogeyman was postponed.

Suddenly, the cat heard something and leaped from her grip, fleeing straight for dark shadows to hide. Lucinda's sense of danger had now returned. She positioned her eyes towards the darkness ahead, hearing approaching footfalls. Slow and tender. She waited, hoping it wasn't her pursuer, until the looming dark figure reappeared.

Instantly, she ran tiredly back to the exit door. But it was locked. She kept pummelling the door and shouting:

"Open up, it's me, Lucinda!"

Still no one came to her aid, but continued to yell, as the footsteps were getting nearer.

"George! Quarry!" She refused to give up. Then her voice rose into a wild panic, "For fuck's sake, help me!"

By now she realised it was only her and it.

Lucinda looked over her shoulder to see -

The figure in a motionless stance, watching her. Like Count Dracula, his cloak covered his legs and body. A dark and menacing figure of evil.

BANG!
BANG!
BANG!

Shots rang out from her gun. She kept squeezing the trigger to fire, until the chamber was empty. But this failed to startle her tormentor. Instead it remained rooted to the same spot.

Lucinda threw the gun at him, but missed him. A bad throw. But she wasn't finished yet. There was one last thing she had to do. Something she dreaded, but it was her only protection. Lucinda opened her mouth wide and released a shrill, while yelping painfully. Then her face stretched, fangs protruding. Eyes changing colour. Back hunching, as her height was extending by many inches. But the transformation wasn't complete, when her claws grew into a monstrous size. Now she was some kind of vampiric creature she was desperate to conceal.

She brayed violently, making her more primal, and standing over 7 foot, she was monstrous and ready for the kill. Each stride was humungous, carefully watching her hunter.

But he didn't seem to be afraid. Instead, he was sullen and calm.

WRRAGGGG!!!

She leaped at him, with her claws aimed for the kill.

BAM!

Lucinda shot back from an impact of a blast, where her back smacked the wall. Then she looked in her horror to see a silver stake impaled through her heart, and her face and body splattered in blood.

Her body writhed painfully, as she only had a few minutes left. As her hands caught grip of the stake, to save herself, it burned her fingers with seeping steam.

Her murderer lowered his crossbow to watch her die slowly.

After a minute, her head dropped down, announcing her death.

Like a ghost, her killer was nowhere to be seen.

As for Lucinda, she was now back in her human guise!

MIKE PATTERSON, MURDERER

By Joleen Kuyper

Mike adjusted his wig carefully. He was very proud of it. The work was exquisite. He'd had to order it specially, it wasn't the kind of wig there was a lot of demand for. He'd been pleased to be able to order it online, anonymously. Mike hadn't liked the idea of having to explain his desired choice to some snotty, young sales assistant. A wig that covered up the fact he was completely bald by making it look like he was only experiencing the initial stages of hair loss.

It was all necessary. All part of the plan. A bald head stood out too much in a crowd. It was too plain. Invited people to examine his other features more closely. He would be the bald man, then the bald man with the big nose, with the thin lips, the thick neck. With his slightly thinning hair, he had enough of a label for people not to notice all that much else about him. A wig like those in the advertisements would also draw too much attention. He needed to be bland in order to blend. He delighted in his own deviousness.

When he was satisfied with the positioning of the wig, Mike adjusted his tie, then smiled at his reflection in the mirror. He let the smile linger for a moment before he turned and sauntered out of his apartment to go to work.

The party was not his scene. Mike was quite happy to be staff rather than a guest. He held no resentment toward the people who routinely got invited to these sorts of things, but he was also devoid of envy toward them. Plus, his black and white uniform added to his guise. No one noticed many details about the waiters, while the guests were the centre of attention.

Mike decided on his mark as he passed out canapés, following the pretty girl with the tray of champagne glasses. A middle aged man, pontificating to a group of people who appeared rather bored. He hadn't seen Mike. Hadn't actively acknowledged him, but neither had he deliberately failed to do so. Mike was simply not on his radar. Just the way Mike liked it.

Mike glanced at the man as he rounded the room again and again with fresh trays. The group around him gradually dispersed, as Mike had guessed it would. Sad and pathetic, Mike thought as he watched the man without looking directly at him. He knew he would be the same, if he hadn't done something to satisfy the urges that had gnawed at him since he was a teenager. That were ignored until he approached middle age. Or perhaps not ignored so much as suppressed. Mike had tried to stop himself acknowledging his secret desire for death. He passed for normal quite successfully, but could no longer hide the restlessness that nagged him as his hair thinned and his waist thickened.

Get a hobby, people told him. Get a Porsche, get a young girlfriend. Mike had opted for the hobby. Golf was never going to be his thing however. Nor darts. As middle age settled with the paunch around his own middle, Mike had finally accepted his need to kill.

He brought the empty trays back to the kitchen and excused himself. Having overheard snippets of conversation earlier, Mike knew his target drove a Lexus. After he left through the staff door, he stood in a dark corner with his eyes on the only Lexus in the car park.

The man left the party toward the very end. Mike was getting tired of waiting. Mostly because he wanted a cigarette. He knew he couldn't risk allowing himself one. The tiny glowing light could give him away. Someone might remember seeing it.

Mike figured he was strong enough to strangle the guy, so he had a thin rope with him, ready to slip round his neck from behind.

He had no pattern. Once again, that could have led to problems. He had no desire to be identified as a serial killer. There was no need for gimmicks. Playing games with the police. Calling cards. He didn't have a method. The issue wasn't how he killed. All that mattered was that a person who was alive at the start of the night did not enter the next day in that state.

Mike checked that no one else was around. The car park was poorly lit, and the guy looked like he'd had a couple of drinks. That wasn't an issue for Mike though. He didn't care if he was saving some kid from being knocked down by a drunk driver. Mike Patterson was not a vigilante. He was under no illusions about that. Mike Patterson was simply a murderer.

The guy didn't have a chance to scream. For all that he was a little heavier than his doctor advised him he should be, Mike was stealthy. He wrapped the cord around the man's neck and pulled. As he held it there, keeping the man pushed against his car with his knee in the small of his back, Mike again considered how pathetic his victim was. This man had not chosen to acknowledge his own darkness, to relive his insatiable urges. He

61

had chosen the car. Judging by his shirt he had also chosen golf. He wasn't particularly successful, but he wanted to pretend otherwise. Instead of acknowledging his dark desires, this man chose a dull facade. Mike was sure that everyone must consider doing the things he did. They were cowards if they failed to do them.

Mike had no specific pattern, but several of his victims were of a similar age to himself. Middle aged. Pathetic. Dull. Exactly how Mike appeared on the outside. Except underneath, Mike had chosen murder. No one else knew, but that didn't matter. Mike knew. He wasn't pathetic. He wasn't a coward. He was free.

He hung on for a few more moments as the guy stopped struggling. Once, he had nearly been caught by that. Strangling a woman with his bare hands, she had stopped struggling. Mike had relaxed his grip only for the woman's eyes to shoot open again. A blow caught him on his left cheek. She'd caught him with her ring, cut him and stunned him ever so slightly. He recovered quickly enough to finish the job, and made sure he kept the ring in case there was DNA on it. Mike had learned a valuable lesson that night. Desperate people might play dead. It's best to be sure. So Mike maintained his grip until he was absolutely certain the former Lexus driver had expired.

He had already figured out his exit strategy. The guy was a little heavier than he'd expected, but he was able to drag him to his own car. A mid range hatchback. Grey. Nothing special. Nothing that stood out. It was easy to load bodies into the boot as well.

Mike never brought bodies back to his own apartment. He disposed of them in various ways. Sometimes he allowed them to be found, like the woman who had hit him. Other times he dismembered them carefully and deposited the pieces in various locations they were unlikely to be discovered. Some classics, like the pig feed factory. The bottom of a river. In the foundations of a soon-to-be-built housing development. It made him smile when he drove past a suburban development where a body, or several parts of several bodies, were buried.

This one was going to be found. Too many disappearances was a pattern in itself. He chopped up the body in an old factory. He knew how to get around the security guard. It was a place he used quite often. It wasn't like on television. Not the only building within a hundred mile radius that was made from a particular type of material. Not the only place a particular kind of dust settled. Not easily identifiable in any way. Just an old factory like hundreds of others, abandoned and left to ruin as the globalised economy kicked off.

He took care to make the job look like it was the first time he'd done it. Appear that he didn't have the precision skills he'd acquired over the past five years. A hatchet job.

Mike wrapped the parts in thick plastic bags and tossed them into the river. Without stones. This one was going to be found. Let the police think they were dealing with an amateur.

Once they were dumped, Mike drove home. Sometimes he created an alibi for himself. Went to a strip club or a bar where no one would be positive he hadn't been there all night. That nondescript pudgy guy who was getting a bit thin on top. He didn't bother tonight. There had never been an occasion to use an alibi anyway. He was never a suspect. Precisely how Mike liked it. He didn't care about recognition. All he cared about was killing.

As he climbed into a hot bath, Mike thought about the night's kill. The memories were the only souvenirs he took from it. Anything else would have been foolish. The memories were safe inside him. They sat comfortably beside his desire to kill. The desire that had not lessened over time. The more it was sated the more intense the next bout of hunger.

Mike didn't mind. He felt no remorse. He didn't care that he killed regularly. He felt nothing except satisfied. At this moment in time, at least. Before he submerged his head in the warm, soapy water, he removed his wig and set it aside carefully. Until next time.

CACTUS FACE
By Joseph Hill

He watched television, the flicker of cartoons loud across his face. She hadn't come back. The sun had set long ago. He was a large boy for his age and the rocker squeaked under him. The long shadow of his mother's saguaro in the glow of the television loomed over him, casting the small apartment in dark.

The cactus started from a scrawny base, reaching out into grasping arms, crowning into a large head. She had bought it the same day she brought him home from the hospital. It hadn't moved from its niche in the apartment since, watching idly over him every day, remaining motionless as he went to school, staring at him, the two flowering bulbs like eyes.

The heavy scent of his mother's perfume still lingered over the apartment, a heady mix of the ocean breeze and desert flower. The cactus was 12 years old. The cone hat from the boy's last birthday still rested on its head.

He knew she was a hooker. She left as dark came, reappearing to give him a soft kiss on the cheek each morning, her makeup smeared on her face. He scrubbed the lipstick off each morning.

She hadn't come home last night. He awoke early and had spent the day in front of the television, his hands making methodical plunges into the bag of cheese puffs in front of him. He watered the cactus once. Nobody came for him. He slept that night in the chair, hands grimy with cheese puff residue, the chair rocking beneath him.

He awoke in the depth of night, his eyes blinking as they adjusted. His mother's perfume was heavy in the air. He blinked again, seeing the outline of the cactus lingering in the corner. The birthday hat was cocked back on its head, the two slowly burgeoning flowers of its eyes bright pink in the night.

He slept again, waking early in the morning as the television shifted from snow to the first wave of cartoons. He watered the cactus once, fingering the withered petals of its flower, setting the hat properly on its head.

The cops broke the door down two days later to find him sleeping beneath it, one arm draped about its base, the spines making pricks in his skin. Social Services loomed behind them, clipboard at the ready.

The boy carried the cactus out of the trailer with him, leaving the door swinging open in the wind. His mother was dead, bludgeoned to death, tossed in a dumpster. He shrugged when the cop told him, the blood from the cactus spines still trailing down his arm.

The boys at the group home hated him for his size and for his slow slouching walk. Geronimo mimicked him, following in his footsteps, catcalls of fat-ass echoing in his ears. He ignored it, trudging from school to the group home. He watered the cactus each day, the thing filling the small room he shared with no one. The birthday hat was gone. The thing had suffered with its journey here, shriveling slowly in the sunless room.

He trolled through school, his words monosyllabic, his breathing heavy, the desks empty around him, his large frame filling out the chair.

Weekends they toiled in the back lot behind the home. The old woman who ran the place yelled at them from the shade of the back porch, sipping at a glass of tea, the cigarette on her lips.

"Cut all them weeds down." The boy swung the machete, the handle small in his heavy fist. Hack and hack, the small brush fell before him. The lawn was close to bare scrub and the dust crept beneath them every time they stepped. Every weekend it was the same.

Except for this one.

"Ma'am?" Geronimo's voice cracked as they all stood expectant before the back porch.

"What, boy?" She spat once, the saliva caking in dust.

"Can I use the machete?"

"You ain't strong enough to handle the blade." She laughed once, the sound barking out across the scrub.

"Let the boy handle it like he always does." Geronimo stood in front of her, waiting.

"Go on now, get to them weeds." She spat once more, the ball of saliva bouncing before Geronimo's feet. The boy hoisted the machete and chopped in the brush. Behind him, he heard the laugh start, the boys circling Geronimo, swirling about him, taunts dancing about his head. The woman smoked on the porch, sipping at her tea. Through it all, as he watched, he saw the eyes of Geronimo on him, watching him swing the machete over and over.

He didn't hear the squelch of the blade into flesh until he was in the room. Geronimo stood with the machete, the cactus in pieces around him, the bulbous head with its dead flowers of eyes tossed in a corner, the arms

65

shredded into spiky flesh. He heard another squelch as a soft cackle crept out of the small boy, the machete ripping deep into the flesh as the cactus bleed in a rush of water.

"Funny, isn't it? Makes you laugh don't it?" The boy whispered. His voice was small over the deep cuts and chops of the blade. He made one last deep gash in the flesh of the trunk and dropped the machete. It clattered to the floor, echoing in the sudden silence. He pulled out the quick of a switchblade and brandished it once at him. The movement was fast and elegant, the knife small and quick as it sliced into his face. The blood welled and he tasted it. It tasted of nothing.

Geronimo skated out of the room, the door slamming behind him, his feet pattering in the halls as he ran. The boy sat on the bed, staring at the broken body of the cactus, the trunk standing like an accusatory finger, the scent of his mother's perfume heavy in the air. Water was thick on the floor, still pulsing out of the gasping trunk. He breathed once, the breathe gasping deep within him.

His mother. She was long dead. He remembered the three of them sitting at the table each birthday.

"Brothers." She said, putting a piece of cake in front of him and the cactus.

"Take care of each other." She said, the cactus small as he was, a young boy of seven.

He remembered his most recent birthday, the both of them casting long shadows over the table.

"Brothers." She said, again, sliding a heavy piece of cake in front on them.

"Billy and Cactus. Born on the same day."

"Take care of each other." She gave him a quick kiss with her smothery lips, the cactus a simple pour of water. He had nodded then.

Cactus was dying as he watched the last pulse of the water bleed out of it. He stood, his hand reaching deep into the shrinking trunk. He cupped the last remaining water and drank.

That night he lay awake, the floor slick with water, the taste of the cactus still in his mouth, the smell of its life still heavy in the air. He stood in the night. A breeze softly blew in the windowless room. His mother's voice trailed through the air.

"Brothers." She said. In the corner, he found the head of the cactus. He pulled the flowers out. His wound on his face cracked as he moved and blood welled again, dripping down his face. It tasted of nothing.

He picked up the machete, still wet with the blood of his brother. It felt warm in his hand.

The head was heavy and dense. With the machete, he gouged out a hole. The blood from his wound dripped into the empty head and mingled with the last remaining droplets of water. He put it on, tasting himself and his brother. It tasted of the desert air and the breeze. It tasted of his mother. He hefted the machete again and raised his hand to his new face, feeling the spines pulse and press against his fingers as he breathed. He walked into the dark, the far edges of his vision clouded by his new face. He felt along the wall, the machete trailing along beside him, cutting the night in slow deep swathes as he used it as his guide. He stumbled once and stopped. Breathing deeply, he felt the cactus conform to the sweat of his face, sucking gently at him, tightening around him. His eyes cleared and he saw the dark. He breathed in the air, tasting it for the first time.

"Brothers." The wind trailed once more as he opened the door to Geronimo's room. "Brothers." He heard as the blade sliced down into the mattress, blood splattering over his new face, jolting out of the warm body, shrouding the room in redness. He chopped again and again, draping himself in the blood of his victim. He smiled once under his new face, the gesture lost under the cactus. He smiled again as he severed the head. He hoisted it to his face, staring at the already dulling eyes. He saw the barest traces of his eyes under the mask as it pulsed in time with his breath, sucking in the night air to his skin. He dropped the head.

"Cactus Face." He said to himself.

"Cactus Face." He said, pushing open the door of the group home.

"Cactus Face." He said once more, feeling the glow of the moon upon him. He walked into the night, trailing down a long dark road that led out of town.

He knew then his place was out here, among the spiny thorns of the saguaro and the whispers of the desert wind. He walked, trailing into the desert, days passing in the cool balm of the night into the hot penance of the day.

A LITTLE BIT OF HEAVEN

By Aaron J. French

Two-thirty in the morning.

Carol opened her eyes to darkness. And a sound—a scratching in the walls. She lay there paralyzed, pulling her mind to consciousness. She listened to the faint scrapes and screeches, the weird tappings up and down the boards. The voices, faint whispering of female sounds, sensuous in nature.

The couple next door—gosh what are their names—Sandy and Jim or something. Freaky art couple. Probably having a threesome.

Wouldn't be the first time Carol heard her neighbors in 2B having sex. They were young, radical, always dyeing their hair and wearing second-hand clothes, listening to whiney, discordant music, and fucking like bunny rabbits.

And yes, Carol, thirty-nine year old divorcee, was jealous of them.

She rolled onto her side, pulling the pillow over her head. She closed her eyes and tried to ignore the thuds and cries. At first she thought she'd succeeded. But once her mind fell silent, the noises returned.

Just don't think about it, she told herself. It's only sex. Nothing to get bent out of shape over. You do not have to listen, because you know what that leads to—to feeling miserable and worthless and hopeless because it's been three years since you got laid.

She'd listened to them having sex before. Had even pressed her ear to the wall, but in the end she just felt sorry for herself.

You don't have to do that this time. You can just go back to bed. You gotta be up in four hours for work, anyway.

Yet some bizarre compulsion goaded her out of bed. She stood in the darkness, the only light a moonbeam pressing through the drapes. It was cold: even this close to winter she insisted on sleeping in panties.

That scraping—which she assumed was the headboard banging up against the wall—had escalated. She moved closer, pressing her naked body to it; the cold surface touched her nipples, stiffening them. She put her ear to the wall and listened.

Moaning. Shuffling. Harsh breathing. Gasps. Carol felt her skin start to tingle, felt that old familiar warmth between her legs. She slid a hand down her panties.

Then she noticed something peculiar. Not one female voice; two. And without the usual grunts of male accompaniment.

On other occasions when she found herself listening, the male— Jim or whatever—had been present. But this time it was two females distinctly, doing God knew what to each other.

Carol felt a syrupy sadness begin to flow through her veins. Started at the feet, moved up her legs.

Why should they have all the fun? What was it about her that kept her single? A failure, not only in love, but in sex too? Goddam it, she wanted intimacy.

Go, a voice whispered. Ask them if you can join.

She almost laughed out loud. She was no lesbian. That one time in college, but that was her and her friend getting laid by the same guy, at the same time, in the same bed. And the other girl never touched her.

Go, the voice insisted. You know you want to. Don't stand there like a coward playing with yourself. Go get some action.

But what if it's just the two women?

The voice didn't answer.

Before she knew what she was doing she slipped into a shawl and crept out her front door into the hallway. Darkness, quietness, and a thin line of light-bulbs stretching away to either end. Nobody around, thank God. She padded to the adjacent door: 2B. It seemed non-threatening, but in reality there was something of ecstasy, of abandon, something society wanted kept behind that closed door, awaiting her on the opposite side.

Should I knock? No. Either they won't answer or I'll disturb their love and then none of this will happen.

Suddenly the loud clatter—so loud it seemed to shake the building —of someone coming up the hall! Whoever it was would see her wearing nothing but a shawl and panties.

Panicked, she tried the doorknob of apartment 2B, found it unlocked, and slipped inside.

Now entering the foyer, beyond which lay the living room with two leather sofas and the flat-screen TV, on but muted, its iridescent images providing the only light in the room.

Carol was frozen in place, unable to move forward or backward.

I could wait. Yes, wait for that person in the hall to pass, then go back to my apartment and forget this ever happened.

Why? inquired the voice. The action is not twenty feet ahead of you. Don't you want it?

A pleasure filled moan echoed through the apartment; she craned her neck, strained her ears. Rustling and bumping from the other room.

Then the great moans of pleasure, larger than life. She was used to hearing them through layers of plaster and wood, so at this vicinity they sounded almost too real, like her fantasies were becoming reality.

She moved down the hall. Closer she got, more noises she picked up. Fleshy sounds like slaps and jiggles, also wet slurping noises. Through the kitchen—down another hall—and there she was standing in front of the bedroom, door hanging loosely ajar.

A crisp blue light streamed out of the doorway, painted the walls with an underwater hue. Looked to Carol like a black light.

She listened. Wet sounds—munching sounds—and the sexual intake of breath; shudders, howls. She was so turned on now that she almost started playing with herself in the hall.

But why do that? Everything you want is through that door. All you gotta do is work up the nerve to go in.

No, I can't do it.

Why not?

She had no reason. Some idea that she was a perfectly good girl who never did anything wrong. Perfect girls didn't sneak into strangers' apartments to have sex—especially gay sex.

But Carol was unable to quell the passions writhing in her soul. And at length she pushed open the door and crept into the bedroom.

Suddenly everything was different. Something akin to a black light was hanging in a wire harness from the ceiling. Swung slightly, its motion enhancing the underwater effect.

Everything was a blur. She remembered reading in some magazine that the mind has the ability to block traumatic events, incomprehensible images, and ideas that one might not want to look at. It can shut itself off, make it so these things don't seem real.

Something like that was happening to Carol as she stood in the bedroom with the swaying black light. She felt dazed, light-headed, similar to the grogginess she experienced upon waking.

The ordinary room—that at least she could see. The armoire with the glass mirror above, the dressers, the paintings on the walls, the crystal lamp on the night stand, even the alarm clock with glowing numbers: three-thirty.

However the scene taking place on the bed was more vague. At

70

first it was all just blurry, a jumble of shapes and outlines, nothing solid, nothing coherent. Only hallucinatory movement, and abstract imagery. But the more she focused, the clearer it became.

Lumps, mounds, jutting appendages, long running metal things attached to the ceiling, an array of items (cutlery?) laid across the bed.

She blinked twice and noticed a figure standing in the corner draped in red, like a monk's habit, hands clasped in sleeves, rope round the waist, cowl shielding his facial features. He stood motionless, and for a moment she thought she was imagining him.

However, once her vision adjusted to the lighting, he appeared more tangible. She could tell by his physique that he was male: firm chest, broad shoulders, bow-legged stance. He merely stood in the shadows, quietly observing.

Her attention shifted to the bed. Some bizarre contraption hung above it, attached to the ceiling, like a swing or a hammock—no nothing like that. Now she made out another figure, also male, this one nude, somehow strapped into the swing. Hooks, like huge fish-hooks, clung to his flesh, holding him up, pulling skin away from bones. The effect made his skin appear fake, so he resembled a latex Halloween costume.

Despite being pinned and mounted like a butterfly in a bug collection, he hung in mid-air, arms and legs splayed, a black leather mask covered his face.

Two women were kneeling below him. They too were nude, both young and voluptuous, one a red head, the other a blonde. These were the ones making the sex noises Carol had heard. Pawing at each other, at the man too, their arms moving rapidly. What exactly they were doing, Carol couldn't tell.

Are they hand-jobbing him? a blow-job? are they massaging each other's nipples? are they fondling each other's breasts?—what are they doing?

Then she saw red, and a dark blackness covering their hands and the man's stomach. She supposed it was due to the lighting, but the more she studied it, the more it resembled something else: liquid—blood, her mind kept saying. But that was ridiculous, why would there be blood—

Suddenly one of the women grabbed something from off the bed. Shiny, metal; it glinted as she rose it over her head and brought it down— (God, is it a knife, could that be, it really looks like a knife). She plunged it into the man's abdominal, causing him to thrash violently. Arcs of dark liquid shot across the room.

71

"OH CHRIST!" Carol exclaimed. And in her mind: That is a knife, they're all knives on the mattress, and oh my God they're stabbing him, they're—

The women turned toward her. Their faces melted into masks of hatred. They picked up more knives, but instead of coming at Carol, they continued to stab the man—over and over—his whole body jerking, his blood splashing forth in waves.

And they were laughing—mad, hellish laughter—demon banshees out of Hell—stabbing and thrusting and jabbing—carving skin from the man's stomach and thighs. The hooks dug into his skin; the chains that held him rattled; his breathing grew fast and labored.

Carol was flooded with terror. Move, bitch, move! she screamed at herself. But nothing got her going. Instead she was like a motionless zombie, a deer caught in the headlights.

Meanwhile, the two women on the bed had dropped their knives and were kissing each other. They must've seen me, Carol thought. And indeed they had, but for some odd reason they weren't acknowledging her. They acted like she was invisible, like she was nothing, a fly on the wall, inconsequential, not even worthy of their time.

I have to get out of here. For Christ's sake, I just witnessed a murder! And the killers are too crazy even to notice that I witnessed! Now, if only I can exit as stealthily as I entered . . .

She assumed control over her legs and was able to retreat a few paces. She was about to run for it when she heard a loud bang. Wheeling, she found the door had been slammed shut; she tried the handle, but it was locked. Who or what had caused it to close was uncertain. There was nobody else in the room.

Someone out in the hall, that Jim guy maybe, or is Jim the one hacked to death up in that swing, or is he the one in the corner wearing the robe? One of those women is definitely Sandy; I can recognize her red hair
—

"Glad you could join us Carol from 2A," remarked a female voice.

She turned and the redhead—Sandy—had crawled to the edge of the bed and was staring at Carol on her hands and knees. Behind her, the other girl was sawing into the man's stomach with a carving knife.

"Sandy, I..." but she could manage nothing else, and it suddenly occurred to her that she was in serious trouble.

"Shhh it's okay, I know why you came." Sandy cupped her left breast and began massaging the nipple. "I know you listen at the wall when

72

Jim and I fuck"—she jerked a thumb over her shoulder—"I know you wish you were getting fucked too."

Carol's fear was augmented by embarrassment as Sandy dragged her secret into the open. She had no choice now but to take responsibility. "So what if I listen?" she said; "you two never had the decency to be quiet."

Sandy burst out laughing. "Well you won't have to worry about it anymore, because Jim is currently having the last sexual experience of his life."

"You're killing him?"

She shrugged. "Your point being? What if I told you this was his idea? That he desired it?"

"I'd say you were full of shit—a lunatic."

"I can't argue with that last part. But it's true. Jim tried everything sexually imaginable, and the only thing that remained was death. Because the orgasm is like a death. Did you know that? I'll bet you didn't. In France they call it "The Little Death," because the human body goes into partial rigor mortis during orgasm—joints lock up, muscles stiffen. The theory is that dying must feel like the best orgasm imaginable. Hence we have Jim." She glanced back to the other woman, who had sliced and carved out Jim's stomach almost entirely, so that blood and ribbons of intestine hung loosely over his genitals.

Just then Carol felt ill, and she doubled over to vomit on the hardwood floor. Afterwards she said, "You're sick, all of you are sick, and I'm calling the police."

She tried the door again but still found it locked, so she kicked at the base, even threw her shoulder into it. "Let me the fuck out!" she demanded.

"Why should we do that?" Sandy inquired playfully.

The other woman had ceased her furious stabbing and Jim's body had stopped jerking. By all accounts he appeared dead, and with his death came a strong smell to the air, something like mold, shit, and stale vinegar.

The blonde, who was grotesquely covered in blood, moved behind Sandy and started fingering her in the rear. Sandy closed her eyes, dropped her head back, and moaned. "We know you don't want to leave, Carol from 2A," she said. "And we know you came over here to get fucked. So let's get on with it already."

Carol tried to remain calm, to think rationally, but whichever part of her brain that was in charge of this faculty was malfunctioning. She watched in shock—as if from outside herself—as she walked to the edge of the bed and allowed Sandy to take off her clothes. In a minute she was naked.

"That a girl," Sandy cooed, running her fingertips across Carol's stomach. It had been so long since anyone—male, female, or otherwise—had touched her in this sensual way, that it felt unbelievable. Sandy's touch was electric, and with each line she traced along her skin, the wetter she got.

She sensed movement; turning, she saw the man in the red robe standing right behind her. She'd almost forgotten him. Her immediate reflex was to stop and put her clothes on, but Sandy pulled her forward into a kiss.

"Don't worry about him," she remarked.

As they kissed, Sandy placed Carol's hands onto her breasts. She began messaging them. The other woman, meanwhile, was busy at Sandy's backside, fingering, licking, and kissing.

Carol tried losing herself in the kisses, in the sweet lip-to-lip tug of war, tried to abandon her reservations and give in to the pleasure.

But when she felt a hand on the small of her back, she jumped, for the touch was cold and unexpected. She pried her mouth away to look, however Sandy jerked her back in place and bent her forward, slamming a tongue down her throat.

And so the hands—which felt oddly rough and callused—moved across Carol's skin, and gripped her hips, and spread her buttocks, and ran clawed fingertips up and down her thighs. She found herself trying to pull away, but Sandy made sure she stayed put.

"Good girl," the woman kept repeating. "That's a good girl."

She was entered with such a momentum that her eyes widened and she gulped in air. She couldn't believe how big he was—either that, or it'd been so long since she'd had anyone inside her. She bit down on her lip, disassociating herself from the pain.

"Just relax," Sandy coached her. "Let it happen—enjoy it. How long have you waited?"

The man in the rob suddenly found her g-spot, and she groaned, "Oh so long! I've waited so long for this!"

"Yes... yes." Sandy stroked Carol's face, smoothed her hair, kissed playfully at her lips, tickled her breasts. Carol closed her eyes and threw back her head—Yes, this is it, this is what I want—fuck me! She slammed her hips backward, thrusting into the man, moving up and down and grinding against him. This excited him, and he began to pump more forcefully.

She was brought closer, dragged moaning and gasping up to the apex, into the heights, of orgasm. She cried out, feeling her insides explode with wetness and warmness.

It was amazing, the most unimaginable, indescribable sensation. The man didn't stop but kept on going, drawing out the orgasm, making it deep and lasting. She could dwell in this space forever. All her problems, all her fears, worries, all seemed to melt away. She couldn't even feel her body, for she was outside of it—her consciousness thrumming and buzzing.

Her joints locked up; her muscles went stiff—I'm dying, I'm dying, I'm dying! Yes, and it feels like Heaven, like I'm being carried up to God!

But not long after her "Little Death" subsided, and she was hurtled back into her material form, she realized the man was not stopping. Nor did he seem inclined to. She felt no sign of his approaching orgasm. He just kept jabbing and jabbing. Carol imagined she was being fucked by a cold metal pole.

Christ, was he ever going to stop? Had he even felt anything? Where was he during that blissful ten seconds of Heaven she'd just experienced?

And now something else: a small, biting pain. Deep in her stomach, where the tip of his phallus seemed to be gorging into her. A gnawing feeling, a rubbing, a chaffing, and a scooping out.

She opened her eyes and found the other women staring at her. Their faces were horribly distorted, like greedy little goblins admiring their kill. "Did it happen?" Sandy asked. "Did you cum?"

"Yes," she answered, "but..."

"But what?"

She craned her neck to look behind her. Her body was rocking back and forth with such intensity that it was making her sick.

The red cowl had fallen back off his head. His skin was pale to the point of transparency, like a snowman. Black rings around his eyes. Black nostrils flat and wide—like a horse's. Bald, smooth bald, without a single hair on his head. Something else... like bone extrusions—poking up through his scalp.

What the fuck are those—horns? For the love of Christ!

He un-blinked his eyes to meet her gaze, his mouth yawning wide and darkly. His pupils were yellow and inhuman, resembling a night cat's predatory glare. He grinned at her, revealing innumerable spindly bone teeth.

"OH MY GOD!" she wailed, kicking, bucking, trying to throw him off. "WHAT IS HE? WHAT THE FUCK IS HE?"

Sandy and the other woman began laughing. "He is your Father!" Sandy exclaimed; "and he's come to make you safe!"

"NO!" she screamed. "NO! GET HIM OFF OF ME!" She fought with all that she had, but the two women overpowered her, holding her down. One of them struck her across the head and she felt the world veer off course.

She dropped her gaze and saw blood pooling around her ankles, running down her thighs. She felt the pain of her insides, the stabbing, poking, and hurting. But the beast refused to stop, slamming into her with as much intensity as ever. Again and again and again—forever.

She lifted her head and screamed at the top of her lungs, the cry reverberating throughout the apartment. And suddenly she felt it coming back, felt it rise in her again, so she grit her teeth and gripped the mattress, waiting for her moment to rise toward Heaven again.

PRESENCE
By Charlotte Gledson

The street-lamp stood like a lonely sentinel in a sea of mist. White wispy tendrils gathered around the rays like a halo, providing a haven of light. A circle of luminosity within the darkness created a boundary from the sinister loneliness that Lilly knew only all too well. She crossed the pavement towards the remaining light that was fifty yards beyond. It served as a beacon of console. The roads were quiet, far too quiet for this early in the evening. The last car had driven by ten minutes earlier. She felt isolated.

Yet she always had. She should be used to it.

She was returning from her auntie's 60th birthday party and as she had not pursued the driving lessons that she had started four months ago, she had to walk the half a mile journey home to the bungalow that she shared. Molly was away again on one of her archaeology assignments, but luckily she had let Lilly stay with her for limited rent, as they had been close friends since high school. Molly was an achiever, Lilly was a survivor.

She crossed the road, but in spite of the mist around the light serving as a nimbus of comfort, her anxiety grew nevertheless. The haze beyond grew denser. She knew that ahead of the street-light her remaining trip was going to be in complete darkness. She reached out for her mobile phone. It was buried in her pocket of her dark military jacket that she had saved up for so long, that had once adorned a top shop dummy in the high street window. As she worked hard at St. Stephen's Prep school working as a learning assistant, she had the funds to treat herself once in a while. And why not? You only life once. However she cursed herself that she hadn't prioritised her funds for driving lessons.

Light rain splattered her face. Strands of brown hair plastered her pale pixie like features. She blinked away drips of light rain, her eyes becoming moist with the precipitation. She turned to her phone and clicked a digit. A faint light glowed. This was better than nothing she thought as she shone the phone just above her head. She faintly searched through the pathetic stream of light as she turned left after the final street lamp had finally disappeared.

She walked into the darkness. Lilly managed to see through the neon sliver of murky light at a distance of fifty inches. She tugged her coat closer to her body, feeling the icy chill that filled the air. Suddenly she heard a noise that was difficult to identify. A dull padding resounded around her. She turned. Strands of soggy hair became flat above her eyes like writhing worms as the rain continued to descend upon her.

She was sure the sounds were footsteps, but the creeping mist behind her had become so thick with dense vapour, it muffled and distorted all sounds. Lilly hovered her thumb over the number nine on her phone, just in case. She knew she may be over reacting, she had always been the butt of many a joke due to her 'paranoia'.

But Lilly knew. That was the problem. She 'felt'. She felt too much. She sensed approaching happiness, pain, horror and joy. She felt she was cursed in a perverse kind of way. But lately she had been using this to her advantage. She actually could feel how others, usually strangers felt about her. If she felt they liked her, that was a huge bonus and she would happily befriend them. Occasionally though, she would sense the hostility, the annoyance of some people, so she kept a low profile. Sometimes she saw behind the fake exteriors of some people and would mould them into liking her. She was able to say the right thing if necessary, manipulate them mentally.

As the footsteps behind her grew nearer, she started to feel a strange aura. A feeling of alarm washed over her. She last had this awareness only two months ago when her Grandmother became rapidly ill. She didn't suffer long. Her death was a kind one, if that is at all possible.

As she experienced this sensation, her skin started to heat up. The warmth rose up from her chest, flooding her neck and face with a flushed prickly glow. However, the surface of her skin was covered in goose flesh. This was not from the touch of the bitter rain, but this surfaced from deep within. Lilly quickened her pace, the faint glow from the mobile phone served no practical purpose now, but she persisted to stretch it ahead of her in the desperate hope to pierce the gloom.

The footsteps quickened behind her. Lilly turned her head as she continued to walk and noticed a dark form take shape behind her. The figure walked methodically towards her.

Coming closer. With a purpose.

She stopped in her tracks; pure curiosity overwhelmed her, though her instinct was to move on. As the outline became clearer, she could now see an individual wearing a large parker coat, a hood swallowing any features that may have been visible. The figure was now quickly approaching Lilly. In a panicked desperate voice Lilly called out, "Hello?

78

Are you following me?"

She stifled a nervous laugh and as she did so, the shape abruptly stopped. So sudden was the halt, Lilly felt even more unnerved. Her body trembled briefly; her fingers grabbed her mobile phone even tighter, her legs felt solid.

Her senses began to swell with fear, her gift, her knowledge felt overpowered with danger.

The figure remained stationary. No face detectable. Silently the person stood eight meters from Lilly's questioning eyes. Only a slice of moon peeked out from the inky sky, which until now had been obscured totally by the solid cloud.

The fur round the hood served as an accentuated menace as the wind faintly ruffled the fibres, leaving a vast void of impenetrable blackness within the hood as Lilly narrowed her eyes in the hope for a glimpse of any discernable features.

Lilly held her breath, her heart accelerated to an unnatural pace, as the intimidating faceless hood glared back at her.

She stumbled backwards catching her heel on the kerb. She continued to gaze into the solitary figure that stood only metres away. Suddenly Lilly's mobile rang. The shrill ring broke the silence like a stark shriek in the night.

Hope sprung from the channels of her mind, yet the figure remained static. Turning on her heel, Lilly started to run. She ran fast. She managed a few metres. Lilly then turned and looked back at the figure once more. It was still stationary, but it was very hard to tell, as her vision was concealed by the ever increasing vapour.

Heart pulsating and mobile in hand, she finally answered the phone, her breathy voice trembling as she carried on running the long deserted road ahead of her. Lilly's footfalls were fast, urgent, she needed to feel secure and this call could be the saving of her fears.

"Hello?"

Silence returned her enquiry.

"Hello?" She repeated, feeling a renewed sense of trepidation.

She was running more rapidly now, her breath out of sync. Glancing in her wake she saw the figure diminish into the fog like a fading nightmare from a sudden awakening.

As Lilly pounded down the isolated road, the town behind her became distant and she yearned to be back in the safe folds of the street life. She again yelled, with so much urgency she was in a state of near hysteria.

"HELLO, WHO IS THIS? I NEED HELP! I AM BEING FOLLOWDED!"

A voice, faint, almost inaudible replied slowly. "Why do you run from me?"

Lilly felt her insides drop and came to a sudden halt. She turned her head tentatively to look behind. The figure was yet again upon her. She could have reached out and touched the vast blank hood gaping out at her. The figure had one hand in the pocket the other up against its hood; Lilly could see the shape holding an object within the hood.

"Who the hell are you?" Lilly screamed.

Eventually after a few heavy breaths and an eerie silence from the caller, courage now took its turn to surface. With sodden hair, chilled body, adrenalin pumping to a degree of defiance, Lilly reached for the hood to reveal her pursuer. But before her finger tips reached the fabric of the parker, she stopped suddenly.

Sliding from the hood, like a turtle's head from its shell, a face appeared from the gloomy opening.

It was a face she knew. It was a youthful face.

Beautiful and beguiling. Lips full, rich and radiant. The eyes a penetrating green, held an unnerving stare. One chestnut lock of hair hung suggestively over one eye.

Lilly felt that her legs had melted into the pavement like ice – cream. She was now facing the caller. She looked beyond the eyes, the eyes that were penetrating her soul with a will so strong, that Lilly felt hypnotised, immersed. She continued to search the gaze that held her.

Her own eyes stared back from the hood. It was her mouth that curled with an expectant grin. Her elfish face with the sallow and opaque complexion that was almost transparent against the weak moonlight.

"What? You are me?" A wavering whimper stuttered from Lilly's dry lips.

For many months, Lilly had been escaping. Running and fleeing from her visions and her nightmares. Now, an understanding descended upon her like a fragile veil of acknowledgement. As she stepped back slowly into the road she turned and faced the car that crashed into her. The sounds of the screeching brakes were the last thing she would hear, the headlights were the last thing she would see, as a mortal being. Her body flew up into the air like a plastic bag.

As it did so, so did her spirit, ascending into the darkened sky like the last fragments of an echo, watching as her body fell to the ground with a dull yet crackling thud. As the back wheels caught her thighs and crushed her feet, boots and bones crushed into mulch. Blood pooled around the shattered and broken body of Lilly Saunders. Daughter, sister, friend and teacher - Deceased.

She watched also the figure, her angel of death; disperse into the atmosphere like steam being released from an open window.

Lilly's time was up. Her psychic talent had held her in good stead but also it was the blight of her life. If only she could have saved herself from herself, but there is no escaping when the tick of life comes to its final end.

DEATH COMES IN PIECES
By Shells Walter

The city smelled of rotten corpses. Sam looked over the cliff at the dimly lit place he used to call home. Things were so different now. If only he had left with the others. If only the war hadn't struck as it did, when it did. He could've lived a different life. He sighed and walked back to his beaten-up car. The door creaked as it opened. One of the last remaining cars left and he managed to barely keep it running.

The car started with its usual sputtering. He hit the steering wheel a few times

"Let's go," Sam spoke to the unresponsive car.

A blasting noise interrupted his thoughts and he looked up out his front window.

Shards of metal floated in the air causing a new deadly wind chime. Sam ducked as the metal cut holes through the window and into his leather seat. Slowly, he raised his head. Some of the metal still hung in the air like a flapping bird. He watched as every little piece remaining dropped to the ground.

Sam looked closely at the smoke remaining from the blast. It inched up from the cliff in black clouds. He opened his door slowly and walked over to the edge. The blast had caused a car explosion, metal shards resulting from the torn up car. After the smoke fully cleared, Sam concentrated on the black silhouetted figures walking the streets below. They were back and there were more of them. He shook as he watched them take one body after another.

One might call them death. They took the bodies and ate them, spitting back any bone fragments. The figures were tall and skinny, almost too skinny to tell they were actually there. The war had brought them. Destruction, chaos, the nuclear elements that ruined this city, all of it, brought them. People feared them and most left after the war started. Sam stayed for his family.

There was still military fending off the intruders, protecting who stayed. It didn't matter though. There was nothing more to defend. Cities were destroyed, houses were as well. A business no longer in existence and food getting even less available-it was becoming the norm these days. And

82

Sam was still there in the mist of it all. The war started by the government over land rights, over stupid land rights.

Sam continued watching as the dark figures devoured corpse after corpse like vultures in a desert. After a couple years of the war, Sam had realized he was but a few who were still alive besides military troops. He wondered in the vast dissolute city now if his family was even alive.

The last puff of smoke flew by Sam and he turned to look at his car. It had gotten him through a year and a half of pounding broken up pavement and war torn areas. Right now, it looked as if the car had severed its time, forever placed in this part of history. Sam pulled at his cell phone. The long slender case unhooked with some pull from his jeans. He didn't know why he looked, but he always checked for a signal-even though he knew one would never come. After another unsuccessful and final attempt, he threw the cell phone on the ground. The cracking noise of the plastic and metal indicated the cell phone's final death.

Sam sighed and brushed his long bangs away from his sweaty forehead. His fingers dried from the heat stuck to his sweaty hair. Shaking his fingers loose, he walked back to the car, patted it on its roof and continued walking in the opposite direction of the cliff. Sam had circled this city as much as he could, but there was always once place he may not have searched.

He often wondered if the rest of the world was like this; everyone gone or dead, shaking buildings, if there were any and a feeling of pure fear due to those dark figures. The internet and television were down. There was no way for Sam to see what was happening across the water. He only thought it must be better over there. The lands now being fought over were military bases. The other civilian lands were destroyed; a combination of the nukes and those dark figures.

The government had once told everyone that things would be okay, bomb threats would never hit here. Sam wondered if the government even knew itself what it was getting into; the fighting over water barriers, over land that they didn't really want, but wanted no one else to have. The first nuke flying overhead and the first scream started the war that would destroy everything Sam knew.

He shuffled his feet through dirt and rock. The narrow path from the cliff was slowly going away-just like everything else. Sam was running out of food. He had a few nature bars that seemed to have with stood anything, but eventually all things die and the bars were no different. He figured he had a couple more days before they totally rotted away. Taking a bite into one of the bars, his teeth ached from the crunch. He took the rest of the bar and placed it in his bag that he carried for supplies.

Sam looked ahead. Many of the trees that still stood only consisted of branches on the ground and some stumps. He sighed. The walk through this area was always bleak, always so awakening to the current situation. The trees became the entrance into another part of the city that was worse than the others. Parts of bodies were laid on rocks. Stones covered any dried blood stains. No one had been through this part of the city for sometime.

He looked around at the decaying buildings, the busted up street lights and the benches that used to be for people to sit, to take in what the city had to offer. Now the city offered death.

The smells of rotting flesh. The parts those black figures had not sucked up yet were scattered in corners and holes. It was a sight Sam remembered seeing in movies, except this was life for him or death in most cases.

"Help me!" A voice cried softly. Sam turned to look at an opened man-hole in the street. He bent down to look inside.

"Hello?" Sam asked. The darkness inside the hole made it difficult for him to see anything.

"Help me, please," the voice continued.

"Where are you? I can't see you," Sam pleaded with the voice. He searched his bag for even a flashlight. He found nothing.

"I'm over here," the voice struggled to say. Sam kneeled in front of the hole.

"I don't have any light. Um, how far down are you?"

"I can barely hear you. I'm all the way down, on the floor," the voice which now sounded like a woman's spoke a little louder.

"Okay, um, I'm not sure what I can do. Um, let me see, wait a second please." Sam stood up and looked around.

A branch or anything that could serve as a connection to get the woman out of the deep man-hole. He finally came across an old pipe that was left from the destruction of building a few feet away. Sam picked it up and checked its length. He only hoped it was long enough to reach down and get the woman out. He walked over to the man-hole and bent down with the pipe in hand.

"Here, I'm going to lower this down to you. Grab a hold of it, I'm going to try and bring you up. Are you injured in any way?"

"I think my arm is broken," the woman responded.

"Okay, this will be difficult, but try and grab this with your one good arm, holding on as tight as you can, okay?" Sam took in a deep breath and lowered the pipe into the hole.

He kept lowering it until he felt resistance on the pipe.

"I got it," the woman yelled up to Sam.

He started to pull the pipe up, shoving his feet against the ground for support. The arms he used to depend on were weak, but he had to get her out. Through some grunts and groans, he managed to pull the woman up. She let go of the pipe and he helped her up.

"Thank you," the woman replied, breathing heavily.

"How did you get in there?" Sam asked, offering her some of his last remaining water. The woman took it and rapidly finished it.

After taking her last gulp, she returned it back to Sam. He nodded and placed the empty plastic bottle back into his bag.

"I was trying to get away from the blasts. A friend of mine and me were anyways."

"Well," the woman continued. "We were running away and thought we had made it past, we did with the blasts, but not the bullets. My friend was shot at and I ran past her. When I got back she was gone."

Sam knew it had to be the black figures that had taken her. The woman continued.

"After that I ran again. I didn't want to come in contact with any more firing. Of course that's when I slipped and fell in there." She pointed to the man-hole. Sam looked at the hole and nodded.

"I've been here for sometime. This area isn't safe anymore," Sam said and reached to the woman's arm to take a look. She pulled back.

"I guess you could say I'm aware of that." She sighed and looked down at her broken arm. A piece of bone stuck out of her forearm area. Sam ignored her comment.

"I'm not sure how long you were down there, but that arm looks really bad. I don't think the military doctors are even around anymore." Sam looked out into the distance.

"I figured as much. The pain has been so bad I've gotten numb to it," she replied.

"We're going to need to get out of this area. Blasts go roughly about every two hours and I would prefer not to be around when they do." Sam started to walk away from the woman.

"Wait, what about me?" She yelled as he kept walking.

"What about you?" He asked back.

"You're going to leave me here?" She pleaded with Sam.

"You're welcome to come along, but there's nothing out there. I've been around this whole city for years, nothing." Sam said turning around to look at the woman and then back to walking away from her.

"I know where there are other people," she said. Sam quickly turned again.

"You're lying," he said back to her. She walked over to him.

"Listen, on the way to this area, we ran into someone who said they were headed across the waters. They said there were other survivors. That's where my friend and I were headed before the blasts started." She waited for Sam's response.

"There's no way. People don't head to the waters. That's the front-line of the war." Sam shook his head.

"No, they said no one is at the front line anymore. There's no more fighting there." She looked at Sam and then ahead at the street.

"Even if I believed you there is at least a mile's time worth of traveling that way and we are in one of the blast zones." He scratched his head.

"Yes, but as before I'm willing to take that chance; I want my freedom to be alive back."

Sam stared at her. He knew that look. The look where there was hope. He had it once too. A little after the war when there was still people, still those that were searching. Soon afterwards they were gone, along with the city. What did come were those creatures and devastation.

"Fine, but I can't have you holding me back. I barely have enough supplies or energy for that fact to move at all," Sam said annoyed. The woman nodded.

"By the way, the name is Ester." She extended her hand from her good arm. Sam looked down at it and shook with his hand.

"Mine is Sam," he said reluctantly.

They walked together through the stones and rumble that encompassed the streets. Dirt got in between his sandals and he shook his foot. Night time had approached and the blasts would be a bit less. The military that was left, took their breaks at this time. Sam wasn't sure what they did, but sleep had to be one thing.

They walked for what seemed to be hours. Sam's legs ached in places that weren't supposed to and his feet formed blisters that hurt when he placed his foot on the street.

"So what's your story?" Ester asked. Sam grunted.

"Why?"

"Just thought we get to know each other with this walk we're doing." Ester tried to smile. The cracks on her lips from dehydration made it painful.

"Fine. I was here before the war. I'm here after the war. My family is dead as I'm concerned. I looked everywhere for them; two years in fact. I stayed, everyone else seems dead and now there's you. Enough of my story?" He turned to look at her.

"Yes, and I'm sorry." Her eyes got watery.

"For?" Sam asked.

"Your family and what you've gone through," she replied. Sam's face softened and he nodded in response.

"Let' see if we can get across the waters, okay?" Sam looked back down the road. A sparkle told him the waters were only a few feet away.

"We're almost there aren't we? I can see it in your face," Ester said. Her eyes widen. She grinned even though it hurt.

"Yes, we are there." Sam walked a bit faster to the waters.

The waters were a mile long in either direction. Across them laid the other city where Ester had said there were survivors. Ester followed Sam close. She looked at her broken arm every so often. It didn't matter to her anymore. She would be free soon.

They approached the bridge that took them across the waters to the other side. Sam looked around and realized she was right. There were no signs of military anywhere; just the guns and shells from what used to be there. Sam walked onto the bridge first. It wobbled under his weight. Ester followed next. They both walked slowly over the wooden patches of the bridge.

After a while, they reached the other side. Sam looked at the smoke filtering around him. His mouth fell open.

"I thought you said there were survivors here?" He turned to ask Ester.

"No, there were, but I took them." Ester grinned. She looked different.

"What are you?" Sam stood back. Fear drowned his eyes.

"I took you here. You're the last survivor."

"But…" Sam sputtered out.

"That's right, now I take you." She twisted around and reached out with long boney fingers. He looked at her and saw a black silhouetted figure in front of him.

He fell backwards on the ground. His hands reached up to try to

87

fight her off. Her claws dug into his legs and his vision faded to darkness.

* * *

"Sam, are you in there?" The nurse asked. The doctor standing next to her took his light and flashed it in Sam's eye.

Uh, what, what happened?" Sam said groggily.

"You've been injured," the doctor replied. "We thought we had lost you."

"I died?" Sam asked.

"Only for a few moments," the doctor said.

"Why, where am I?"

"You're at the hospital son," a military general replied.

"What?" Sam asked again.

"Son, you were hit by a blast." The general approached Sam's bedside.

"But I thought, the black figure, I was dead." Sam looked at him confused.

"We didn't find you right away. We had looked everywhere for survivors. "The general shook his head.

Sam leaned up and placed his back against the hospital pillow.

"Take it easy, not too fast now," the doctor said helping Sam.

"My legs, where are my legs!" Sam yelled.

"They got taken in the blast son. I'm so sorry," the general replied looking way from Sam.

Sam turned and looked outside the window. All he saw were flames and smoke. The war had just started.

THERE'S A LIGHT

By A.E. Churchyard

"In the velvet darkness of the blackest night,
Burning bright,
There's a guiding star,
No matter what or who you are.

There's a light
Over at the Frankenstein place
There's a light
Burning in the fireplace..."

Lisa turned the CD player off with a disgusted noise, "How can you listen to such rubbish Frankie?"

"Because it's funny Lisa. Then again you wouldn't understand that would you." I sighed and flipped the CD Changer to something a little more Lisa-ish.

"Are you saying I have no sense of humour?" Lisa grinned at me.

I shook my head, "No, I suppose I just have a weird sense of humour that most people don't understand."

Listening to James Blunt wail on about some girl being beautiful, I thought "I like this song, but Rocky seems somehow more appropriate for the drive." We weren't going far, just to Olivia's nineteenth birthday party at Hilltop Manor Hotel.

Lisa fiddled with her dress, staring out at the woods that lined the road, "Why did it have to rain? It makes everything seem so much more spooky up here."

I grinned, "I like spooky." I changed gear to cope with the steep road better.

"Like you said before, you're weird. Why on earth is Olivia having her birthday party up at Hilltop? I know she wanted to have a ball, but that place is the pits." Lisa pulled a leaflet out and grimaced, "Celtic House would have been much more the thing."

"Careful Lisa, you're showing your money prejudice again. Olivia's parents couldn't afford Celtic House." I stifled a giggle at the sneer on Lisa's face that turned to horror, as she registered what she'd said.

"Don't tell Olivia I said that! She'd be mortified. Oh, now I'm going to feel guilty all night."

"I won't tell her." I laughed.

"It's straight over the crossroads and up the hill." Lisa peered at the map on the leaflet.

I stopped at the junction, "Of course it's up the hill. Why else is it called Hilltop Manor?" Lisa made a face at me. I changed down to first and concentrated on my driving.

Just as we saw the gates of the Manor in the headlights, the car spluttered and lurched, "When I borrowed Mike's car, he said it was fine, so why…" my thought was interrupted as the engine gasped again, before coughing itself into silence. I slammed on the brakes, the car shook and there was a "Snap".

Jamming the pedal to the floor with both feet, I executed an emergency stop; it just slipped into the gap as the car rolled backwards down the hill.

"The Brakes have gone!" Lisa screamed "We're going to die! We'll smash into a lorry at the crossroads, I know it!"

I ignored her and pulled on the handbrake hard. It slowed us down a little, but then there was a second "Snap" and it became worthless as well. I resorted to trying to steer the car in reverse.

When we did hit the crossroads, I swung the car around so that it was side on to the hill and used the last of the momentum to run it into a large oak tree on the right hand side of the road. There was a hiss and a thump as the airbags activated, pushing me and Lisa into the back of our seats. I blacked out from the force of the blow.

I came to as the air-bags deflated. Dazed, I listened to the rain drumming on the roof for a moment, "You OK, Lisa?" I asked.

"A bit scared and bruised, but nothing broken. What about you?" she tried the door, "Damn, it's jammed."

"I'm OK. I think we'd better get out of here though. I ran the car head first into a tree and we can't survive the crash just to die in the resulting fireball can we?" I pulled my legs out from under the crumpled dash and scrambled over into the back seat, blessing my decision to wear a trouser suit.

"Ha-ha, very funny." Lisa pulled her long red velvet dress up, so that she could climb through the seats.

We grabbed our coats and bags, pushed the passenger door open and jumped out, dashing across the road to shelter under another oak tree.

I looked over at the car, water dripping down my face, "I'm going to kill that brother of mine; he told me the bloody car was fine!"

"I'll hold your jacket while you do it." Lisa said, putting hers on over her wet dress and pulling the hood up, "Have you got Recovery?"

"Thankfully yes." I pulled out my mobile, looking up the number, "Shit. No signal! Putting it away, I put my jacket on, grateful for the warmth that the thick leather gave me.

"I'll try mine." Lisa said. She fiddled with it for several long moments.

"Well?"

"Nothing. Maybe it's the trees around us." She put it back in her bag.

"Well the Hotel is only just up the hill. Why don't we walk up there to get help?" I zipped my leather jacket up, slung my rucksack over my shoulder.

"But it's raining! I spent all afternoon in the Salon having my hair done. I am not getting soaked to the bone after spending a hundred and thirty pounds on it." Lisa wrapped her long velvet coat around her.

I blinked "A hundred and thirty quid on your hair?"

She ignored me, "Besides, we're at a junction." Lisa tossed her head towards the road that ran around the hill, "That goes to a village so if we stay here, there's bound to be someone come along soon."

"You're hoping aren't you? I still think that going to the hotel is our best chance."

"Not unless it stops raining."

Lisa's stubborn streak was kicking in, so I humoured her, "How about this. We wait for half an hour. If no one comes along in that time or the rain stops, we go on up to the hotel." Lisa nodded, pulling her deep hood closer around her face. I sighed with relief at an argument defused and sat down on a convenient rock.

An hour later, no one had come past from any direction. The car was smoking furiously and I had an inkling that the only reason it hadn't exploded, was the rain that still fell. It felt like it was stopping so I stood up. "Lets go."

"It's not been half an hour yet." Lisa protested.

"It has by my watch and I think that if the rain stops, the car will explode. So let's get out of here before it does."

"I'm cold. I don't want to go anywhere."

91

Looking up at the sky, I tried to keep my temper. A bright spot peeked through the clouds as they began to clear away, showing a bright blue, full moon. It shone down on the junction giving it an eerie feel.

"There, it's stopped now. Lets go. You'll warm up faster if we move." I grabbed Lisa's arm and dragged her to her feet.

Lisa followed, hugging her coat in around her. As we moved into the moonlight, she looked up, "Isn't that lovely? They say that full moons are magical you know."

"Crossroads are supposed to be magical as well, so let's hope we get some good magic from both and make it up the hill in one piece." I quipped. Lisa giggled and I felt better at forcing her to move.

We moved into the centre of the crossroads as the blue moonlight brightened around us. It almost looked like a wall, the darkness beyond was so deep.

According to the map it wasn't far from the crossroads to the hotel. In fact, I could remember seeing the gates of the hotel in the headlights, "So why is this taking so long?" I thought as Lisa started rambling on about her shoes, how much they had cost and how badly they were getting ruined.

"Shut up and walk Lisa." I snapped.

Lisa stopped talking to me in a huff, so when she said, "Can you see that?" five minutes later, I almost jumped out of my skin

"What?"

"There's a light up there." Lisa pointed up hill and slightly to the left.

Unbidden, the Rocky Horror song popped back into my head and I began to sing softly, "...There's a light, Over at the Frankenstein place, There's a light, Burning in the fireplace..."

"I hope that they do have a fire burning. I'm freezing." Lisa shivered, "But it's the Hilltop Manor Hotel not Frankenstein's place."

"I know that dummy, it just reminded me of the song, that's all." I rolled my eyes.

The road petered out into a dirt track lined with remnants of gravel crunching under foot.

"You'd think that a Hotel would have sorted this out. This drive is disgraceful." Lisa complained. I nodded, concentrating on my footing, "And the outside of the Manor looks terrible!"

I was too tired to respond.

We climbed the steps of the portico over the front door and while Lisa adjusted her dress, I knocked on the door.

It swung open to reveal a tall thin man in a butler's outfit, "May I help you?"

"Um, we've had a car accident down at the crossroads and our mobiles aren't working. Is it possible that we could use your phone to call for help?" I asked, unable to keep the shiver out of my voice.

"Oh you poor dears! James, don't keep them standing out there in the cold, fetch us some hot drinks and I'll take them into the library." A woman wearing a thick woollen dress, pushed the butler aside and gestured us in.

"Very good Madame." James replied.

Behind us there was a flash of lightening. Moments later the sound of an explosion rolled over them. Turning, I saw a mushroom of flame and smoke rise through the trees, before the rain began again, harder than it had been before.

"And there goes my CD's and Mike's car." I murmured.

"At least he'll be able to collect on the insurance" Lisa patted my shoulder.

I shook my head, "I'm only third party on other cars. I'm not sure he'll get anything at all."

"Come on in girls." The woman shut the door and ushered us through into a room lined with books. There was a large open fire that warmed me almost immediately and a maid took our coats.

"Sit down, sit down. James will be back with a nice warm drink for you." The woman said.

"We're sorry to impose on you like this Miss...?" Lisa said, moving towards a large comfortable looking sofa.

"Oh, I am sorry, where are my manners?" the woman flapped almost visibly and Frankie suppressed the urge to giggle, "I am Lady Annabelle Price."

"I thought that this place was a hotel?" I muttered to Lisa.

She ignored me, "I'm Lisa De Cristani and this is my friend Francis Tyson."

"Just call me Frankie, I hate being called Francis. We really are sorry for interrupting your evening." I held out my hand to the lady, but she just smiled.

"Nonsense Child, you needed help and I am glad that I was here to give it to you." The lady said, "Please call me Anna, I haven't had visitors up here for such a long time."

There was another crash of lightening. The lights flickered for a long moment before becoming steady again.

"I do hope that wasn't the transformer. We have such a hard time with the Electricity up here." Anna said, pouring us a steaming cup each.

Lisa sipped and sighed.

"Taste good?" Anna asked, smiling.

Lisa nodded and sat down on the couch.

I smiled politely, "I'm sorry if I'm being obtuse Anna, but I was sure that Hilltop Manor was a Hotel. One of my friend's was supposed to be having her birthday party here."

"Hilltop House has never been a hotel Francis." Anna sounded rather offended and Lisa was quick to try and distract her.

"I think that Frankie might be in shock, Anna. Can I use your phone to call my mother to pick us up?"

"Oh. Of course dear, it's in the hallway. I'll show you." And Anna bustled away, with Lisa following.

Having finished my drink and almost dozed off, there was a huge crash of thunder over head. Almost immediately the lights went out and lightening brightened the room.

Putting the cup down on the tray, I found my way to the door and looked out, "Lisa? Did you get through to your mum?"

"No, the phone line went dead as soon as the power did." Lisa replied with disgust, "And my mobile is still out."

"Oh dear." Anna sighed, "James? What is the weather like out there? Any chance of you getting over to Hilltop Manor and asking them for help?"

"No Madame. The Gardener just informed me that the road has been washed out by the torrential rain." James appeared from the back of the house carrying an oil lamp.

"See? This isn't the hotel at all." Lisa hissed at me, "We must have taken a wrong turn in the dark."

I shrugged.

"I think that it would be a good idea for you girls to stay the night here and go over to the Manor with James in the morning." Anna said.

We exchanged glances, "Is the weather really that bad?" I asked the butler.

"Yes Miss, it is. The road down the hill has become a veritable river." James turned to his mistress, "Shall I have the Lilac Suite prepared, Madame?"

Anna nodded "Just the thing. Tell Marie to assist the girls in dressing for dinner." She looked at Lisa, "I'm sure that you'd like to get out of those damp clothes and have a bath."

"That would be lovely." Lisa's eyes lit up.

The water was hot and bubbly, the towels soft and fluffy and it felt just like home. Except that something still niggled, "Anna is a really nice person." I said to Lisa as we luxuriated in the warmth.

"What else do you expect from a Lady?" Lisa's face was obscured by the bubbles, but she had her 'money' voice on.

"I could have sworn that we didn't take a wrong turn." I continued, trying to work out what was bothering me, "But this isn't the hotel that Olivia said it was."

"What are you trying to say Frankie?" Lisa pushed herself out of the foam and leant on the edge of the bath.

"I don't know, there's something about this whole evening that is bothering me."

"Forget it Frankie! And don't mention it in front of the Servants. It wouldn't do for them to go running to Anna about it." Lisa closed her eyes and lay back.

I tugged at the neck of the dress that Marie had put me in. "Why do we have to wear these again?" I asked the maid.

"Madame said it was more appropriate. Your other clothes will be cleaned for you." Marie replied, "It's time to go down now."

"I'm starving. I wonder what's for dinner?" Lisa said as she left the room.

I started to follow her, but Marie held me back, "Miss, please listen." She whispered, "Don't eat the meat. Vegetables, fruit, drinks they're fine, but don't eat the meat, Miss!."

"Why?" I felt the niggle return, "What's going on?"

"I can't tell you miss! No one in this house can go against Lady Anna." Marie said before she screamed and convulsed. Her eyes bulged, then her whole body expanded and burst in a cloud of red globules that drifted into the dressing room fire, lighting like little sparks.

I took a deep breath, fighting a wave of nausea, "Frankie, m'girl there is no doubting it now. Something weird is going on around here." Still shuddering I went downstairs.

The house was blazing with lamp and candlelight. James met me at the foot of the stairs.

"This way Miss Francis, Miss Lisa and Lady Anna are in the sitting room waiting for you." he said.

"Thank you. Um, Marie seems to have disappeared." I told him, wondering what he would do.

"That happens occasionally Miss." He replied, "Do not worry, Lucille will attend you after dinner." And led me into the sitting room.

"Where did you get to Frankie?" Lisa asked, her 'money' voice even more pronounced.

"I had a problem with the laces, Marie helped me sort them out." I told her quickly.

She accepted the excuse, "Try this punch, it's gorgeous." She waved at a bowl of deep amber liquid, sat on the sideboard.

"Yes Francis, do have some punch." Lady Anna smiled and a maid quickly brought me a tiny crystal cupful of it.

"...Vegetables, fruit, drinks they're fine, but don't eat the meat..." Marie's voice echoed in my mind and the urgency in it made me think that she was telling the truth. I sipped the punch carefully. It was fruity and sweet with a faint touch of mint. "This is lovely Anna." I said.

"An old family recipe." She smiled again, mouth closed.

It hit me that I hadn't seen her show her teeth when she smiled. "Lisa hasn't been smiling properly either, maybe she broke a tooth?" I thought, then dismissed it, "Nah, she would have told me, she's not that vain."

I sat down beside Lisa, "May I ask what is for dinner?" I asked Anna, trying to seem casual.

Lisa frowned slightly at me. Anna didn't seem to hear anything odd though.

"The starter is watercress soup, followed by a roast with all the usual trimmings and a lemon mousse for desert." She replied.

I breathed a little easier, "I ought to mention that I'm Vegetarian."

"What on Earth is that?" Anna looked confused, "Some kind of new-fangled diet?"

"It means that I don't eat meat. Haven't you heard of it?"

Lisa's eyes widened and she began to open her mouth. Before she could say anything, a maid came into the room and Anna turned to look at her.

"Yes Jennifer?"

"Madame, Cook has a problem in the kitchen and would like your opinion on something." Jennifer bobbed a little curtsy.

"Very well. Please excuse me girls." Anna smiled and followed the maid.

96

"Vegetarian? Don't eat meat? What on earth are you talking about!" Lisa hissed at me.

"I am now. Look when I was upstairs Marie told me not to eat the meat. Everything else is fine, just don't eat the meat." I tried to put the same urgency that the maid had used into my voice.

"Don't eat the meat? Don't be daft Frankie! I swear that all those odd movies you watch are going to your head" Lisa twirled a finger beside her ear.

"I am not going nuts. It ties in with the way this place feels. When was the last time you had a land-line die on you in a storm?" That seemed to make her think, I followed up on my advantage.

"This place feels wrong. I don't know why, but it does. No one smiles properly and it's not every day that you have someone burst like a bubble in front of you."

"Burst like a bubble?" Lisa's eyebrows shot up into her fringe.

"Is everything all right girls?" Anna asked as she came back in.

"Oh, err, perfect. The punch really whet my appetite." I managed to answer while I waved my cup.

Lisa nodded "Everything is fine Anna."

"Good." She smiled, again without showing her teeth. I wondered if she had such bad teeth that she was ashamed of them.

"Lady Anna, Miss Francis, Miss Lisa," James appeared at the door as if he had been teleported, "Dinner is served."

The table was laid with sparkling crystal and silver cutlery that glowed in the candle light. A fire burned in the grate and warmed the whole room. The soup was lovely; well seasoned and with the bread roll, filled me up nicely. Lisa kept throwing strange looks at me and sipping at her spoon in a very dainty way, breaking her roll into tiny chunks.

"Have you been to Finishing School yet, Lisa?" Anne asked her, almost ignoring me.

"Unfortunately no. My Father and Grandfather wished me to, but Mother refused to allow it." she looked at Anna who smiled at her sympathetically.

I frowned, "Lisa's mum has never refused to allow her anything. What's going on?"

The soup bowls were taken away and the main course brought in on a wheeled trolley. The maids served the vegetables, then stood back as James uncovered the Roast.

I took one look at it and nearly screamed, "That's a human torso!"

97

but held it back, even though the shape of the ribs and chest could only be human. I felt incredibly sick and it must have showed because Lisa did a double take at me.

"Are you all right Francis? You've become very pale." She asked.

"You never call me Francis! Can't you see that something is wrong?" I felt like saying. Instead I swallowed against the nausea and shook my head, "I'll be fine. I'm just not keen on the sight of meat."

Anna smiled at me, "Eat what you can my dear. I assure you that it is very good. We farm our own cattle, so this Roast is as fresh as they get."

I stared at her, "You farm your own Cattle?"

"Oh yes. Hilltop House is a well known Meat Producer." Anna was very proud of the fact, her whole bearing showed it, "My husband is actually away selecting breeding stock." Anna smiled at the butler, "James, would you carve please?"

I had to sit there and watch slices being carved from the Joint. If it had been pork I would have said it was perfectly cooked. I looked down at the vegetables on my plate. They suddenly became much more appealing.

"Is the gravy made from the meat juices?" Lisa asked, "That's how my grandmother makes it."

"Oh yes. Cook makes all her own stock. It might interest you to know that this roast came from a young heifer. Her milk had dried up so I had no choice, but to have her slaughtered."

James paused, "Would you like ribs or breast, Miss Lisa?"

"Breast please, James." Lisa replied.

I gagged and pushed my chair back, "I'm sorry but I can't eat any more... I'm feeling ill."

"Oh dear." Anna looked concerned, "Maybe a lie down would help? Lucille can attend you."

I nodded and fled back to the suite. My last glance at the table showed Lisa eating the meat and complimenting the cook on her seasonings.

Lying on my bed I decided that I had to get out of this place. Lisa came into my room to check on me at ten.

"Are you OK Francis? Lady Anna was most concerned."

"Since when have I been Francis to you? I'm fine. I just had enough with the soup that's all." I tried to blag it, but the nausea I felt when I remembered Lisa eating the meat came back and I went white.

"You need something in your stomach. How about some meat broth? That roast was lovely, so tender and juicy." Lisa had a dreamy, far away look on her face, "It'll make you feel better."

"NO! Lisa didn't you recognise the joint?" I had to know if she'd twigged or not.

"It was pork of course." Lisa shrugged, "Very juicy and tender."

I closed my eyes in horror, "It was a human torso, half of a woman's chest! Please don't tell me that you couldn't see that?"

"What are you talking about? I think you must have caught a chill from being out in the rain," Lisa sighed, "I'll ask Lady Anna if we can stay a little longer. Besides, I really would like to look around the grounds. She's offered us a tour you know."

I stared at my friend and something about her face seemed wrong. I made my mind up to find out what was going on here and escape to tell the authorities, even if I had to leave Lisa here to do it.

She left my room and Lucille brought me a cup of warm milk, "This will help you get better, Miss."

I drank it automatically, "First thing in the morning, I am out of here." I thought as I fell asleep.

I woke up wondering if last night had just been a really bad dream. Staring up at the rafters, I wrapped the blanket closer around me, straw tickling my nose. "Straw tickling my nose?" I sat up. I was in an animal stall.

There was sawdust in a deep layer beneath the straw, so it wasn't all that cold; instead of the thick cotton nightdress that Lucille had put me in, I wore a green linen shift dress. When I tried to stand up, I fell over.

I felt a smooth, soft binding when I explored my legs with my hands and thought, "I'm tied up!"

"That's it, I'm getting out of here!" I tried to say aloud. To my horror I found that I couldn't speak. I tried for several minutes to say something, but not even a mumble came out of my throat. It felt sore and there was a bandage around my neck.

Using the side of the stall, I manoeuvred myself to my feet and half – hobbled, half – hopped across to the gate that closed it. I found I could look out over it, but wasn't tall enough to reach over and unlock it.

I tried anyway, hauling myself up onto the gate and leaning over. I could see now that the stall was one of about fifteen in a huge barn; there was no sign of anyone else. Then voices echoed around the building as a door opened and I dropped back into the stall, lay down under the blanket and pretended to sleep.

The voices came closer and I recognised Anna and Lisa. There was a man's voice too, deep and seductive. Every so often Lisa would laugh at something he said. Their footsteps told me how close they were to my stall and I prayed that they wouldn't look in.

I heard the footsteps stop.

"Here is my latest acquisition, my Lord." Anna said, "She's a little undernourished at the moment, hence the fact she's in here with the calves."

The man looked into the stall. I didn't recognise him and assumed that he was Anna's husband.

"She's very tall for a heifer, my wife. Where did you find her?" he asked.

"Liselle brought her in. It's quite a tale." Anna looked over the gate at me and smiled, "You see, we'd opened the portal to the Cattle World so that you could come home. It happened to coincide with a road junction and Liselle went out to see if you were on your way."

Lisa... Liselle, smiled down at me too and I realised what was wrong with her face; her nose was too long and her eyes were green not blue, "How could I have missed that?"

"I found a car had crashed into a tree there, so out of curiosity I looked inside. One of the occupants had died on impact, a long branch through her chest. A pity really, she was quite plump and succulent. This heifer had been driving and was unconscious. I pulled the other body out of the car and absorbed her friend's memories by draining the carcass' blood. Then I cast a Glamour on this one and woke her up, pretending to be her friend. From there it was easy to bring her back to the house. " Liselle explained.

"I had to lull her into being relaxed though, "Anna took up the story, "So I had to treat her as Human." She shuddered, "The thought of having a heifer at my table was difficult, but I managed to get through the experience. Unfortunately she recognised the roast that James was carving and fled upstairs, feigning sickness. From there it was easy to drug and prepare her. We removed her voice box first thing this morning."

I surreptitiously touched my throat with a finger. When I slipped my finger under the bandage, I felt coarse stitching in my skin.

The man unlocked the gate and came towards me, putting a pair of rubber gloves on. I scrabbled backwards into the wall, terrified.

"Ah, she's awake and I would say that she's recognised you, my wife." He laughed. Anna laughed too.

Liselle just smiled, "She is actually quite intelligent father, for cattle. She'd recognised that there was something wrong before we'd even gone down for dinner and somehow managed to get one of the maids to confide in her.""

"Hmm." He prodded at my breasts and hips, "Nice ample Mammeries, with a good set of hips. Might make a good breeding heifer, once we feed her up a bit. Intelligence would be good for producing bulls as well, I'm fed up with having dumb bulls that have to be shown how to service the heifers."

"Good milk?" Anna asked, "I had to slaughter Marie yesterday, her milk had dried up completely. She made a nice tender roast though."

I flinched and wriggled as he poked and prodded lower. I gasped, more an animal sound than a human one as he prodded somewhere that no man had touched.

"Hmm. Needs to be broken in before she can be bred. I captured a young bull, about sixteen who hasn't been bred either. This heifer is obviously old enough, so we'll match them up." he stood up stripping the gloves off, dropping them into a bin just outside as he shut the gate behind him, "We'll feed her the contraceptive for this one time. Prep and send her for soul extraction. We can't have it getting in the way." The man took a deep breath and grinned. His mouth was full of sharp peg like teeth, "Well done, my girls."

Anna and Liselle smiled at the praise and Anna put her hand on his arm, "Come Husband. Let us look at the cattle you have brought home."

He nodded and they walked back the way they had come. Liselle stayed, leaning on the gate and looking at me.

"I'm almost sorry for you Francis." She said grinning, showing the same peg teeth as her father, "If it's any consolation, I wish you could be my friend. I think we'd get on well. Ah well, I'd better go and see the foreman about your soul extraction. I might even request your soul to be my personal assistant, once your memories have been altered."

I stared up at her, too scared to do anything, but cry.

"Aw, don't cry little heifer. Believe me, it's nothing personal. I mean we all have to eat don't we."

Acknowledgments

Lyrics taken from "There's a Light" - "The Rocky Horror Picture Show" by Richard O'Brien

FAMILY LEGACY

By John Miller

The last words of Doctor Luther Frank:

Science had nothing to do with what lay on the gurney in my laboratory. Two floors down, in the sub-basement where I had worked non-stop in my laboratory for five years, it lived. Just like in the movies: It lives! And in living, it wrought forth my mind's greatest nightmares, fashioned from strands of evil tucked deep inside my soul, unbidden until now. Until it began to jerk with spasms on the gurney, once the first currents of electricity jettisoned through its dead limbs. While my family—and especially my wife, Elaine—had laughed and laughed, while I became the butt of so many inside-jokes, their derision couldn't keep me from my unholy work. For there is a kind of purity in death, in understanding and animating it, which was something the Family didn't seem to comprehend. Not even when my creation broke free from its straps and lumbered about the mansion, filled with my rage for having been doubted for so many years. By my great wrath that damnable monster struck down my family members one-by-one, taking especial slow treatment with my wife, Elaine whom had bantered me the most.

I found her in our bedroom, a mushy puddle with jagged bones jutting toward the chandelier in the ceiling, her face still intact and locked in a rigor-mortis scream of pure terror and agony. By the time I found her, my creation had already destroyed the rest of the family, had already killed grandma and grandpa, Uncle Bill and Aunt Josephine, both of whom had suffered greatly while in each other's arms. The monstrosity of my hands had bear-hugged them slowly, until their insides oozed from their mouths in a final death-kiss-gurgle. I returned home from having gone for staples and dead cadavers, and the twang of copper pennies gushed over me upon entering the mansion. And then I saw the great bloody footprints and I knew… I knew.

It took gassing the entire mansion to put the monster down. How I laughed that it lived. At the same time I cried at my loss—a mixture of elation and terrible sorrow. Although my Family had angered me, I never once wished their demise in such grisly fashion.

Well, maybe Elaine—but that is another story.

After it fell unconscious, I took a dolly and wheeled it to the stairs. It thumped painfully on the way down, first two flights of stairs to the basement, then another two flights of stairs to the sub-basement. By the time I used pulleys and levers to hoist Ernie up to the gurney, he had several head wounds, so he shouldn't be too much trouble. I bound him with chains and leather straps and duct tape—anything I could find. Enough to keep God Himself on that table. Enough to hold Ernie fast until he rotted, until I could catch my breath to figure out what I must do.

I sat in this kitchen where Grandpa Frank hung from the ceiling. Ernie had struck him so hard that Grandpa Frank had splattered against the ceiling. The constant *drip, drip, drip* wasn't from the faucet. And here, where you and I sit, I contemplated my next move.

All I had ever wanted was to earn the respect of the Family. Once they had a different name, and once a great man had built himself a monster. A woman wrote about the event, and our family was hounded throughout the ages, ridiculed and taunted, until we moved so many times, having finally changed our names to Frank—we'd dropped the last part of our last name.

My wealth came from the Family. They had so many patents and inventions, most of them regarding bioengineering and genetic research, specialities that the first great genius of the Family had pioneered. When I came along... well, I just didn't belong. My interest in all things arcane only angered the Family. Grandpa Frank nicknamed me the Psychic, and Aunt Josephine ran with it.

Have you heard about the Family Psychic? she'd ask when I returned from the library with occult tomes and medical books. He's going to raise the dead like our founder. I would walk past the Family's jibes and taunts, refusing to have anything to do with their hollow Science.

Our Founder's name was Dr. Frankenstein, as I'm sure you've guessed by now. And his Science wasn't just an earlier form of bioengineering and genetics; it was so much more than that. And while I tried to convince the Family of this, while I tried to show them those Eastern Medicinal principals our Founder had studied such as acupuncture, kundalini, chi energy and elixirs, the Family would hear none of it.

It's not respected Science anymore, Aunt Josephine would argue. Alchemy is no longer taught in the universities, and we are no longer known as Frankenstein. Don't try to animate dead dogs, for the past is dead.

And so it was. But I could not unleash my terrible hold on long

103

abandoned secrets. Don't you realize why you've never raised the dead? I told Grandpa Frank once. Don't you see it's because you've left the Founder's secrets when you forsook the occult? He slapped me hard enough to knock me down, and it happened right before the entire Family. It was the last time I ever mentioned my ideas again, but they derided me more than ever afterward.

Don't tell me you've never tried it, I blatantly told Grandpa Frank when he tried to stop my shipment of cadavers from the Body Farm. The Body Farm was a large refrigerated warehouse that shipped cadavers to medical universities so that students could operate on corpses, getting a feel for how the liver lay in the body, for how the small intestine entwined like serpents in the gut. They shipped cadavers out all over the nation, in the name of Science. And since the Franks had a sterling reputation in the world of Science, it wasn't so unusual to have bodies shipped Federal Express to our house. Grandpa Frank, I remember signing for bodies as a child, bodies you yourself ordered from the Body Farm. I didn't know what I was signing for back then... but I do now. And I know what you were doing.

Watch your tongue, boy, he told me. But he stepped out of my way, and I wheeled the iced box containing the cadaver down the stairs via the dolly, feeling the weight of Grandpa's eyes upon my back. After the first flight of stairs to the landing, I turned to take the next flight of stairs to the basement. I looked up and saw Grandpa Frank's face. He was sad, so terribly sad, as if he knew that possibly I was on the right track; as if he feared for my safety, for the safety of the whole Family.

What is that idiot Psychic doing now? Aunt Josephine asked when she came into view.

Leave him alone, Grandpa Frank said. And God help us all.

Now, with the Family and their teasing all gone, I sit with you in the kitchen, realizing that Science has nothing to do with what moans in the sub-basement. This is what I have worked for, lived for, this living piece of animated flesh sewn together from various cadavers. I have recreated life in the similitude of our Founder. Am I not like he now?

When Grandpa Frank saw my creation, he screamed, demanding that I kill it immediately. Before it claims us all, you fool! But Aunt Josephine cried when she saw it. She pinched my cheeks saying, Oh, how we underestimated you, boy. You'll be famous like our Founder. She hugged me and wept. Over her shoulder I saw Grandpa Frank's face, a look of abject horror. It was as if he were looking ahead at the future, looking at the Family still lying in the same exact spots where Ernie had killed them. But

104

Aunt Josephine had only praise for me: How could we have doubted you, boy? How could we have taunted you? Over her shoulder, I saw Grandpa Frank crying just like Aunt Josephine. Only his tears weren't from overwhelming joy.

Now, as I tell you this tale, Grandpa Frank drips from the ceiling behind you. A monster moans in the sub-basement. I can hear his moans from here, where we sit, you and I. Together we might be able to go down into depths of this madhouse, down into my Family's insanity. Together, you a gardener, having worked for the Family for... what? Ten years? Okay, eleven then. You and I, together, Scientist and gardener, we can descend into my Family's darkest secrets and slay the beast.

You have to do this, you see. If you don't, I'll have you deported. You have no Green Card. An illegal. That's why Grandpa Frank hired you, you know. Hahaha! You should have seen the look on your face when—for the first time—I invited you inside our mansion. Didn't you suspect it would be for something bad? I mean, after all these years, never once were you allowed inside, not even when Aunt Josephine broke her leg. Do you remember how she screamed for you to Stay the hell out of our house? Even though you were the one to call 911, even when you were the one who sought to help Aunt Josephine, she still hated having you come inside with your gardener's stink, despite her agony of shattered femur.

So why did you enter with me? Was it curiosity? Was it, a sense of adventure?

Well, you'll receive adventure and then some. You stay right here. I'm going to the emergency locker in the basement. There are special weapons there for emergencies such as this. We need guns that can kill a thing already dead, guns that were invented by Grandpa Frank before I was even born.

I know why Grandpa Frank invented those guns now. I know why he never got rid of them. Because he knew that genius ran in the family, and he knew that one such as I would come along. They all did. All of them knew the truth, that Science outside the realm of mysticism is just a hollow belief system comprised of lifeless computers and godless technology, and that only by adding the supernatural can we ever hope to raise the dead.

I now know, deep in my heart, that certain members of the Family have been raising the dead throughout the years. They used the original notes of our Founder, some of which have been destroyed, the occultic parts of those notes, the forbidden parts. But the majority of those arcane studies have been handed down from generation to generation, photocopied and

105

saved to computer disks. And here, in this very house, lives and breathes a creature out of nightmare, a creature we hear even now, moaning like someone damned in hell. A creature formed from my Family's Science.

You will see how he moves, how that body crafted from various dead pieces twitches with spasms. He will seem clumsy but he moves surprisingly fast, and Oh so powerful! Powerful enough to take your head off with but one swipe of his hand. But fear not, for as I said he is chained secure. But just in case... just in case I warn you.

Now that you know the truth, are you ready? Are you ready to go down and destroy my Family Legacy? It seems odd that, after all this time —after working so hard to create this monster in order to win my Family's approval—I am now trying to destroy my life's work.

Let's go.

A NEW DAY

By Alva J. Roberts

"You want some coffee?" Mary's voice echoed into the small bathroom.

Alex looked up, the pounding his head had lessened. He stood with a groan, walking out of the bathroom. He felt miserable. The coat from his Santa suit was missing, he must have left it in the bar.

As he stumbled from the bathroom, looking over into the small dining room. Mary sat there with a newspaper and a pen, doing a crossword puzzle. Another woman sat next to her with a book. They both wore sweat pants and t-shirts. It was the first time he had seen Mary out of her elf costume. Last night his co-workers from Santa's Village had invited him out for a drink, he must have overdone it.

Alex looked down at his own beer-stained shirt and felt his face go bright red. He ran his fingers through his hair. This wasn't the best way to make a first impression.

"Finally. I can take a shower. If you're gonna bring home strays, Mary, at least you could keep 'em in your room." The woman with a book walked past Alex. She was taller than Mary, with dishwater blonde hair.

"That was my room-mate, Jenny. You aren't looking to rosy this morning, Santa. How you feeling?"

"Horrible," Alex admitted as he sat down next to her. "Sorry about…well whatever I did last night. How'd we end up here?"

"You couldn't stay awake long enough to tell me where you lived, and there was no way I was letting you drive." Mary sounded like she was trying to hold back a laugh.

"I don't drink much. It was really nice of you to bring me here. I am sorry."

"All in being good Santa's helper. You think you can tell me where you live today?" She asked with a smile.

"Yeah, but you don't have to give me a ride. You've done enough."

"It's Sunday, and I don't have to work. The only plans I have are finding a really bad movie on TV and vegging out. I don't mind giving you a lift."

Mary grabbed her coat and purse and they walked to the door. The door creaked loudly as she opened it. A blast cold winter air swept into the room. She turned to him with a smile.

"You do owe me lunch sometime for the ride."

"More than happy too. It is the least-"

A scream cut Alex's sentence short. They ran outside to see what was happening. Abandoned cars littered the street and the snow was red with thick pools of blood. Screams echoed through the streets, but their source was hidden. The sound of a dog barking and a helicopter overhead joined the clutter of noise. Alex's breath made a huge cloud in front of him, as he shivered from the cold. Nothing was moving, the snow covered suburban street seemed eerily still.

The sickly odor of death filled Alex's nostrils. He turned to see a man walking towards him, his arms outstretched. His skin was a grey color, with fresh, red blood dripping from his hands and face. A large chunk of flesh was missing from his throat and old dried blood surrounded the wound.

"Holy crap!" Mary screamed running into the house.

Alex was just a step behind her. He slammed the door shut behind him.

"What was that? What was that? Damn! I'm going to call the cops!" Mary said out of breath.

Alex looked around the room, finally picking up a chair to use as a weapon. He knew what it looked like, he had seen plenty of bad horror movies. The man could have come straight out of a zombie movie. Fear churned inside his stomach. It was impossible!

"It's busy! What the hell, how can 911 be busy?" Mary screamed.

There was a loud thumping at the door. It sounded as if someone was trying to beat it down with something thick, wet, and meaty. A crash and a scream came from the bathroom.

Mary ran to the door, turning the handle and banging her shoulder against it.

"It's locked."

"Out of the way!" Alex yelled running over and kicking the door as hard as he could. The door-frame shattered and splinters of wood flew through the air.

Jenny lay on the floor the shower curtain wrapped around her prone body. Another gray skin figure crouched over her. Blood pooled beneath her body, and spattered the walls. The grey-skinned man looked up at them. Jenny's blood drooled from the corners of his mouth and covered his naked body. His eyes had the glaze look of a dead man.

Without thinking, Alex ran forward smashing the chair into the man, knocking him to the ground. Alex kept swinging the chair, smashing it into the man again and again. Thick black fluid ran from the his body to join Jenny's brighter red blood. The chair shattered, but Alex kept swinging the broken pieces.

"What the hell's going on?" Alex asked no in he stumbled from the bathroom, out of breath.

There was another crash at the door. Wood splintered and a large crack ran down the door panel. Alex could hear a huffing grunt on the other side of the door.

"We need to get out of here! Through the back!" Mary yelled.

Alex dropped the shattered chair, picking up one of the splintered chair legs. It was about an inch thick. It felt reassuring to be holding the two foot chunk of solid oak.

"Where do we go?" Alex asked breathless.

"I…I..don't know. The school. All the windows are real high. We can barricade ourselves in a room. It's only a couple of blocks away."

"Sounds good," Alex said, his voice hollow and numb with shock.

They inched their way through the back door. The neighborhood was quiet. The screams were gone the dogs had stopped barking. The silence was eerie and unsettling. Alex's hands shook as he tried to look brave in front of Mary.

They crept their way to the alley, the only sound the crunching of the snow under their feet. Mary had a six-foot tall privacy fence around her yard. Alex stuck his head out through the gat, looking both ways down the alley. He saw more pools of blood, steam rising from them in thick clouds, but nothing moved.

"We'll stay low, and run like hell," Mary whispered.

Alex nodded in agreement. He wrapped his arms around himself, shivering from both the cold and the fear. The icy alley provided insecure footing, and Alex slipped and slid his way along, his baggy red Santa pants threatening to fall down as he walked.

They stopped when they reached the street. Alex moved forward in a crouch, peering around the edge of the houses. He gasped for air and swallowed hard, trying to keep from being sick. There were hundreds of the gray-skinned creatures in the street, flocking around a tipped over bus. Alex saw an older bald man try to crawl his way through a window of the bus to disappear in a cloud of splattered blood as six of the things converged on him.

"Come on, don't look. Just run. They're distracted, but god, don't look at it," Alex whispered in a tight voice on the brink of tears.

They sprinted as fast as they could over the layer of ice that covered the street, no longer trying to hide. Instead, they were trying to out run the monsters. A few of them gave chase, howling incoherent screams of hunger, but the zombies were even more unsteady on the ice than Alex. They slid and fell, only to grope their way to their feet. Mary and Alex turned the corner and the school building loomed in front of them.

A white car came skidding around the corner, its driver wearing a look of pure terror. Four of the gray-skinned men were holding on to the speeding vehicle. Alex grabbed Mary, throwing her out of the car's path.

The back fender of the car hit Alex, sending him flying. The world tumbled and spun in slow motion, and then the ground came smashing up and the world went dark.

"Alex! Alex! Are you okay?" Mary leaned over Alex's prone form.

A group of about thirty people stood behind her wearing looks that ranged from concern to apathy.

"Yeah, I think so."

Alex stood up, looking around. His body seemed to throb in time with the beat of his heart and his muscles barely obeyed his commands. They were in a hallway, lined with blue lockers. A thin gray commercial carpet covered the floor.

The people in the crowd ranged in age from about three years old to an older woman the Alex thought had to be 90 and wore a mish-mash of clothing. One of the women stood self consciously adjusting a nightgown. Mary had not been the only one who thought the school would be safe.

"They helped me carry you in, while those things ate the people in the car," Mary said.

"Thank you," Alex said turning to the crowd.

He received a murmur in reply. The group separated the excitement over. Alex leaned against the wall taking deep breaths. His headache was a thousand times worse, and he wished he had not gone out drinking the night before Doomsday.

"Damn, this cannot be happening. I have a degree in Library Media Science and I work as a frickin' Santa Claus at the mall. I'm not some kind of zombie hunter from a crappy movie."

"Me either. I don't even make the Santa grade. I'm just an elf and a part time chef at an Italian restaurant." Mary looked as exhausted as Alex felt. "They say the things are all going to the park. No one knows why."

Alex leaned against the wall, grateful for the safety the building offered. The school had been a good idea, it was a safe place to think about what should be done next. He stared at Mary, and then glanced over at the other people in the hallway. Her auburn hair framed her face in tight curls, he had never realized how pretty she was.

"We can't stay here. The only food is a candy machine. Even if we still have water, it is only a matter of time. I'd rather die doing something than in a damn High School. I couldn't stand my own, and I'm not going to die in someone else's," Alex said after a few minutes.

"You're crazy! I can't believe you want to go back out there."

"We need to go to the park, maybe we can figure out what is causing this. We're going to die. We might as well die trying to stop Armageddon," Alex asked, ignoring her statement. "Excuse me! Does anyone know how far away the park is? I'm from the city and I don't know the suburbs very well."

They all looked at him as if he was crazy, but one of the young men drew him a map. It was only about twelve blocks, but it might as well have been twelve thousand miles.

"I have to get there, maybe we can stop this. Does anybody have a car I can use?

Blank stares met his question, followed by looks of pity. They must think he was losing it. The group glanced at each other and shifted their feet. Alex tried to look confident, people responded better to confidence.

"I don't know about everyone else but I want to keep my car in case I have to run," an elderly woman said after a few minutes.

"Me and Steve tried to make it to his jeep. His keys are lying out in the parking lot. They got Steve," one of the boys wearing a blood spattered letterman jacket said, his voice numb and hollow.

"Okay, I'm going for Steve's jeep." Alex said.

"Alex, you are crazy. You couldn't pay me enough to go out there," Mary replied.

"Think about it Mary. What other choice do we have? We can sit around waiting to die or we can do something. Maybe we can stop this." Alex said.

"There's a fire exit in the gym that leads right to the parking lot. It'll lock behind you, though," the blood-spattered boy said, his voice gaining a little more life.

"Hopefully I won't need back in," Alex said.

The gym was dark, Alex felt like he was entering a cave. The only light came from the open door. Most of the people followed him to the fire exit. Alex felt strange being the center of attention. It was always a feeling he hated.

Alex made a slight detour when he saw the field hockey equipment piled against one wall of the gym. He scurried over to pick up a hockey stick before walking over to the exit.

Alex stopped, staring at the door like it was the gateway to hell. Maybe it was. Fear churned inside him. It was easy to talk about the best way to die, but when it came down to it, he wasn't sure if he could do it.

He breathed in deeply.

Everyone was staring at him, staring at the crazy man.

"Wait. I'm coming too." Mary said. "You're right. I'd rather die fighting than starve." Her voice cracked as she spoke and her hands were twitched, but she held a hockey stick, and her eyes shown with determination.

The fire exit opened with a squeal as the long unused hinges protested the movement. Alex and Mary took off at a sprint through the parking lot. None of the gray-skinned zombies were in sight. Alex's eyes kept darted everywhere, looking for the monsters. Cars were parked haphazardly in the icy lot, pools of frozen blood colored the dirty ground.

The zombies seemed to come from nowhere. Alex smashed his club into one and then another. Mary hit one in the kneecap, Alex heard its knee shatter from the force of the blow. More and more of the creatures came. Alex could tell he and Mary were slowing down, their momentum lost to the ghoulish onslaught. The jeep was only another dozen steps, but Alex didn't know if he was going to make it.

Mary let out a scream and dropped to the ground. She's hurt, Alex thought as he tried to make his way to her, smashing zombies from his path. One of them grabbed onto his t-shirt, the cloth tearing and shredding.

"Come on! I got the keys!" She shouted, jumping to her feet.

One of the zombies bit Alex's arm before he could smash its teeth out with his elbow. His club fell to the ground. All thoughts of fighting the creatures vanished as Alex sprinted the last few steps, shouldering a zombie out of the way to hop into the passenger seat.

The Jeep lurched to a start. Mary threw the vehicle in reverse, thick black fluid spraying outward as she backed over zombies. More monsters grabbed the sides of the Jeep before Mary could get it moving forward. The tires spun on the ice as they sped out of the parking lot.

The Jeep raced through the streets, dodging abandoned cars. Mary swerved onto the side-walk and weaved her way around light poles and trees. The Jeep slid and skidded all around. We are going to die Alex thought. The half dozen creatures holding on to the jeep rolled off, but a glance behind them said they were attracting the notice of hundreds of the decaying undead.

Alex dove into the back of the Jeep, hunting for a weapon, any kind of weapon. He found long pieces of steel rebar and grabbed one. The half-inch thick round steel rod felt cold but reassuring in his hand. Blood ran down his arm, from his wound, and dripped from his fingers.

Mary drove straight into the park, her speed increasing. They hit a snow bank driving up the frozen ice, and the jeep flew through the air smashing through a fence and landing with crunch and squeal in the middle of the icy basketball court.

Alex rolled out of the car his make shift club ready. He wasn't expecting what he saw. A huge man, over seven tall, cloaked in shadows that hung like living tendrils from his body. Alex felt overwhelmed, as if his mind couldn't truly comprehend what he was seeing. In his hand he held a long black knife that seemed to be made of the shadows.

"They have sent more. How many fools can you find? I will not be stopped in the time of my rebirth!" The man's voice sounded like cracking bone. "When will they realize it is too late? Listen mortals, and look upon those who have already been sent before you." The ominous man gestured to the fence. Hundreds of human heads lined the top of the fence, all wearing expressions of incredible pain.

Alex looked uneasily at Mary. She gave him a smile and floored the Jeep, running it straight at the giant. The huge man smiled slightly, then with a flick of his wrist, a bolt of lightning jumped out of his fingertips, smashing into the front of the Jeep. The vehicle flipped through the air and rolled away. God, I hope she's okay, Alex thought, staring uneasily at the man,   Alex felt like he might throw up, what the hell was he going to do?

"Oh mighty lord," Alex said, his voice holding all the reverence he could muster. "It was foolish of us to think of attacking you."

Alex glanced to the side of the court. Thousands of the zombies were gathering, subject to the man's will. Alex dropped the rebar and knelt to the ground.

"Alex, no!" Mary shouted, her arm limp and useless at her side. Blood ran from a cut on her head as she stumbled her way out of the wrecked Jeep.

"Make it quick, great lord," Alex whispered.

"As you wish." A blade made of darkness itself struck deep into Alex's chest. He fell forward, his eyes glazed and unseeing.

"Now for you." One Death turned striding toward Mary.

Mary picked up a rock, throwing it at the giant. The rock skipped away without touching him. Mary looked around for a weapon as tears welled up in her eyes.

A foot of steel rebar blossomed from man's chest. Alex stumbled forward, his skin gray, and his hair faded and lusterless.

Mary stared as the zombie of Alex fell forward. All around the park the zombies dropped, as if whatever magic animating them failed, with their lord's death.

"Alex? What happened? Alex? Please be alive," Mary called uncertainly.

"Some of the dead out there were old, so it I guessed that no matter how you died you would come back, I was just hoping that I would still remember enough to kill that bastard. I'm lucky he killed me with magic, it looks like everything his magic did is reversing. Not everyone is so lucky," Alex said, standing. His chest wound slowly closed.

All around the park thousands of bodies lay in the snow, a massive heap of frozen, dead flesh. Alex could only imagine how many had died elsewhere. Billions, he was sure. The world would be a different place.

A new beginning was coming.

114

POCKET GIANT

By Gary McKenzie

"Mommy!" Nicki screamed as she pulled the covers over her sweat soaked head.

Her father, Bruce, bolted upright in his bed. His dreams of finally telling off his ignorant boss rapidly faded from his groggy mind. He glanced at the alarm clock. It read 2:06 am. Wordlessly, he nudged his wife, Gerrie.

"Nicki wants you," he hoarsely whispered.

"It's your turn," she said without even opening her eyes.

"But she called for you," Bruce insisted.

"It's your turn," Gerrie repeated as she rolled over and snuggled even further under the covers.

"Mommy!" the shrill voice again echoed throughout the house.

"You know, I have to get up early for work," Bruce whined. He waited momentarily for a response. There was none. "All you have to do tomorrow is the laundry." The only response he received was a weak imitation of a snoring sound.

Having lost the battle of wills, Bruce swung his legs out of bed and placed his bare feet on the cold wooden floor. Its icy touch jump-started the flow of adrenaline to the rest of his body. Sitting on the edge of the bed, he looked around the moonlit room for his slippers

"Where the hell are they?" he mumbled to himself. "I could have sworn that I left them right here." As he prepared to look under his side of the bed, Nicki called out for a third time.

Disgusted that he had been rudely awakened, he started to run his fingers through his sleep-messed hair when Gerrie nudged him off of the bed. Taking the obvious hint, Bruce trudged out of the bedroom and down the dark hall to his four year old daughter's room.

He flicked on the bedroom light, momentarily blinding himself. As his vision returned, he looked at the shaking mound of covers in the center of the bed. Skillfully manuevering around the piles of dolls and toys that littered the floor, he made his way to the bed where little Nicole hid in fear.

"What's the matter, pumpkin?" he asked as he removed the covers from her head.

"I want Mommy!" she sobbed as an alligator tear ran down her freckled cheek.

"Mommy's asleep," he said through gritted teeth. He brushed the hair out of Nicki's eyes. "But I'm here."

"I'm scared," she meekly said.

"Scared of what, darlin'?"

Nicki looked around the room cautiously and then leaned forward to whisper in her father's ear, "The Pocket Giant."

A look of shock and confusion crossed Bruce's face. "Pocket Giant?" He had been prepared for a ghost, a monster, even the Boogey Man, but a Pocket Giant? "What's a Pocket Giant, honey?" he asked as he tried not to laugh.

"A monster," she whispered.

Bruce and Gerrie had done their best to protect Nicki from all types of horrors; no monster movies or scary stories before bedtime. They had even gone so far as to tone down the villains in fairy tales. When her older cousins, Doug and Mike visited, they were kept under constant adult supervision so that they wouldn't scare her.

"Where did you hear about this Pocket Giant?" Bruce asked now that his interest had been piqued.

Nicki had no reply. She dropped her eyes and pouted.

Pulling his daughter close to him to give her a sense of comfort, Bruce asked again. "I'm only trying to help you, pumpkin. Who told you about this Pocket Giant?"

Raising a hand to her father's ear, she whispered, "He did."

"Who did?" he whispered back.

"The Pocket Giant."

"The Pocket Giant told you about himself?"

Nicole nodded; her eyes wide with fear.

"Pumpkin," Bruce whispered, "why are we whispering?"

"So he doesn't hear us."

"You mean this Pocket Giant is here in the room with us?"

Nicki nodded again and clutched the blankets closer to her.

"Well, what does it look like?" Bruce asked.

"I don't know," the little girl answered. There was a hint of shame in her voice.

"If you didn't see it, then how do you know it's really here?" Bruce asked, trying to get some type of logic into the conversation.

Nicki remained silent. She hung her head and stared at her flower-

116

covered sheets.

"She's only four years old," Bruce reminded himself. Seeing that his daughter was about to cry, Bruce decided to cheer her up before the dam broke.

Standing up and doing a brave and gallant knight impression, Bruce lowered his voice and spoke out loud, "Come out, vile beast! Come out yon evil Pocket Giant, so that I may slay thee!"

"No, daddy!" Nicki yelled in terror. "Don't let it get you!"

Bruce broke down and laughed. "Nicki, there's no such thing as a Pocket Giant. Heck, up until tonight, I've never even heard of one. Monsters aren't real, and even if it was real, I'm your daddy. It's my job to protect you and Mommy. As long as I'm around, I won't let anything bad happen to you."

After a few moments of looking at her father in awe, Nicki let out a meek, "Really?"

"You bet, pumpkin." He reached down and hugged his daughter close to him.

Nicki held her father tightly. He would be her hero.

Releasing his protective embrace, Bruce leaned Nicki back into bed and pulled the covers up to her chin. He looked down at his daughter who lovingly looked back at him with her blue eyes.

"Is everything going to be OK now, pumpkin?" he asked.

Nicki nodded but there was still a hint of fear in her eyes.

"Would you like me to check your room and make sure that there aren't any Pocket Giants lurking in the shadows?"

A smile grew across Nicki's face and she vigorously nodded.

Bruce smiled back at his little princess and proceeded to kneel beside the bed and check underneath for any creatures of the night. Other than some board game pieces, stuffed animals, and dust-bunnies, there was nothing waiting to spring upon him.

"All safe under here," he said and gave her the thumbs up sign. His back cracked loudly as he rose up, making Nicki giggle. He then made his way across the room toward the closet.

"This is what it must feel like to walk across a minefield," he thought as he made his way across the littered floor. Toys, dolls and books blocked a direct path to the closed closet door.

"OK, pumpkin, this is the only place left for me to check," he said once he made it to the door. "After I check in here, it's sleepy-time, all right?"

Nicki nodded, held her breath, and watched.

Bruce turned the doorknob and pulled the door open. A darkened figure lunged at him from the top of the closet. The shadowy, round object hit Bruce in the forehead and sent him sprawling backwards. The dark blue ball bounced to the ground and rolled into the hallway. By the time he noticed that it was only a ball, Bruce had stumbled back and stepped on a bunch of jacks with his bare feet.

Nicki, seeing her father flailing around like a mad-man, pulled the covers over her head and screamed at the top of her lungs.

Bruce fell on top of a pile of stuffed animals, which were stacked up in the corner of the room. He sat there and laughed, thankful that his fall had been cushioned by Tommy the Tiger, Superkitty, and Eggbert: the Unbreakable Egg.

"Honey, Daddy's all right," he said when he saw his frightened daughter trying to hide.

Nicki slowly peeled the covers off of her head and saw her father sitting among the smiling stuffed animals. He sat there laughing with two jacks embedded in the bottom of his foot. She had no choice but to laugh along with him.

Soon after, Bruce tucked in his daughter and gave her a goodnight kiss.

"Love you sweetie."

"Love you too, Daddy."

"Are you going to be all right?"

"Yes."

With a sense of relief, Bruce switched off the lights and made his way down the hall, careful not to trip on the dark blue ball, on the way back to his bedroom. The only sound throughout the house was Gerrie's snoring, which was loud enough to wake the dead.

"Great, how am I supposed to go back to sleep with all of this noise?" he thought. Then something caught his eye. He noticed that one of his slippers was back beside the bed.

"Hmmm. Maybe I just didn't see it in the dark. The covers could have been lying over it," he reasoned to himself. "Well, I might as well find the other one, since I'm awake."

He bent down to look under the bed and suddenly cringed when his knees and back simultaneously cracked, making a sound like popcorn popping. Lifting the covers off of the floor, he peered into the darkness for his other slipper. Seeing nothing, he plunged his arm into the pitch black

118

shadow, hoping to feel his lost slipper. Nothing.

"Oh hell," he said under his breath. "I'll just look for it in the morning."

As he started to get up, his missing slipper slid across the floor and stopped next to the other one. He was about to tell his daughter to get back to bed when he looked at the silhouette standing in the doorway.

Two glowing red eyes stared at him from a rather large head that perched on top of a scrawny, hunched over body. The creature couldn't have been much bigger than a regular house-cat. A rat-like tail whipped about behind the strange, shaggy humanoid.

Before Bruce could react, the Pocket Giant leapt over the threshold with its small, powerful legs and latched onto Bruce's face. Its tail whipped around Bruce's neck, forcefully closing his windpipe. No air could get in and no screams for help could get out.

The Pocket Giant's face was mere inches from Bruce's. He stared into the hypnotic red eyes, which contrasted against the pale blue skin of the creature. The rest of the beast's face was covered with thick bushy, eyebrows, beard and moustache. It opened its unusually large mouth, revealing many tiny, yellow, needle-like teeth and putrid breath.

Bruce tried, with all his might, to pull the beast off as he struggled for air. The troll-like creature, with its razor sharp claws, continued to hold on to its victim. It skillfully moved around to the back of Bruce's head and rode him piggyback-style.

Bruce felt faint as the tiny teeth penetrated the back of his neck. The monster's venom coursed through his veins at record speed. Within seconds, Bruce's legs weakened and he fell onto the cold wooden floor with a sickening thud. Gerrie continued to sleep throughout the entire assault. As Bruce's vision blackened, he saw the Pocket Giant looming over him. The tiny beast appeared to be growing larger and larger.

"I've got to warn… Gerrie," he thought. "Must… save… Nicki," then, everything went black.

* * *

Bruce woke up surrounded by darkness. The pain in his neck had subsided. "Where am I?" he thought. "What the hell just happened? Oh my God, is Nicki all right?"

He went to stand but couldn't get a steady foothold on the terrain; it was lumpy and unstable. It shifted and collapsed beneath his weight. To his

119

bare feet, the terrain felt like a burlap sack. It was as if he was trapped inside a giant bag. The only source of fresh air seemed to come from above.

As he gazed up into the starless sky, a blinding light assaulted his vision and slightly illuminated the rest of his strange prison. Before he knew what was happening, a gust of wind sent a large, web-like bush tumbling his way. The weightless monstrosity fell upon Bruce. It immediately became secondary once he heard his wife's voice echo around him.

"So, did your father scare away the Boogey Man last night?" Gerrie asked.

"It wasn't the Boogey Man, mom. It was the Pocket Giant," Nicki answered.

* * *

"She's all right!" Bruce thought. "My baby's all right! But where are they? What's going on?"

* * *

"Where is Daddy, anyway?" Nicki's voice thundered.

"I guess he went to work earlier than usual, honey. I'll tell you what, as soon as I'm done with the laundry, we'll go visit Aunt Bonnie and Aunt Linda. OK?"

"Goody!" Nicki shouted. "I can tell them how Daddy saved me from the Pocket Giant and then how he fell on his butt."

* * *

Bruce felt the stomping of Nicki's feet as she ran to her room to get ready for her day out. It was like being caught at ground zero during an earthquake.

* * *

Gerrie hummed a tune as she reached into the hamper. She grabbed a handful of socks and underwear and threw them into the laundry basket.

* * *

120

The strange world that Bruce was in started to collapse around him. The weird walls that surrounded him buckled and closed in, while the ground shook and rose up, throwing the helpless father off balance. Above, the sky went from light to dark to light again within seconds. It was as if a lightning storm had magically passed.

* * *

Gerrie reached into the hamper and pulled out a pair of Bruce's jeans. She carelessly threw them into the washing machine.

* * *

Bruce felt himself go weightless as the ground below him dropped, leaving him floating in the air. Gravity just seemed to quit, and then, just as suddenly, it reappeared sending him crashing to the unstable ground. He looked up and saw a large, flesh-colored arm pass over the opening of his prison. And then things really got freaky. He saw Gerrie's face. It hovered above him, taking up the whole sky.

"Gerrie!" he yelled as he frantically waved his arms from side to side. "Honey, it's me!"

Gerrie turned her head, clueless to her screaming husband, and then disappeared.

"Why doesn't she see me?" he thought. "Wait a minute, why was she so large? What the hell is going on?"

When Gerrie reappeared in Bruce's version of the alien sky, she had a yellow cup in her hand. Looking down into Bruce's new world, she poured a thick blue liquid from it.

"Oh my God!" Bruce screamed. "She's doing the laundry! Of all the times, why now?" He frantically looked around his surroundings. Reality had finally dawned on him. "That's a piece of lint!" he said as he looked at the giant web-like tumbleweed. "This ground and the sides of the wall… I'm inside of a pocket!"

He tried to climb the unstable walls of the pants pocket but couldn't get a good grip or foothold. Above, Gerrie pushed an unseen button and left Bruce's view.

A roaring of water started as the washing machine kicked into its first cycle. Bruce fell to his knees as his eardrums burst from the deafening sound. Some of the blue liquid seeped into the pocket containing Bruce. It pooled under his feet, trapping him like a dinosaur in a tar pit.

121

Hopelessly gazing up out of the top of the pocket, Bruce saw his wife's face for the last time as she closed the lid of the washing machine. As the lid closed, he noticed a small figure clinging to the ceiling above Gerrie's head. It was the Pocket Giant. Its tiny needle-like teeth shined through its raggedy facial hair as it smiled down at Bruce. It withdrew one of its claw-like hands from the ceiling and waved.

"Noooo!" Bruce yelled as the lid slammed shut. He sat, a defeated man, and waited for his soap-filled, sudsy death.

GRANDPA JACK O' LANTERN

By Ken L. Jones

Old Simon was an elderly man who lived on the outskirts of the little town of Delbert , Iowa. His ramshackle farm was a place of wonder to the neighborhood children and a source of idle gossip to the adults in his community. It was whispered that the old man must have an independent source of wealth because he had never been known to have held a job. His eccentricity was further enhanced by the fact that he rarely came to town. When asked why that was he would only vaguely reply that he "had everything he needed out at my place."

Simon's spread was as inexplicable as its owner. To even call it a farm these days was something of a misnomer. It was lately less a cultivated acreage than it was a gigantic wild pumpkin patch! The thirteen solid acres of land that surrounded the ancient house and barn were legendary in the countryside for they yielded no ordinary pumpkins. Indeed most of the townspeople agreed that they had never seen anything quite like them before. It was said that Simon could have easily sold his cash crop at a huge profit but he never charged anyone a cent for them delighting instead in giving them away for free.

Although most adults could barely tolerate the old eccentric the local children were Simon's steadfast friends. He loved to visit with them and tell them stories after they tired of frolicking in his pumpkin patch and the old deserted barn next to it. Even though the neighborhood youngsters liked to visit "Grandpa Jack-o-lantern's" place as it had been nicknamed anytime of the year they found it most irresistible at Halloween time. It was obvious to the whole countryside that this was Simon's favorite time of the year too. Every October he joyfully carved and gave away dozens of unusual Jack-o-lanterns which he always sculpted with an ornate dagger whose hilt resembled a human skull. Simon often told his young visitors that the odd looking knife was a family heirloom and he would get a faraway look in his eyes when he talked about it.

Bobby Whitaker and Jayne Rusk two of the old timer's most constant visitors had come straight from the local grade school this October 30th to get their treasure from their beloved friend.

123

"Oh, Simon that Jack-o-lantern is even more wonderful than the one you made me last year." lisped Bobby appreciatively.

"How did you ever learn to make something that pretty?" Jayne asked in wide-eyed awe.

"Well my paw learnt me some o' it but I guess ya might say I comes by it natural like being a Druid an' all! Guess that's why I likes Halloween so well since us Druids invented it," he said as a grin sprouted across his toothless mouth.

"Druids! You's always talking them and I don't rightly know what they is exactly," said Jayne with more than a little exasperation in her voice.

"Wal, if ya promise not to tell another living soul about I guess it will be all right if ya knows. Ya see afore anyone came to America the Druid folk was a great people. My pa learnt me that they's the lost remnants of ole Atlantis itself and the only ones what still exactly remember any of the old time ways. Us Druids is special kinds of folk who lives with nature instead of apart from it like most other human beings does." Simon said his voice full of pride and reverence.

"So is it like Christianity or what?" Bobby asked hesitantly.

"Wal, maybe a bit so" Simon said with downcast eyes.

"Well are you a Christian or isn't you?" Jayne asked rather testily.

Old Simon just spit a wad of chewing tobacco on the ground in reply then went back to his carving in gloomy silence. Then after an awkward eternity he sent the two children and the objects of their quest on their way home fearing that he had said far too much.

Bobby was sullen and quiet at the dinner table that night but after much prodding from his mother he told her something of what Simon had said and about how much it had upset Jayne. About this time his father Jason who usually ignored the boy became intrigued and began questioning him at length about all this. About two minutes into this interrogation Bobby was sorry that he had ever mentioned it in the first place because he had never seen his father get this angry this fast! Mrs. Whitaker was clearly upset too and tired to calm her husband down.

"Now Jason dearest, Old Simon's just a might touched is all he's so gentle and loves all the children. Why lots of folks wouldn't have had enough food on the table during the war if it hadn't been for his free pumpkins and "Grandpa Jack-o-lantern" still gives them to us for free for our baking..."

"Grandpa Jack-o'-lantern! What kind of a fool name is that for a full-grown Christian man? That old blasphemer isn't going to get away with poisoning youngin's innocent minds! We church elders are meeting tonight and I aim to bring this to everyone's attention there!," he angrily declared as he slammed the front door behind him leaving his wife and son in tears.

Later that night the executive council of the Full Gospel Church of the Holy Ghost decided to pay an official visit to old Simon's place. As a full orange moon rose over the seemingly endless pumpkin patch several battered trucks pulled up to the farmhouse there. The right Reverend Georgie T. Muller and his elders were the personification of righteous anger itself as they moved menacingly towards the front of the building.

Simon did not look up from his pumpkin carving as the mob approached his shadowy dilapidated front porch. "Evening Simon," announced Reverend Muller theatrically. "We're here to discuss the winning of a soul for the Lord!"

"And which Lord would that be now?" the old man asked as he chuckled gratingly.

"I figured you'd say something like that!" hissed Jason Whitaker his face a twisted mask of rage now. "Tell us more 'bout these Druid fairy tales you poison our children's minds with "Grandpa Jack-o-lantern" and then you can explain why none of us can remember you ever attending any church for as long as anyone can recall!"

"Always thought what a man believed was his own business." Simon replied with just a hint of sarcasm in his voice.

"Godless blasphemy is the business of the whole community!" screeched Reverend Muller.

"Seems to me that how a feller feels 'bout religion ought to be his own concern leastwise I recollect old Tom Jefferson saying something to that effect," Simon replied still carving away nonchalantly on the fifty pound Jack-o-lantern at his feet.

"Were not going to argue theology with you all night old man let's get back to this Druid hogwash and why you fill our children's heads with it!" Jason said trembling with volcanic anger now.

"Well boys alls I can say is that thems as what bothers a Druid often times comes to regret it," Simon softly answered as he stopped his artistic endeavors and slowly looked each man straight in the eye in turn to show them that he wasn't afraid. For a brief moment Simon pitied these men whom he had known since they were little boys until one of them produced a rope from behind his back as they all in unison started inching towards him menacingly. "Wal now I sure as shooting hoped it wouldn't come to this." Simon sighed regretfully as he rose to his feet and held the

125

knife above his head as the air around the old front porch began to hiss and roil as he began chanting in a forgotten ancient tongue.

When Halloween arrived the next day it was a somber joyless event much like it had been during the dark days of the recent great second World War. The countryside was baffled by the sudden disappearance of so many of its prominent leaders as well as that of the old beloved pumpkin carver too. Yet despite it all the children still managed to don their home-made costumes and the streets were populated by diminutive hobos, pirates, and spooks. But despite its forced jocularity clearly something was missing. Without Grandpa Jack-o-lantern Halloween just wasn't as much fun anymore. The community eventually forgot Old Simon but they never stopped talking about the six strangely familiar looking Jack-o-lanterns that he left behind on the rail of his front porch that fateful Halloween night so long ago.

PRICE TO SELL

By Kevin L. Jones

Adam Fletcher looked over at the clock on the night-stand and let out a frustrated sigh. It read 2:46 AM . He had never been plagued by insomnia before he had purchased his new home. The last few nights that he and his wife Ashley had occupied their house he had been kept awake by strange noises that he could not account for. Earlier in the evening he had thought that he had heard someone or something walking up and down the stairs but when he had got out of bed to investigate he could find no one in the house but his wife and himself. Most troubling of all though was the barking dog. Once it got going it would go for hours. The obnoxious animal sounded quite close but as far as he could tell none of his immediate neighbors even owned a dog. Adam thought back on something that the realtor had told him while he and his wife were still looking at the house. He had said that the home's previous occupants had died there and that's why the asking price was so low. Given all the unusual sounds that he had heard over the last few nights Adam had to wonder if the house was haunted but not being a superstitious person he banished these thoughts from his head and he was finally able to drift off to sleep.

* * *

Adam awoke the next morning and rubbed his bloodshot eyes. He stumbled wearily into the bathroom and took a long hot shower. When he emerged he felt somewhat human again. He went downstairs and his wife had hot coffee and scrambled eggs waiting for him. He kissed her on the cheek and sat down and began to eat. While they were having their breakfast Adam asked her if she had heard anything odd last night.

She replied, "Nope didn't hear a thing slept like a baby." Adam grunted and finished his meal in silence.

When he was done he stood up and said "Well I guess I better mow the front yard. It looks pretty cruddy." Adam got his mower out and poured gas into it and he was about to get going when he noticed one of his neighbors was outside working in their yard too. Adam walked over to him and introduced himself. The old man shook Adam's hand and told him his

127

name was Bill Wilkins. The two talked for a while about this and that and then Bill told him that he used to own a construction company and that he had built most of the houses on their street including Adam's place. Bill asked how he liked his new home so far.

"Well," Adam replied, "I like it just fine except I've been hearing a lot of weird noises at night."

Bill looked troubled and was silent for a moment and then said "You might think I'm an old fool but sometimes I think that house is cursed."

This made Adam a little uneasy and he asked him what he meant. Bill looked at Adam's house nervously and said, "Well for starters there was a young fella' named Gerald that used to work for me. He just up and died when we were building the house and no one could ever explain why. Then there was Mary, a few months after she moved in she just went plumb loco. Her husband had to put her away. Then a few months later he killed himself. Had him a little neck tie party in one of the closets. Everything was quiet for a good long while after that until about two years ago. A young couple moves in the guys name was Josh Underhill. He was a big stupid looking idiot covered practically head to foot in those ridiculous looking tattoos that all the young folks seem to have nowadays. His wife I think her name was Amy or something was a real dumb ass too. She was the skinniest thing I ever saw. She looked like she had the "aids" or something. Anyways they was a couple of dopers and one night Josh kills his wife with a meat cleaver and chops her up and feeds her to his pit bull. Don't get me started on that mutt of theirs. Even their dog was a freak. It would bark all night at nothing. The damn thing used to keep me up all hours of the night yipping his head off. The way I heard it that big idiot Josh went around bragging about what he'd done to anyone who would listen. Like it was something to be proud of. Eventually the sheriff's department got wind of it and carted his butt off to jail and now there is you and your Mrs. I hope you have better luck than most of the people who have lived there because you seem like nice folks. "

Adam laughed nervously and said, "Me too! Surely not everyone who has lived in my house has had some crazy thing happen to them?"

"No not everyone there was a guy named Clint Davis who lived there for years and so far as I know never had any problems with the house although he was a long distance truck driver and was hardly ever home."

"Well, that's at least a little encouraging", Adam said.

"Yeah" Bill replied, "Don't let me put a lot of silly notions into your head I'm sure everything that's happened there has just been a coincidence." After a few more minutes of idle chitchat Adam said his goodbyes to Bill and then got back to mowing his yard.

As he worked Adam thought about all the disturbing things that Bill had told him. He wondered if he should mention any of this to his wife. He mulled it over for awhile and decided not to tell her. After all what did it matter the house was perfectly fine and Adam didn't believe in life after death anyway .

* * *

Later that evening Adam and his wife went out to the movies. Then afterwards they had dinner at a nice Italian restaurant. The young couple came home and had a few more drinks and then went upstairs and made love. For the first time since moving in Adam was actually able to fall asleep right away. A few hours later he was awakened from his peaceful slumber by a dog howling like a damned soul. The racket sounded closer than ever. Adam woke his wife up and said "There's that dog again!"

Ashley let out an exasperated groan and replied, "Honey its just some mutt having a bad dream go back to sleep."

Adam whispered, "No listen to how close it sounds." Ashley sat up in bed and said, "Yeah it does sound really close. Almost like it is coming from right outside our backdoor."

Adam got out of bed and said "Wait here. I'm going to go downstairs and check it out" He went down to the kitchen and got a flash-light out of one of the drawers. He walked over to the sliding glass door that led to the backyard. He peered out into the darkness but could see nothing. He tried the back porch light but when he flipped on the switch nothing happened. Adam thought to himself that the bulb must be burned out. He reached for the glass door handle and cautiously slid the door open. As soon as he stepped outside the barking stopped. Adam listened for a moment but could hear nothing but crickets chirping. He was getting ready to go back inside when he heard something moving around in the bushes. Adam turned on his flash-light and pointed its milky beam at the source of the noise. He went weak in the knees when he saw the huge brown pit bull step out of the bushes. The ferocious looking dog was sickly looking and its ribs were visible beneath its filthy matted fur like it had not eaten in a very long time. As the beast snarled and took a few step towards him Adam stepped back inside and quickly closed the glass door behind him and watched as the dog

129

approached the glass. It stared right at him. The animal's breath fogged up the corner of the door and it sat down like it was waiting for something. Totally unnerved Adam fled the kitchen and rushed up the stairs two at a time and slammed the bedroom door behind him. Feeling a little silly for being so afraid of a dog he laughed at his own skittishness.

Adam said, "Honey there is a big ass dog in the backyard!" He then turned on the bedroom light and felt panic well up inside him when he saw that his wife was not in bed. He looked around the room and he could see her hand sticking out of the partially closed closet door.

Adam said, "What the heck are you doing in there?" as he approached the closet. He could tell something was terribly wrong. His heart raced as he slid the door open and he could not believe what he saw. A belt was tied to the metal rod inside and the other end of it was wrapped around his wife's throat. Adam's mind almost could not comprehend what he was seeing. He looked at his wife and her face looked slightly blue. Her head hung at an odd angle. He untied the belt and her lifeless body hit the floor with a thud. He turned and left the room shutting the door behind him. He slowly descended the staircase and sat down on a couch in the living room. He looked out into the kitchen and could see that the dog was still waiting by the back-door. Adam stared at the animal as it walked straight through the glass door and entered the kitchen. He looked at the door and it was still closed and the glass unbroken. He shut his eyes tightly and began shaking his head and hysterically repeated , "This can't be real I must be dreaming." Every fiber of his being told him to flee for his life but as the dog approached him he just sat there in disbelief. The dog sniffed Adam's feet and licked his toes. Adam screamed as he watched in horror as the beast unhinged its jaw and began to swallow him like a cobra gulping down a rat. In a matter of seconds the demonic vision devoured Adam entirely. Its hunger satiated for the time being the hell hound left the house and vanished into the darkness from which it had been born.

* * *

Bill sat on his porch wishing that the hot weather would finally end but it was a vain hope considering it was the middle of August. He rubbed a cold can of beer against his forehead as he looked at the for sale sign in front of the house next door. The realtor had put a sticker on it that read "priced to sell". He shook his head and muttered to himself, "Who would be stupid enough to move into that death-trap?" He opened his beer and took a long gulp and hoped that having a few cold ones would help him get some sleep. Bad dreams had kept him awake all last night. Several times he had though he had heard Josh's pit bull barking but that just couldn't be. After Underhill had killed his wife animal control had taken the mangy mutt and destroyed it. Bill took another sip but almost choked on it when he saw a U-Haul truck pull into the driveway next door. He began to weep softly and whispered "God help me I wish I had never built that damn house in the first place!"

PHASES

By J. Derris Ward

I used to be a day person. I waited tables, went to school when I could afford it. But the joint I worked at closed down, and the money I'd saved ran out.

So did my girlfriend. Said something about wanting a life with someone going somewhere. It crushed me somewhat. She needed a man who takes charge and leads, not a boy that runs away from real life.

I looked around at the work available for nine-to-fivers. I even tried a few place; banks, coffee shops. Nothing suited me. Maybe it was the people. Maybe it was the mornings. Whatever it was, I was having more and more of a hard time getting up just to face the thankless general public. It suddenly hit me, as I tried to apologize to the business suit complaining about too much foam but instead threw the 145-degree latté in his face, that I might be out of my element.

So I took a job working nights.

Nothing fancy, just a job pushing paper. Invoices. That sort of thing. After the days business was done, I'd come in and take care of the rest. Boring. But I worked alone, and the extra money for the late shift was nice.

I got used to it. Never waking up to an alarm clock, never being nagged by some woman with not enough of her own life to worry about. Living off fast food and a slow pace.

So one night, driving home at three in the morning, I was passing a Jack in the Box when the hunger struck me. I needed a Spicy Chicken Sandwich.

I flicked my wrist and glanced down at my watch for no real reason since I already knew it was about three in the morning. They'll probably have their shake machine taken apart, so it'd be useless trying to get an Oreo shake to go with the sandwich. That's always annoying.

But at least it's a nice watch. It tells me the date, the day of the week, and even the phases of the moon. That's why my ex-girlfriend bought it for me, because I'd always wanted a watch that told the phases of the moon ever since I'd read about the one Arthur Dent had in one of those Hitch-hiker books.

It's a full moon tonight, which I knew from looking at the sky when I left work, but it gives me a geeky thrill having a watch that also knows that.

I drove along the private drive to the speaker and waited politely to order my sandwich. A girl came on and took the order through the static. She asked if I wanted anything else and, in a moment of gluttonous whim, I ordered two tacos. She told me my total and I drove around.

A rickety old van covered in scratches was parked at the window when I pulled up. To save gas, I turned off my engine. With my windows down and the car off, I could hear the conversation at the window very well.

"I'm sorry, sir," the cute drive-thru girl said. She had a slight lisp that wasn't unattractive. "We have to cook all our meat to at least medium-well. It's store policy."

A pale, wizened hand rested on the windowsill, the fingers thrumming in a slow intermittent rhythm. "I understand you have policy," the driver said. His voice was old and foreign, but I couldn't place it. Eastern European? A similar frailty to the hand echoed in his precise, controlled speech. "But my companion is a very picky eater, and anything above rare makes her quite the cranky."

The girl at the window smiled, but it didn't touch her eyes. The tone of her voice was friendly, but of someone resigned to dealing with difficult people. "I really wish I could help, but we have to cook the meat through, sir."

"The thing is, you see – " He was interrupted by a commotion from the back-seat. He turned around and yelled into the back of his van, slipping into a language that I didn't understand.

He turned back to the girl, and took the bag of food. "Yes, is fine. Must go now." He thanked her, and pulled forward a couple of car lengths and stopped.

I turned my engine back on and pulled up to the window. The drive-thru girl was waiting and said, "Hi, it'll be four dollars, forty-three cents."

I handed her my debit card. Her fingers brushed mine as she took the card. Her hair was reddish-yellow and not just blonde, and it flowed in curvy rivulets around her moon-shaped face. "Evening. A real particular customer that last guy was, huh?" I said, trying to chat her up a little. I chuckled nervously. Gimme a break, it's hard to meet women working the hours I do.

She rolled her eyes and smiled with a mouth full of dental work

133

and fillings, but this time it's with her whole face. She had deep laugh lines and bright, friendly blue eyes.

I glanced at her namet-ag: JENNA. "Yeah, geez, what am I s'posed to do, give out undercooked meat? Doesn't anyone remember that E. coli business from the nineties?"

She turned around and grabbed a brown bag from a co-worker. "You want any taco sauce or anything?"

"Yeah, taco sauce would be great. Extra spicy, if you have it."

"Oh, I keep it spicy!"

I laughed in spite of myself. It was strange. I hadn't laughed in a few months at least. I looked at the girl again, and started feeling my pulse quicken just a bit as I quickly tallied her good qualities: sense of humor, lovely face, interesting curves...

And hey. She worked nights. "You usually doing the graveyard thing here?"

She slumped down on the counter in an exaggeration of exhaustion. "Yeah. I'm a slave to the night. Barely conscious, and just a hair above comatose." She rolled her eyes up into her head and stuck out her tongue.

I was smitten.

I said goodbye, not wanting to linger too long and made plans to eat several more chicken sandwiches in the near future. I checked my rear view mirror. There was no one behind me and I was starving, so I pulled out a taco. I start moving forward, eyes wandering to the rear view for another glimpse of her.

I looked forward and hit the brakes abruptly. The van was still parked a car length in front of me taking up the whole path.

I pulled the car up to the van. I don't think he noticed my polite inching forward, so I pushed the horn for a split second in the honking equivalent of a polite cough. I don't want to seem rude, but this is a horrible place to do a bag audit.

I pulled out a packet of extra spicy sauce. The guy was still blocking me and I noticed, with just a little bit of horror, that the van was rocking up and down.

Oh, my.

I got out of my car. If there are old people getting nasty in the drive-thru at Jack in the Box, I'm going to lose my freaking mind.

I walked to the driver's seat, praying I didn't see anything wrinklier than that guy's hand. I eased the taco out of the wrapper and opened a corner of the sauce with my teeth.

I looked in the driver's window of the van, but there was no one at the seat. I heard groaning from the back though, so I walked around to the sliding door on the right and prepared my ass-chewing face as I mentally rehearsed to tell these old people there's a four-hour window for Viagra, and you don't have to start as soon as it gets hard.

I opened the van door.

Inside, I could see what was causing the moaning. The old guy was sprawled across a dilapidated mattress with several shreds in the surface and springs poking out, but thankfully the body of a woman was in front of him blocking any geriatric bits and pieces that might have flopped inappropriately into view. She was facing away from me, and had the hairiest back of any woman I've ever seen.

She wore a yellow sun-dress with white polka-dots and it was obviously a few years late for a leg shave. Her head was bobbing and swaying over the old man's waist.

The metallic scape of chains on the van floor screeched in my ears. There were two of them attached to manacles on her wrists. I looked towards the back. I saw two more broken chains hanging from the walls.

Jesus, kinky seniors.

"Alright, Esther," I said. "Enough with the gummer. Let's move this van so I can get out of here!"

Her head stopped moving. I heard a growl, a low feral sound. A shiver that had nothing to do with the cold night ran up my spine. The hair on my neck and arms stood straight up.

My stomach sank. Every muscle in my body seized as I realized something here was very, very wrong.

Esther slowly pulled her head back from the old guy. He wailed in a gurgle. His entrails were exposed in a bloody mess across the mattress. He lifted his hand towards me. It was shaking.

"Please..." he managed with an effort. Blood dripped out of his mouth. "Kill me..."

My jaw dropped, and so did the taco. The she-wolf slowly turned her head; I saw a blood-stained elongated snout. She pulled her lips back in a vicious snarl, her fangs dripping with spittle. I caught her gaze and we both stared. She turned on me completely and reared back, getting ready to pounce.

I screamed. She jumped.

I was finally able to move, and I tried to back away in a panic. I fell

135

backwards and instinctively squeezed my fists, bringing them up to cover my face. I'd been holding the taco sauce packet that I'd barely torn a hole in, and the force of my squeeze made the sauce shoot out like a fire hose.

The sauce flew true and landed directly in the beastess' eye.

She howled in sudden pain as she blindly leaped from the van, sailing over me and landing in the bushes. She whimpered loudly, scratching frantically at her eye.

I rolled over and scrambled to my feet. I looked around desperately, and saw the open window of the drive-thru as Jenna stared back at the scene.

I ran to the window. "Stand back!2 I shouted. She did, and I jumped at full speed through the tiny window.

I scraped the hell out of my stomach but I cleared it. I hit the red-brown tile of the kitchen floor. I stood up, rubbing my bruised elbow, and the night crew was staring, gape-jawed. I turned around and (maybe uselessly but just in case) slid the service window shut.

"Dude," said a pierced and tattooed grill cook. "Was that a... werewolf?"

I looked at him. Suddenly confronted with the question, it derailed me, and I rejected the idea vehemently. "Don't be stupid. A werewolf? What are you, five? There's no such thing."

A flash of fur and polka-dots streaked by the window. The beastess hit the wall. The drywall cracked, obviously about to crumble. "What are we going to do?" the grill cook said, his voice trembling. Fear was taking the night crew, and I felt it overpowering my own mind. It was high time for me to get the hell out of there...

Jenna shrieked and grabbed my arm, babbling unintelligibly. I threw my arm around her.

Something about her turning to me for protection caused a change. I probably would have been the one to run any other night, but now... I was in charge. It was someone else's turn to run tonight.

The fry cook shrieked in a high tone. He turned and ran to the lobby, going around the counter and running to the locked front door.

I ran to the counter. "No, don't open the door!"

He pulled a ring of keys out of his pocket and, trembling, tried to shove one in the keyhole. "I ain't gonna get ate!" he screamed, a deep-rooted Southern accent surfacing. He finally put the key in the hole and unlocked the door. He threw it open wide and ran. The keys jangled as they hung abandoned in the lock.

I sprinted to the door. I cracked it open a few inches. I saw a freight train of brown fur, and I slammed it shut again. I twisted the key, snapping it off in the lock. "Oh, hell!" I muttered.

I looked through the window in the door but could barely see. I wasn't able to see around the wall, but I think the fry cook ran around the building back towards the drive-thru speaker, a blur of brown and yellow nipping at his heels.

I could only imagine what was happening to that poor soul, but it turned out I didn't need to. I went back to the kitchen where the others were staring at the speaker of the intercom system that was hooked up to let the cooks hear the orders as well as the drive-thru person. We heard the fry cook screaming "Oh, sweet Jesus!"and snarls, and the sickening sound of bones crunching.

No one said anything for several dreadful seconds. "Maybe this means she's not hungry anymore," the grill cook said, his eyebrows raised and he looked repeatedly at all of us.

The wolf hit the wall again. It exploded with enough force to knock huge chunks of mortar through the air. I ducked as a block rushed through the space where my head had just been.

It may have missed me, but it hit Jenna directly in the face. She was knocked over backwards from the force of the blow. She hit the ground hard. She gingerly held her hands to her face. Blood gushed from her mouth, and several teeth lay next to her. She tried to scream but could only gurgle through the mess of her mouth. She turned over to let it flow out of her airway.

I wanted to do something for her, but there was no time and she was conscious, though crying and wailing as she looked at the blood gushing from her nose and pooling on the floor.

She'll be okay, I hoped.

"Is there any other way out of here?" I asked.

"No. We don't even have roof access," said the grill cook.

I looked at him, his apron slicked with the grease of raw hamburger. "Where's your raw patties?" I demanded.

He stumbled over words, unable to speak. Another slamming against the wall rocked the building, and it brought his senses back. He opened a waist-level refrigerator and pulled out a metal pan. "Here's some. B-b-b-but why do you need it?"

I shot my thumb toward the shattering wall. "Sounds like she's still hungry after the fry guy," I said. I grabbed several patties and mushed them

137

into a big ball of beef. "You got a better idea?" I said, shoving the ball of meat at him. He shook his head.

The wolf hit the wall again, finally busting it. All the employees scattered and I started flailing backwards. I took a few steps, then slipped in the pool of blood and landed on my ass by Jenna, still numb from terror.

The wolf's nostrils flared several times, smelling the air. She had her eyes shut tightly. "That extra spicy sauce must be a real bitch," I said absently.

Her head snapped towards me.

I grabbed one of Jenna's teeth and jammed it into the raw hamburger meat. I threw the wad of food at the wolf. Her nostrils flared as she tracked the meat-wad. She jumped forward, snapping her jaws on it in mid-air.

The wolf choked the food down in one gulp. She lowered her head to the ground and prepared to charge us. It was obviously not enough to sate her hunger.

I closed my eyes in silent prayer, and braced myself for an attack...

That didn't come.

I opened one eyelid. The wolf was still in her pounce position, but her face was twitching. She stood straight again, pained. She took a few drunken steps, staggering backwards. Her head twitched. Her eyes dilated. She convulsed and fell with a loud smack against the tiled floor.

All of the hair started to recede into her body, revealing the pale skin of a late-teen to early twenties thin blonde woman. Her dress was torn but still functional for modesty's sake.

The kitchen was stone silent, save for my breath. I gasped, my heart thudded in my ears, pounding the staccato rhythm of passing terror. The employees crept out of whatever cover they'd found during the commotion. I brought my left hand up to wipe the sweat off my brow, but stopped as I saw it covered in blood.

"Someone call 911!" I barked, rushing to Jenna's side. I told someone to get a first aid kit. They brought it to me and I started taking care of Jenna's face. She had passed out, but it looked like she'd be okay.

The grill cook stared at me. He asked, "What did you do? To stop that thing?"

The words took a moment. They were swirling in my brain, looking for somewhere to connect. I focused my attention on swabbing Jenna's wounds with disinfectant, and the distraction was enough to let my mind catch up. "Well," I said, hesitating. "I shoved one of Jenna's teeth in

138

the meat I gave it."

"Why? That's ridiculous." Some of the crew nodded in agreement.

My cheeks flushed red. "Uh, this'll sound stupid, but I saw she had fillings. In her teeth."

The cook stared at the still body of the blonde woman. "Silver fillings?" he hazarded.

I didn't say anything. The thought was too ridiculous.

But it had come to me at the critical moment. And it apparently worked. I looked sideways at the still body of the woman nearby. Damn, she didn't look dangerous now. She just looked like someone's sister. Someone's niece. Someone's ... granddaughter?

"The old man!" My pulse exploded as my heart jump-started again. I scrambled to my feet. I tried to run, but had to slow down on the rubble of the recent hole in the wall.

Please, oh please, still be alive ... I almost tripped running around the back of the van, but I caught myself on the ladder attached to the rear. I rushed to the door, still wide open.

I looked inside.

It was empty.

I shuddered. I turned around, my eye catching the light far up in the sky. Two distinct black clouds rimmed with soft grey covered most of the moon. The steady wind pushed them aside, letting the eye of night shine bright.

I felt a chill run deep into the marrow of my bones as, somewhere in the distance, I heard the low, melodic echoes of a howl.

INCARNATION

By E.W. Bonadio

The airborne attack was swift and sudden. Twenty-two members of the Islamic terrorist group had been killed by strategically placed cruise missiles fired from a missile frigate stationed in the Arabian Gulf. Those that survived the early morning onslaught managed to slip away from the ruined camp. Now, all that remained was the aftermath of death and destruction. For Major Jonah Diggs, the insertion of his Ranger team was the only thing left to accomplish. He was there to clean up, document the kills, collect intelligence and then supervise the extraction of his team back to the U.N. camp.

"Not long now Nazir," he yelled over the roar of the chopper's turbine driven blades. Looking down at his wristwatch, Diggs continued, "Just a few clicks to the west."

Holding onto his loosely fitting helmet, the Egyptian shifted uneasily in his seat. He nodded briefly and grabbed onto a handhold just above his shoulder. Just then the helicopter pitched to the left then banked right cresting the hilly terrain into the valley below. It was a basic evasive manoeuvre to counter an ambush of RPG's or small arms fire. The Egyptian officer knew that if they were to encounter hostiles it would be as they descended into the valley. Nazir released his grip and pointed with his free hand to the remains of the camp. "There it is Major, just in front of us now." Rich plums of black smoke rose from the smouldering ruins, distinctly marking their objective. As the choppers approached the landing zone, Diggs could see the main camp structure, a mud brick building, ringed by several tents and a few vehicles. Nearby, a stand of indigenous trees stood among tall grasses and an ancient watering hole, the lifeblood of the camp.

"Here we go," Diggs yelled, "lock and load." Nazir smiled thinly, shaking his head at the bravado emanating from his counterpart.

The two U.N. designated helicopters swooped down and landed on the desert floor between two ridges. Diggs's small force was in Egypt, just a few miles from an ancient ruin near the western bank of the Nile River. The major's mission objective was politically sensitive, and he was thankful for the Egyptian government's help and the five Arab soldiers under the command of Nazir el Ghazi.

"OK, everybody out," Diggs commanded from his jump seat. Nazir's men were the first to clear the landing zone. Under orders, they trekked over to the roofless one story hut where many of the terrorist bodies lay. As the helicopters ascended turning away from the camp, Diggs' immediate task was to secure the camp and he went about it coolly, placing men at strategic fire points. After a thorough search of the camp, the Egyptian found Diggs rummaging through a semi-collapsed storage tent. Nazir strolled into the tent and the major could see in his eyes that the main objective was lost.

"Sorry to say that there are none left alive, major. They must have took the wounded and left only the dead. My men are gathering the bodies now for identification and disposal."

"Too bad," Diggs countered, "I was hoping to catch one still alive. We need INTEL." Leaving the Egyptian's side and sliding out of the tent, major Diggs looked around for his ranger squad leader. Finding him taking a smoke break with an Egyptian soldier he barked, "Sergeant Pennington, get two men to search the area near that vehicle." He pointed to a partially wrecked red Toyota truck sitting a few yards from the camp's ancient cistern. With a quick salute, Pennington dropped the smoke crushing it with his boot heel, calling out as he jogged away, " Smith... Gordon, come with me." Arriving at the truck, Pennington rummaged through the cab. The others rooted around the ancient watering hole flipping over sheets of metal and examining barrels and boxes strewn around the area.

Minutes later, Pennington returned to Diggs carrying a satchel under his arm. "Gordon retrieved this from a spot near the well, sir... Bet one of the jihadists dropped it while booking from the camp." Diggs grabbed the bag and investigated. Opening the flap he peered in, then dug deep into the canvas pouch. "Shit son, all you brought me was stone tablet...some pictures on it. What is this stuff?" Pennington shrugged. Looking back to the Egyptian officer, Diggs bellowed, "Nazir, come over here will you." As he approached, Diggs threw the heavy package over to him. "Got any ideas what this is?"

Temporarily caught off guard, Nazir blinked. Quickly, he brushed a thin layer of sand and dirt from his face. Opening the satchel, the Egyptian pulled out the tablet. "It's Hieroglyphics, major, ancient Egyptian writings etched into stne."

"Well, what do you suppose the terrorists want with it?" Diggs queried.

Nazir shook his head slowly. Then a thought came to him.

"Mohammad, come over here," he shouted in Arabic. A young Egyptian soldier helping with the collection of the dead dropped his end of a badly burned body and raced over to his superior. With a sharp salute, he clicked his heals saying, "Reporting as ordered, sir."

"Mohammad, what do you make of this?" The young man took the satchel and pulled out the stone tablet. He shook off the dirt and sand covering the inscriptions and studied the pictures. "Oh Allah be merciful," he declared, "It's the spell of regeneration." Nazir shook his head. "You meant the book of the dead."

Mohammad did not want to counter his superior, but he knew that Nazir was mistaken. "No sir, not quite. This is a banned spell, purportedly used by a high priest who rebelled against the Pharaoh Ankhenaten. It was supposedly a gift from the God Anubis, created to raise a personal army of the dead. But the priest was executed before an army could be raised to challenge Pharaoh. That was over three thousand years ago. Only the myth of that priest ever existed. That is until now."

"That doesn't make any sense," Diggs said. "How'd you know… could you really read this stuff?"

Mohammad smiled shyly, "Yes sir, I was a university student, but I got called into the Army last June. My specialty in school was ancient Egyptian mythology and writings."

Nazir bit down hard on his lip. "Major, I have heard of a cult in this region of Egypt. It's headed by an IMAM who wants to bring back the dead to help fight off the invasion by Westerners. It could be that…"

Diggs stopped Nazir in mid sentence. "Now hold on Captain. You mean to tell me that they were trying to raise the dead to fight us?" Nazir's lips pursed as he tried to come up with an intelligent answer. "Well Diggs I must confide, when the tablet was being translated I heard a faint groan coming from over there." He pointed to the well. "It was as if one of the dead had begun to come back to life. But the noise stopped."

"That's ridicules," the major challenged, "But I'll give you this, those dead corpses over there would certainly like to be the first ones reincarnated." He pointed to the mud brick structure where nearly two dozen dead terrorists lay.

Nazir was not laughing. "I tell you major, if the spell of the ancients is spoken properly and the power of the one that controls this spell is strong, there are some that believe they might rise to fight again."

"Is that so?" Diggs grabbed the stone from Mohammad. Laughing out loud, the major said, "Let's test that theory." He studied the tablet for a

142

moment, then gave it back to the Egyptian soldier. "All right son, just read it out for us just as it is written" The young Egyptian looked over to his leader. Nazir reluctantly nodded his approval and Mohammad began to translate in Egyptian. After a few words, Diggs stopped him. "No son, in English…say it in English. I want to understand the words."

"By the light of RA and the staff of Anubis, I call upon the gods of our forefathers. My brother, rise up to live and fight again." Mohammad fell silent and then suddenly, as if in a trance, he began to collapse. The Egyptian captain held him by the shoulders, keeping the boy from collapsing. Mohammad had properly chanted the spell of awakening and it had nearly consumed him. Shaken by the experience, Nazir protested, "I want my people out of here by nightfall. You may stay if you wish, but I would not trust this place now that we have dishonored the past and our ancestors."

Major Diggs laughed. "So you are afraid of a little ancient hocus pocus are you? Ok, I'll have your men extracted within the hour. My team is staying tonight. We'll show you that your ancient rites don't scare American rangers. Besides, we have to RECON the area and finish the mission."

Two hours later, Nazir and his team were on a chopper heading back to the U.N. base camp. The Egyptian took the stone with him, promising Mohammad, "You are not to blame for the words you spoke, but I fear that we have inadvertently awakened a terrible thing, an evil hidden for centuries. The stone will go back to the authorities. I will make a report and see to it that the tablet reaches the museum of antiquities in Cairo."

Mohammad agreed, "There is no other choice but to place it into the hands of our learned men. I am glad that we have retrieved such an important artifact." Mohammad accepted the task of protecting the tablet on their trip back to base. But the young soldier refused to unwrap the stone to show it off or explain the dread that came over him as he read the spell. He vowed never to speak the words again in any language.

Fearing the terrorists' return, Diggs re-set the perimeter around the camp. The bodies of the dead Islamists lay stretched out in front of the burned out hut. Five of the rangers had bunked inside the hut. Two sentries secured the eastern perimeter and similar pairs lay north and west of the hut. Major Diggs took up residence in the bed of the Toyota truck at the southern edge of compound.

At midnight, the carnage began. One by one, the terrorist bodies came to life and they lay in front of the building waiting for the command to take action. When fully reincarnated the terrorists received orders and they fell on the unsuspecting rangers in the hut. No shots rang out, but the muffled death throws of the rangers in the burned out hut alerted the sentries on duty. As they stared out through night vision goggles they had no idea of the threat from behind. Unseen attackers wielding rocks, shovels and other makeshift weapons dispatched the sentries until only Pennington remained on the perimeter.

Diggs and Pennington were still alive. The major lay sleeping in the back of the Toyota. Pennington had taken temporarily residence in a tent halfway between the truck and the hut. Dead silence filled the air around camp and as Pennington roused to relieve himself they came at him. Leaving the tent, he noticed three reincarnated terrorists. Holding a bayonet within striking distance, the lead one struck. In the Toyota, something stirred within Diggs, rousing him from sleep. The feeling of certain doom channeled by Nazir's fears and his own bad dreams forced Diggs awake. Lines of sweat poured down his brow and his eyes opened just in time to hear the muffled screams coming from the tent. Something was terribly wrong and instinctively, Diggs bristled. He dared not call out for fear of giving away his position so quietly, he pulled out his combat phone. Diggs pressed the call button. "Gordon… Pennington… anybody there?"

The last living Ranger released the button and waited. Suddenly, something caught his attention as strange sounds began to sift through the air. Crawling out from the darkness of that ancient pit, the reconstructing body of the priest pressed on to complete his own mission. Echoes of falling debris with occasional splatters of mud plunking into the water drew his attention and Diggs sat up. The entity was alive, ascending from his watery grave. The evil entity had festered in his dark prison for centuries and his incarnate soul longed for a day of reckoning. Thrown into the cistern by Pharaoh's soldiers, he had long ago decayed until nothing was left but minute particles of dust and DNA. It was an unfitting end to his human form, a body that could be reconstituted only by the properly spoken recitation of the spell. Pharaoh's soldiers had foolishly thrown the tablet down the well along with his broken body. How stupid, he thought, to have left the means of my regeneration so close. All the evil entity needed was someone to retrieve the stone and speak the words of regeneration. By the time he reached the lip of the well his human form had only partially reconstituted. Now he needed a donor, someone whose life essence could bring the body completely back to its original form, this time as the immortal champion of dead souls.

In the truck, Diggs locked and loaded his trusty 45 automatic. It had served him well in previous actions and he knew how to use it. Reaching over the side of the truck bed and gently lifting his head above the rail, Diggs looked for signs of life. Through night vision goggles he spied shadowy forms moving forward toward the Toyota. Peering over to the hut, he saw the bodies of his rangers, now devoid of life. The regenerated attackers had laid them to rest in the same spot where they were displayed that afternoon. Diggs threw off his night vision goggles and squinted and his eyes adjusted to the darkness. He could make out their faces better as the undead closed in on his position. Each of the walking re-animated killing machines had but one purpose now, capturing Diggs so that his life form could be used to help fully restore their new master.

"Goddamn zombie bastards," he shouted. Instinctively, the pistol fired - bam, bam, bam...one by one they dropped in a heap. When the magazine emptied, Diggs drew another clip and quickly shoved it into the butt. Again, shots rang out in rapid-fire succession. The zombie attackers continued their methodical assault against Diggs's well-placed fire until the last of them hit the ground, dead for the second time that day.

Drained by the experience, the major fell back into the Toyota's bed. Diggs mind raced uncontrollably. He tried desperately to understand what had happened. Fearing for his life Diggs rolled over onto his belly and grabbed for his field phone. Whispering into it, he said, "May-day, may-day, come in GREEN DRAGON 4, this is BRAVO DELTA 6, over?" There was no answer. After a short silence, he called out forcefully, "GREEN DRAGON 4, this is BRAVO DELTA 4, we have casualties and need assistance. Request a transport and support, over?" This time they answered. "Negative, no can do, sir. You'll have to hold out 'till 0-700 hours." It was night-time in the Egyptian desert and help would not come until morning.

Diggs sat up in the bed of the truck and listened for sounds of activity. Instinctively, he felt an evil presence in the darkness near the ancient well. He pointed his pistol, ready to shoot at anything that moved, but the blackness of the night left him unsure of whom, or what was still out there. It could be one of my men, he thought. Diggs hoped desperately that he was not alone, that another ranger had survived the zombic attack. "Hey out there...Bravo team...is that you?" A low grunt, followed by a wisp of shadowy movement made Diggs realize that something was heading in his direction.

"Hello, Bravo team, report or be shot," he challenged. Still, there was no answer, just the sound shuffling forward in the desert night. Sweat poured down his cheeks as Diggs drew a bead in the general direction of the noise. Then he moved it off-center and fired two rounds. POW – POW!

The ploy did not work and the phantom intruder edged closer to the truck. Fear gripped at Diggs and he hyperventilated close to the point of blacking out. Catching his breath, he dropped down into the truck's bed and fumbled nervously with his ranger flash-light. Pulling it free from the webbing, he pressed on the rubberized switch – nothing. "Goddamnit!" he exclaimed. Banging it twice on the rail, he clicked again and the light flickered on. His next move was both daring and tactical. With his 45 automatic in his left hand and the illuminated flash-light in his right, Diggs pulled himself up over the truck's railing. Again, he flicked it on.

The beam from the flash-light focused on a grotesque form, that of the mummy priest and Major Diggs screamed. The sound reverberated among the ridges ringing the camp. Nazir was correct. They had unleashed an evil on the world, one that was bent on using Diggs as its host. It was a hideous monster, a demon from that ancient well of time reeking of pure hate and malice. For over three thousand years the creature waited patiently for its freedom. Now, because of a chance encounter between a few misguided Islamists and the unsuspecting foreign infidels, it was back among the living, back to seek revenge.

Now partially restored by the words of Mohammad, the mummy was still regenerating. But he needed fresh blood and life fluids that only the living possessed. Confronting Major Diggs at the truck, it regarded the unbeliever. It could sense his life force. It was strong in the Major and the priest was glad to have spared him. Diggs would be the mummy's first sacrifice. The priest would require others to keep his newly regenerated body viable and as with Diggs, he would choose them well. The terrorist leaders had been useful servants. They would continue to be of use to him. Digging up the tablet in an attempt to use it for their evil purposes had been foolhardy. They possessed no such power. The prophecies and stories of the tablet of regeneration were certainly true, but not as the terrorist leaders had hoped. The priest's banishment to the underworld had been useful as well and his malice grew with each passing year. The hate inside drove him to what he was about to do. The terrorists killed by the infidels had provided the muscle needed to rid the camp of the intruders. Now only Major Diggs remained, and the mummy meant to make quick work of him.

The next morning two Army helicopters arrived, bringing in twenty-six additional soldiers from the U.N. base camp near Cairo. They found nothing but death and destruction. During the search the soldiers found Major Diggs sitting up in the bed of the truck, his lifeless eyes set

146

deep into hollow sockets. The Major's desiccated body barely filled out his once proud uniform. The essence of his body was gone, replaced by a shallow shell of clothes, bone and skin. The officer in charge of the rescue reported to base, "We found Major Diggs. He looks like a three thousand year old mummy." No other sign of life remained in the ruins of the terrorist camp.

Miles from the camp the completely regenerated form of the priest rested at an outcropping overlooking the Nile River. The hard work of re-incarnation was now behind him. Wearing traditional Egyptian garb taken from a Bedouin sheep-herder, he watched as small sail-boats navigated the river. The stone tablet of regeneration was safe in Cairo, hidden away in a museum vault. The incarnate needed to finish what had been started nearly three thousand years before when the world of man was young. He yearned to understand and learn from the advances made in weaponry and other tools of war. Only then would his power be complete.

Within the week the priest arrived in the ancient capital city. Assuming the form of an Egyptian scholar, one selected from a list of Egyptologists currently on the museum staff, he readied himself for the task. Strolling up the steps of the museum building the incarnate had come to reclaim his army. With the tablet safely in his hands he expected nothing less than dominion over the graven fools who tried so ineptly to use its power.

THE DISAPPEARERS

By Jeffrey B. Burton

Banning's head lifted as he fought the drowsiness. He opened his eyelids mere coin slits, and felt as though his eyeballs had been rolled across a sizzling iron. He leaned his head against the back of the chair and squeezed them shut.

"Stings at first." A voice across the room whispered.

This must be a nightmare, Banning told himself. As if his problems weren't already unpleasant enough, they now invaded his sleep.

"It's not a dream." The voice, low as a distant train rumbling on the edge of Banning's consciousness, read his mind.

Banning forced his eyes open. Blurry, like staring through warm, oily water, the light slivering into his brain. A candelabrum, silver like found in antique stores, sat in the middle of some elongated dining room table that'd seen more pleasant days. Four white candles burning low—the only light in what appeared, and smelled, like a dank cellar—felt like razors across his retinas. Banning slumped lethargically in a high-back chair at one end of the ancient dinner table. He couldn't move, felt as though his hands were nailed to the wooden armrests.

"You'll feel better in a minute." Again, a quiet susurrus from the other side of the room.

Banning squinted toward the voice, but only made out a smear of white at the far end of the table. He tilted his head sideways for better viewing through the kaleidoscope of candlelight and pain. He did his best to filter, to focus on the unknown voice.

Grandpa?

But Banning's grandfather has passed away a quarter of a century ago, back when he was a five year old boy. In fact, the only vivid memory Banning had of his grandfather was from the old guy's funeral—grandpa lying there in the black pine coffin, waxy, slightly bloated, and white. It had left an indelible impression on him at so young an age. Somehow that image, buried for decades, sprung to the forefront of Banning's thoughts as he strained to make out the figure across the table.

"Where?" Banning's throat was sandpaper. He cleared it and tried again. "Where am I?"

148

"Consider it a weigh station after such a hasty exodus," the voice replied slowly, heavily. "You've come so very far, Albert Banning, so very quickly."

He knows my name, Banning thought, fighting his way through the grogginess to piece together the events of last night. Banning remembered the Jack Daniels, of course. Hard to forget as Mr. D. had become a part of his nightly ritual, helping to numb Banning to sleep after each hard day's drive since he'd departed St. Peter, using only gravel roads and back ways to put as many miles between himself and the latest mess he was in. Banning remembered taking a long piss into the cheap motel's bathtub—a wider target—before sprawling onto the sweaty sheets of the twin bed. Banning remembered a noise. Remembered sitting upright, a frosty breeze across his face, knowing someone was in his room, someone right there in front of him, touching him, a steel grip, an aborted scream . . . then darkness . . . then here.

The intense fatigue caused his mind to grind away in slow motion —must be burning off whatever drug this old bastard had given him—likely made more damaging in combination with all the sipped whisky from the night before. Banning gradually came to an epiphany. Banning's epiphany was a resounding: Oh Shit! But this creep couldn't possibly be a bail bondsman—why would a bounty hunter bring him to wherever in hell this place was? Banning's follow up epiphany was slightly more substantive and consisted simply of: The Girl's Father!

"I didn't do it," Banning blurted at the strange figure, much in the same manner he had two months earlier when that goddamn tight-ass Hadrian Houtz, the school principle, had summoned him out of the American History class he taught to immediately come see Houtz in his office. The girl told pounded through Banning's brain on the long walk past the cafeteria, down rows of lockers, and finally into Houtz's office only to be caught marginally off guard by Principle Houtz, an unsmiling attorney representing the school district, and a plain clothes from the St. Peter Metropolitan Police Department.

The dead-grandfather-like figure remained frozen in silence at the table's end.

Banning closed his eyes again. He'd initially fought the charge, said the girl had made it all up because he refused to make her goalie on the school soccer team of which Banning was the head coach. Banning even got a union attorney, but then that Lolita bitch came forward with the notes he'd thought destroyed, a cell phone tape of them arranging times, and some

149

freedom-extinguishing DNA of his on that goddamned soccer jersey. Evidently, the girl's mom, cold witch that she was, strongly and vocally wondered about the stain, and, after a feeble attempt at saying it was only melted ice cream; the dumb little whore broke down and spilled all the beans to mommie dearest. Yup, just more of Banning's great fortune to have a Monica Lewinsky clone on his soccer team.

Even more of Banning's luck that the girl's parents had gamed the school system's technicalities. The little tramp had been able to advance one grade, meaning that she was only fifteen when their affair had first begun last spring and, in this state, the age of consent was sixteen. Meaning that Banning was looking at a statutory rape charge. Meaning that Banning had been immediately suspended—oh hell, why quibble over semantics— he'd been shit-canned. Meaning that Banning was out on bond, meaning that his due process had almost ground to a halt, which ultimately meant incarceration in Banning's near future. High School Teacher Beds Minor screamed the St. Peter Sentinel. And to make matters worse, the national news had picked up the AP dispatch, and bit hard on the story. Fucking CNN.

But events continued to spiral south and now his current scenario could make his ducked court appearance seem like a stroll in the park. It was obviously the bitch girl's dad, but the guy was in real estate for crying out loud, he sold condos. He must have some kind of connections. The girl's dad must know some Tony Soprano wannabe who could arrange whatever the hell this was . . . kidnapping, assault or . . .

"Who are you?" Banning's trembling voice broke the long silence.

"Just another lost soul, Albert Banning." The old man's voice, both ancient and distant, echoed about the dark cellar, chilling Banning from all sides. "I too have a taste for forbidden fruit."

Taste for forbidden fruit? What the hell did that mean, Banning wondered—that girl was 15 going on 30, with tits out to Montana —I'm no god-damned paedophile. So the bitch girl's dad hired this pervy looking freak to mete out some kind of twisted payback? Oh Jesus, now there's a happy thought.

If anything, Banning was the victim, he'd been the one raped by the news media, prying into every aspect of his personal life and broadcasting it to a salivating world. They'd even dug up that thing in Rochester, but at least that Rochester student had been seventeen and that girl had some class. She'd clammed up all the way down the line, just as Banning had at the time, even though there were several witnesses that saw them necking in his minivan at that strip mall parking lot. Mercifully, the school district gave him the "JFL" option, that is, the just fucking leave and nothing will be filed option. Not so with hard-ass Hadrian Houtz and his rabid pack.

"What do you want from me?" Banning asked the dead-grandfather-like figure, noticing that movement had now returned to his hands and that he wasn't secured to the chair after all.

"You made it all so easy for me, Albert Banning."

"I made it easy?"

"'Why Albert Banning must be a thousand miles away,' all will say. And good riddance, all will think. Some may look—at first—but not terribly hard. In a week, you'll be old news. In a month, Albert Banning, you'll be forgotten."

"How did you find me?" Banning began curling his fingers into clenched fists.

"I've a special talent for the disappearers, Albert Banning. For tracking those who've fled to the shadows." The voice became louder, like a rusty chain dragged over cold and unforgiving stones.

"Whoever hired you, old man—whatever your game plan—forget it." Banning could now freely move his legs. Things were beginning to look up. "I'm innocent, goddammit. I've got witnesses on my side."

He figured it'd be best to keep the creepy old shit talking. Banning was six-one and one-ninety. Once he got a little more feeling back, breaking this geezer's face would be highly satisfying, kicking his teeth out a great release from the hell of the past months. "The attorneys are already cutting a deal. I'll even get some money from the school district for what they've done to my . . ."

Banning stopped in mid-sentence as the dead-grandfather-like figure began to move for the very first time, slowly extending an arm, raising an ungodly long forefinger, and pointing straight toward Banning's chest. Caught off guard Banning looked down and noticed some small droplets of blood on his breast pocket. Banning pulled down on the pocket, dragging the wrinkled shirt downward, gasping when he noticed all the black and tacky blood about his collar, more blood than any minor injury would suggest.

"Good God!" Banning's eyes stung with tear as he ran his fingers slowly across the base of his throat until he found a flap of shredded skin, and then the open wound. "What the hell have you done to me?!"

"Done, Albert Banning?" The dead-grandfather-like figure crossed the table in a heartbeat, suddenly hovering over Banning... white, waxy and

151

not even remotely human. "Whatever made you think I was finished?"

And the last thing Banning saw was the thing's tongue darting across a pair of spiked teeth, dripping saliva and possibly something more . . .

BAD TEETH
By Marc Lyth

The shapes scuttled toward the silent moonlit house. They were tiny, none of them more than a couple of centimetres tall. There were thirty two of them. Quite how they moved was difficult to say. They had no muscle to move them; they simply... moved. Each had twin-pronged bases and used those almost-but-not-quite-feet to shift themselves. Their top halves varied, with some rising to a single point, some flat with a long sharp crown and others were wider and flatter topped. All of them shone bone white in the moonlight.

A mouse started and ran as they skittered past it. Sensing the motion they turned. Two of them jumped and pinned the mouse's tail between their pronged "legs". The mouse struggled to free itself but it was too late. It was surrounded. The sharp ones rushed in and slashed at the underside of the mouse's jaw. The blunter ones battered it from the sides, cracking ribs and breaking one of it's legs. The pointy ones aimed themselves at the eyes.

Blinded, crippled and bleeding, the mouse was dead in minutes. A passing black cat with a triangular white bib would have a surprise snack later on that night.

The shapes continued toward the house. When they reached a step they didn't even slow. As if gravity worked sideways they simply "walked" up the stair like so many mutated and partially dismembered spiders.

They were soon at the back door of the house, pausing only to scare a bird into flight. They slid silently under the wooden door into the kitchen. If they could talk they would have been giggling like schoolgirls. Instead they jumped up and down with as much glee as their expressionless forms could allow before splitting into separate groups and skittering to the different areas of the kitchen.

One group found the dustbin and spent time tearing holes in the bin liner. When the bin was emptied later in the week it duly split, emptying its contents over the kitchen floor, further adding to the distress of the family.

Another group climbed onto the table and tipped over the salt and pepper shakers. When they couldn't quite tip the box of cornflakes they moved to the edge of the table and somehow, without any noise audible to

153

human or animal, called another group up to help them. This third group stopped their attempts to cut through the TV aerial cable and quickly scaled the table legs to join in.

With the reinforcements the group on the table now managed to tip the cornflake box and proceeded to crush as many as they could into the tablecloth, brushing a pile off the table in the process for the remaining shapes on the floor to crush into the carpet. A carton of pure orange juice was their next target and it was rapidly spilt over the table.

This achieved, they jumped off the table, landing in the spilt cornflakes, crushing more into the carpet, before they all rejoined and crossed the floor to the hallway.

A sleeping family could be heard upstairs, gentle snores and the creaks of a bed as the daughter tossed and turned in her sleep. The shapes giggled their silent giggle again and started up the stairs, making a point of scratching the paintwork on the skirting boards as they did so.

At the top of the stairs they separated again and scouting groups entered each of the three bedrooms. After a few moments of their strange communication, the groups left the rooms where the parents and the daughter lay sleeping and converged on the son's room.

They climbed onto the bed to join the scouting party already present and watched eyelessly as the boy lay sleeping in the slight breeze from the open window. He lay on his back with his mouth open. Under his pillow was his upper left bicuspid and a note for the tooth fairy. The shapes crept under the pillow and nudged the bicuspid. It twitched and giggled noiselessly when it saw the teeth surrounding it.

Silently it joined them as they climbed the pillow and surrounded the boy's head. The thirty three teeth on the expanse of soft cotton examined the sleeping form in front of them. He twitched as the teeth climbed his face.

The canine teeth aimed for his nose. They were thin enough to squeeze up his nostrils and drop down the naso-pharyngeal tube to the back of his throat. The boy's own bicuspid followed them, sliding down the back of his nose to join them on the boy's uvula, pushing it down over the top of the windpipe. Another dozen of the teeth entered the boy's open mouth. They gathered together at the back of his throat, adding weight and bulk to the blockage.

The boy woke and tried to cry out but the blockage was too much. The weight of the teeth in the back of the throat stopped even the gag reflex from clearing his mouth. The remaining teeth on his face sniggered

154

noiselessly and played a game of bucking bronco, trying to cling on as the boy twitched and swatted at his face, desperately trying to cough. After a minute or two of struggling he lay still, his lips a cyanosed blue.

The teeth crawled slowly out of his mouth and nose to examine their work. His old bicuspid resumed its spot under the pillow.

A woman's voice from the next room – " Gary , are you OK?" – was followed by a man's voice - "He's just having a bad dream.". This in turn was followed by the woman's voice again – "I'm going to check on him" and the man - "He's quiet now, why do you mollycoddle him?" The woman again - "I'm going to check that my son is OK. I don't need your permission."

As the sounds of the woman shuffling in her slippers approached the door, the teeth scuttled to the window. They climbed out and slid down the ivy on the outside of the house into the garden. A cry sounded from the room above, the woman calling for her husband to come and help now, call an ambulance, please god call an ambulance.

The teeth skittered back across the garden to the gate and onto the street. They debated noiselessly and started downhill.

The man at the bottom of the road stopped as if he'd sensed something. He shone his torch up the hill directly onto the scuttering shapes. "Vair you are" he said, then knelt down with his hand outstretched.

The teeth, grudgingly accepting they'd been caught, dutifully filed toward him and onto his palm. He opened his toothless mouth wide and tipped the teeth into it from his hand, using his tongue to direct the teeth back to their correct places.

He walked off down the hill again, pausing at a shop window and grinning at his reflection. An ambulance siren sounded in the distance. You'd be a good looking guy, he thought to himself, if you didn't have such bad teeth.

MAYONNAISE – THE REAL STORY

By Neil Leckman

We were outside playing and Chuck's mom called us over to the porch.

"I made you boys a couple of bologna sandwiches and there's some kool-aid for you too."

We both ran up the back porch shoving at each other trying to be the first one inside. The back porch was one of those screened in porches; there was a washer and dryer as well as some shelves for cleaning supplies and storage. Chuck's mom also kept a bunch of jars out there that she used for canning. It was cooler inside his house. His mom had set two plates with bologna sandwiches on the table. Next to them were a couple of tall glasses of Kool-aid. They were so cold that water drops were forming and sliding down the outsides of the glasses.

"Be right back" I ran down the hallway to Chuck's bathroom. I really had to go badly. When you're a kid it seems like you can hold it almost until you pop. However when you get that message that your time has come, you'd best be moving along. A couple of minutes later I walked back into the kitchen.

Chuck gave me that quizzical look, as if to ask "Is it safe to go in there?" His Kool-aid was half gone and his plate was empty. Sitting down I grabbed my Kool-aid and took a big swallow. As I was reaching for the sandwich he asked me, "Did I ever tell you where Mayonnaise comes from?"

"Nope, don't think so."

"You know that shelf on the back porch that mom keeps stuff on?"

"Sure."

"She always keeps a bunch of mayonnaise jars out there too, but I ain't never seen her buy any mayonnaise at the store. When we run out, she cleans the empty jars, then puts them on the shelf on the porch. A couple of days later, when I check, they're full again."

"So? She goes out and buys some when you're not around" I say.

"No she doesn't. The jars get refilled right there."

"Bullshit! You're telling me that your mom makes the mayonnaise!!"

156

"Not mom, something else. If I'm lying, I'm dying."

Taking a bite out of my sandwich, I looked up at him skeptically.

"OK, so who or what fills them?"

Lowering his voice almost conspiratorially and leaning closer he said, "I snuck out one night, and hid out in that space between the washer and dryer. After a couple of hours I fell asleep. The sound of the screen door squeaking open woke me up. It was pitch black, so I couldn't see a thing. I just heard this sniffling, shuffling noise like something large went over by the shelves. I could hear the sound of the jars being moved around. I knew that this had to be the secret to how mom got her mayonnaise. Standing up I turned on my flash-light and shined it where the shelves are. Do you know what I saw?"

"Nope" I said through a mouthful of food.

"This seven foot tall half snake, half lizard monster. It had a long tail that it dragged along behind it. Its body was green and covered with all of these really nasty oozing pus covered yellow sores. The sores were all red and swollen around the edges and white stuff was seeping out of the tops. It turned away from me and picking up one of mom's clean jars placed it next to one of those sores. Then it squeezed that sore with one of its claw like hands real hard. White stuff slide out of that sore and filled the jar. All I could do was stand there and stare at it while it filled the rest of the jars. When it was done it turned and for one brief second it looked at me. Its eyes were like a cats eyes but bloodshot. The look in them was almost like the monster was going to cry. Then it shuffled back out the screen door and was gone."

I spit my piece of sandwich into my hand and put it back on my plate, "That's disgusting!!" I said, taking a big drink of Kool-aid to wash down the now sour taste in my mouth.

Standing up Chuck walked over and grabbed my unfinished sandwich and sat back down eating it.

"Sucker! Oh, man, that was classic" Sitting there laughing, Chuck looked pretty pleased with himself. To this day I can still remember as we ran inside through the back porch. I had glanced over at that shelf. There, on the floor in front of where the jars were, had been a big slimy looking footprint of some kind. Say what you want, from now on I eat all my sandwiches with mustard.

157

DARKNESS WITHIN
By Ash Krafton

She waved at the approaching headlights as if she signalled a plane, her hands sweeping wide, desperate arcs. When the car slowed she lunged toward it, throwing herself against the fender as if to prevent its escape.

Still sobbing, partly now in relief, she pulled open the door. A rosary hung from the rear-view. A sweater folded over the console. The driver's expression was a mix of compassion and confusion as she clambered into his sanctuary.

"Please, drive!" She nearly choked trying to rush out the words. "As fast as you can!"

"What are you doing out here alone?"

"Just go!"

He pulled back onto the road, watching the rear-view mirror, then glanced at her. "You're bleeding."

"I'm alive. Alive, right? I can't believe it."

"Somebody hurt you?" He stretched to reach into his pants pocket, tugging free a handkerchief.
"Here."

She pressed it to her head, checked the bloody smear, and pressed it again, harder. "Yeah. You can say that. How fast can you get to Wilkes Barre?"

"Forty minutes. Why there?"

"Lights. Lots of lights."

"Somebody back there doesn't like lights?"

Her tone sounded black like a well: hollowed and a long way down. "*They* don't."

"Who?"

"*Them.* They're like water and shadow and I thought they'd never end."

"I don't understand."

"They drip onto your skin and creep over your face and pour inside--and--I never want to go back." She was babbling and she knew it but it was hard not to sound crazy. He looked like such a nice old man. He'd never understand. "Those shadows. They were so deep."

158

"You're afraid of shadows?"

His words could have implied teasing, but his expression and tone did not. Didn't matter, she thought. She knew nothing could ever be black and white again. The window was cool against her forehead and the trees lining the road spattered past. "Forget I said anything."

"When we flip a light switch, the shadows disappear." He used a cautious, careful tone that made her think of hands, palm-side down and gentle. "That's easy, isn't it?"

She shook her head. "Not when you're strapped down."

"Strapped – " He faced her, the lines of his face reminding her of her dad: concerned, protective, outraged. "Do the police know?"

She barked a harsh laugh. "Who do you think did this? Those things couldn't be real. But they were. And the good guys--they were the ones using them."

"You weren't just attacked, were you? You were."

"Yes."

He let the implication hang in the air. "And you weren't the only one."

"Nope. My entire class was quarantined. Said it was swine flu but we weren't sick. They sealed off the campus, made it a medical ward. Rats in a trap."

"Anyone else make it out?"

"How many others did you pick up?" She craned her neck to look in the back seat at no one.

"Everyone else – just broke, opened up, and the shadows spilled back out. Not me. I drowned in them."

Her eyes felt cold, making her shudder. The shudders travelled and multiplied, causing her to bite her cheek. Pain and a thin taste of pennies. "I saw things. So dark inside. So dark. Felt capable of doing *anything*. No boundaries. No one should ever feel like that."

"Like?"

"Full of – I don't know." The words were heavy, as if they weighed upon her. They were a load she'd carry until the end of her life. "What's the opposite of *mercy*?"

He flicked up his high beams, illuminating more than just the chipped yellow sign: Dangerous Curve. He checked his mirrors again, drummed his fingers on the wheel.

"Mercy is overrated, dear." The driver drifted to the berm, the parental lines of his faces shifting into un-crossable chasms before

159

solidifying into granite splits. He hooked his tie and tugged it loose. "Where did you say you went to school?"

The door lock clicked. His eyes held shadows as he grinned and turned the car around.

GETTING HOME
By David Bernstein

Marcus awoke in pitch darkness. Pressing the illumination button on his wristwatch, he saw the time was two am. One of the crewmen was suppose to wake him at nine and bring him food. He was ravaged. He finished off a bottle of water and began working his way toward the front of the shipping container.

He had been abroad on a business trip in Spain and had been robbed of his passport and wallet. With no proof of who he was, except for a duplicate debit card he'd left in his room, he would have to wait at least a month before his situation was sorted out. In the meantime he was told to enjoy an extended vacation.

A day after the mugging, his wife called his hotel room and told him horrible news. She'd been dizzy with headaches, finally going to see a doctor and it turned out she had a tumor in her brain. The MRI revealed the cancer was most likely operable.

Unable to wait, desperate to be by his wife's side, Marcus began withdrawing large sums of money over the next three days. Through a business associate, he was able to acquire passage on a cargo ship. The freighter would be at sea for four days while traveling to Florida with a few stops along the way.

Now, he worked his way in complete darkness, save his wristwatch, banging his knees, shins, arms and head on cargo. The captain had insisted he stay in the container rather than below deck where boarding patrols would search more thoroughly.

Marcus made it to the other end of the container. Feeling for and finding the handle, he turned it, cracking the door open. Fresh sea air assaulted his nose as a gentle breeze cooled his skin. He listened, hearing nothing. He pushed the door open further, stepping out, the large metal hinges squeaking loudly, breaking the silence.

The breeze died down, leaving the air still. Marcus licked his fingers, holding them out. There was no air present indicating the ship wasn't moving. He closed the squeaky door, before heading out of the cargo area.

As he rounded a corner he came upon a dead body. Its stomach was torn open, entrails hanging from the cavity. Marcus froze, stunned, before breaking out of his stupor and began yelling for help. A horrifying scream sounded in the distance, port side, making him re-evaluate his decision to call for aid.

He worked his way starboard, finding the ship's railing and began heading toward the bridge. A dark lump lay ahead. As he neared, he saw it was another crewman. The man's chest had a hole where the heart should have been. Four large gashes, like claw marks, went across the face, the man's right eye missing. A side-arm lay in a holster on the man's belt. Marcus, avoiding the bloody deck as best he could, plucked the weapon from the body. It was a Sig Sauer P226, a common weapon used by U.S. Homeland Security and Navy Seals. Marcus had fired them while in the National Guard. He crept along, following a trail of blood that lead into the first level of the bridge's tower. The steel door was open, light coming from the inside.

He entered the doorway, guardedly. Smears of blood continued across the room and up a flight of mesh stairs. The crimson trail glistened under the lights, the blood was fresh. A gunshot echoed from above. Reluctantly, Marcus crossed the room, placing his shaky foot on the first step and climbed.

By the fifth step he stumbled upon the crewman's missing eye lodged in a gap in the mesh work. Continuing up the stairs, he found a clump of fur attached to a chunk of torn flesh wedged into the mesh railing. It looked canine. He continued upward, halting when he heard a woman's scream followed by a gunshot and a howl of agony.

"Hello?" Marcus yelled.

"Who's there?" a man replied.

"Marcus Riggs."

"You alone?"

"Yes."

"Get up here fast."

Marcus hurried up the stairs. After two more flights he entered the bridge.

The room was low lit, a single lamp hanging, swaying back and forth. Blood pooled on the floor in different areas like rain puddles after a storm. Parts of the control panels were damaged and smoking. Two bodies lay slouched in chairs. One, the throat had been ripped out and the other was missing its head, nowhere to be found.

"Hello?" Marcus whispered, seeing no one.

A man's head, with a white, neatly shaved beard, popped over a U-shaped control area. "Over here," he said. Marcus ran over, slipping on syrupy blood, but regained his purchase. Rounding the control wall, he saw the captain and a young woman holding an AK-47 machine gun. She had dark hair, radiant skin even in the dim light and emerald colored eyes. Marcus squatted next to them.

"What the hell is going on?" he asked.

"Keep your voice down," the young woman said. "They'll hear you."

"Who?" Marcus asked.

"The werewolves," she said.

Marcus frowned, shook his head. "Werewolves? Come on. Are you serious?"

"Dead," the Captain said, his eyes beady and red. Something crashed outside making all three flinch.

"There's no such thing," Marcus said. "Must be dogs."

"And what kind of dogs could cause that?" the captain said, pointing to the headless corpse in the chair. Marcus followed his gaze before turning away.

"I just can't bring myself to believe in werewolves, but if there are such beasts, what the hell are they doing on this ship?" His heart began pounding, his mind racing, as the possibility of such mythological creatures dawned.

The captain lowered his head. One of the control panels sizzled, sparks flying outward. "Had a client," he said. "Offered me a large amount of cash to transport him and four of his buddies to the states." Marcus eyed the captain. "What? You thought you were the only stowaway?" The captain laughed. "You guys are my retirement fund." He cleared his throat as if embarrassed. "We were under strict instructions, not to open the container until we reached Florida, when the full moon would be gone." The captain pulled a flask out of his back pocket, offering some to Marcus who shook his head. "Suit yourself." The man took a long swig before returning the flask to his pocket. The young woman had been watching the door the whole time.

"And?" Marcus asked.

"One of the crew, instead of opening your container, opened theirs by mistake." The captain looked haggard, shaking his head.

"That explains why no one came to feed me," Marcus said.

"Mike, the crewman carried in the food, while Pedro waited at the

163

container's door. Pedro ran screaming when he saw wolves standing on hind legs, ripping Mike to pieces. I came out of my room, crew members gathered around. Pedro told us what happened. We all thought he was drunk." The captain swallowed, his face grave. "Until we saw them emerge from the container. They separated, running wild, gutting every crewman they encountered. Me and my niece came up here and have been holding out since."

"We've got guns," Marcus said. The woman turned, eyes fierce. "Bullets don't kill them, they only slow them down and make them ugly until they heal and come back."

"Will the ship move?" Marcus asked.

"No, the controls are damaged," the captain said.

"Lifeboats?" Marcus asked.

"What about them?" the girl asked.

"If we can get to them, we can get off this ship."

"You're crazy," the captained barked. "We're not going out there."

"Uncle Jack," the woman said. "We can't hold out forever. Soon they'll be no crew left and we'll run out of ammo. We'll be the last meals left."

"We can wait them out," the captain said. "Once the full moon is over they'll change back."

"No," Marcus said. "I don't think we can wait. The moon can look full for about three days and we don't know how long they'll be . . . werewolves." He looked at the woman, then at her gun. "And from what you've told me, I don't think we have enough ammo to keep them busy."

"He's right," the woman said. "My name's Melissa by the way." She held out her hand. Marcus took it.

"Marcus," he said.

"Good to meet you," Melissa said.

"Enough with the pleasantries," the captain complained. "Let's get moving if we're going to do this."

"I'll lead," Melissa said.

"No," her grandfather said, pulling at her arm.

"Guys," Marcus intervened. "I've got military training. Let me take the machine gun and lead the way." He thought about giving the captain the handgun, but Melissa looked more in control. "Melissa, take my gun."

They exchanged weapons and came out from behind the terminal. One of the werewolves, a hulking mass of fur and sharp teeth, appeared in the doorway. It stood seven feet tall, growled, and charged at the group.

Marcus opened fire, jumpy at seeing one for the first time. The first bullet hit the creature in the sternum, the second in the face. It fell to the floor in writhing, howling agony. A fireman's ax hung from the wall in a glass case. He smashed the glass with the butt of his gun and tore the ax free. He approached the downed beast, raising the ax over his head, almost hitting the ceiling. He saw its eyes amongst the grizzled bullet wound on its snout. They looked human, with irises, pupils and all. He brought the axe down on the monster's neck, severing its head from its body. The howling immediately ceased, the room becoming quiet. He kicked the head out the door. It rolled, bouncing over the stairs' edge and into the ocean. He turned to the others.

"That one isn't coming back," he said, flatly.

"Guess that's one way to make sure they stay dead," Melissa said. The headless werewolf corpse began shaking, then shrinking. The hair receded, revealing the body of a naked man, blood pooling from the severed neck.

"That's the final stage," the captain said. "We'll know they're dead when they turn."

Outside on the mesh walk the night was still, save a pleasant breeze that seemed as if it didn't belong. They made it down the first flight of stairs. Screams broke out from somewhere below, breaking the silence and sending a chill down Marcus's back.

Halfway down the second flight, a growl sounded from above. All three turned to see a werewolf descending upon them. Melissa and Marcus raised their weapons and began firing. The beast was struck multiple times, but kept coming, its face in a snarling rage. The captain, at the rear of the group, shoved Melissa and Marcus out of the way.

The two tumbled down the stairs, weapons flying from their grasp. Marcus recovered quickly and looked back to the werewolf standing over a downed captain, claws raised. It sunk its maw into the captain's throat, blood gushing and began tearing at his stomach.

Melissa had been knocked silly and was woozy. She tried getting up, but stumbled. Marcus was glad she hadn't seen her uncle's nasty demise. He scooped up the AK-47 and Sig Sauer.

"We need to leave now," Marcus said, grabbing Melissa's arm and tugging her away.

"What . . . what about my . . . uncle? she asked.

Marcus wanted to be gentle with her, ease the words, but there wasn't time. "I'm sorry," he said. "He didn't make it."

165

"What?" she said, tears beginning to flow.

"I'm sorry. The werewolf got him. We can't help him now. We have to move." Marcus looked past Melissa, eyeing the way they'd come, checking to make sure they weren't being pursued.

"He's dead?" she asked, not grasping his words. "We have to go back, check."

"We have to move, Melissa. He's dead and saved our lives doing so. Let's not let that be for nothing."

Marcus pulled the weeping girl with him. They hurried to the other side of the ship, away from the werewolf and toward the lifeboats. He'd known where boats were, having asked a crewman before boarding. It was something the National Guard had instilled in him.

A werewolf sat, with its back to them, hunched over feeding on a crewman. The sucking and gnawing sounds of flesh being devoured would stay with Marcus forever. He raised his weapon. Melissa sniffed, her nose runny from crying.

Marcus cringed knowing the sound was too loud. The werewolf's ears went up and it spun around with lightening speed. Marcus pulled the trigger making sure to fire in short bursts, conserving ammo. Bullets riddled the werewolf as it drew closer, making Marcus pull the trigger faster. The creature kept coming until Marcus was able to hit the beast in the head. It slowed, but kept coming, its face jutting this way and that. Finally a bullet found its way to the beast's eye, destroying it. The creature howled in pain. More bullets shattered its teeth and ripped apart the inside of its mouth. The werewolf fell backwards, holding its head in its clawed hands. Marcus ran up and put two more bullets in its head. The beast fell still, a twitch here and there.

"Help me push this thing over the side," he said. Melissa ran over and together they managed to shove the heavy, bloody werewolf over the railing. It fell, splashing into the ocean.

"Two down," Melissa said.

"Lets hope we don't run into any more. I think I've maybe a shot or two remaining. Plus whatever you have left in the pistol.

They headed forward, stepping around the mangled crewman's body, blood seeping all over like some Rorschach test. They had no choice but to step in it, leaving a crimson footprint trail behind.

They crept forward, quickly, but silently. An open doorway stood on the left. Marcus watched the entrance, while Melissa passed by.

They finally made it to the first lifeboat. It looked like someone else had the same idea, but didn't quite make it. The lower half of a crewman, strands of loose flesh and intestine sprouting from a pair of jeans, lay near the boat. Marcus looked around, but the upper region was no where to be found.

Marcus and Melissa worked together to peel off the lifeboat's cover. Melissa climbed in, Marcus following. Each boat was equipped with an S.O.S. beacon that would send out radio signals where nearby ports or ships would pick up the transmission. Marcus pressed the button on the S.O.S. box.

Next he lowered the lifeboat using the manual crank. It wasn't too noisy, but made him and Melissa cringe with each turn of the crank. Howling from above made them jump, each looking overhead for falling werewolves, but none came. Marcus cranked faster.

They hit the water after what seemed like an eternity, relief flooding through Marcus like sipping a cold beer after a long day of work. He had no idea how far out at sea they were, but had confidence someone would pick up the radio signal and rescue them.

They got out the paddles and began paddling away from the large vessel. The lifeboat came equipped with bottled water, enough for a few days.

As they began to gain some distance, at least enough to ensure no leaping werewolves would reach them, Melissa spoke.

"I feel a little better now. Those things were awful."

"I can't get far enough way from that ship," Marcus said. "Want some water?"

"Sure."

Marcus rose from his seat to hand Melissa a bottle when a loud splash erupted from the side of the boat. Furry, clawed hands gripped the side of the small dinghy, rocking it wildly. Marcus flew sideways, bashing his head on the side. Melissa, who had been sitting in the boat, screamed as she tumbled over the side into the dark salty sea.

Marcus tried regaining himself, shaking off the pain in his head, when he felt a sharp, singing pain in his calf. Turning he saw the werewolf climbing into the boat, its arm outstretched with pieces of his flesh and pant leg on its claws. He scrambled for his weapon. Grabbing it, he turned firing point blank into the monster's forehead. It let out a single howl before dropping back into the sea.

He heard Melissa splashing in the water, reached over the side and pulled her in the boat.

167

"Where the hell did that come from?" Melissa asked, breathing hard and water-soaked.

"I think it was the one we threw over the side," he said, breathing hard himself.

"Who knew a werewolf could swim?" Melissa joked.

Marcus's ankle ached where the beast had scratched him. He used the lifeboat's first aid box to disinfect the gash before bandaging it.

A day later they were rescued by a merchant vessel and brought to Puerto Rico. A U.S. Coastguard station took them in, where they were questioned about the incident aboard the freighter from Spain. They were told nothing of what was found on the ship and all their own questions went unanswered. Some high ranking military officials came in, making them sign non-disclosure statements, silencing them while the investigation was foregoing. They were free to go home.

A month later, Marcus was back with his wife in their home. Things were good; his wife's surgery went well, the tumor removed successfully.

As the month neared its end, Marcus's energy level soared. He thought it might be his new workout routine. He began ordering hamburgers less and less cooked, always having liked his meat cooked well-done.

"What's gotten in to you?" his wife asked one night as he tossed and turned restlessly in bed.

"I don't know. I feel so damn good, energized."

Marcus lay in bed for the next hour, unable to sleep. The shades were drawn, making the room dark with nothing to look at. Finally, he got out of bed and decided to find something to eat in the kitchen, he was ravished.

The kitchen was bathed in the bright glow of moonlight. Marcus felt a warm tingle in his head, feet and arms. He walked to the sliding glass door leading to the porch, opened it and stepped out. Looking upward, he saw the moon, its glow intoxicating. The euphoria turned to agony as pain racked his body as if he was being electrocuted. His skin split as the bones stretched, growing thicker and longer. His mouth elongated into a snout and long pointed teeth lined his gums. Fur sprouted from his skin as his nails grew to six inch claws. He howled at the moon.

Fully transformed, Marcus leapt from the porch, running into the cool night air, his hunger for meat, insatiable.

168

DINNER IS ON THE TABLE
By Chris Dean

Blake Fischer suddenly understood his mistake and his heart grew cold. He stared at the machete and he stared at the plate, and then he stared at the cruel black eyes across the table. And he knew he'd been a fool to come there.

He watched the spoon dip into the undulating shimmer of red and gray, clicking on the plastic plate. A slimy silvery heaping rose, jiggling as it caressed the other man's ruby lips for a moment. The pink mouth sucked and the spoonful was gone and sliding down into his gullet. Blake looked at the floor, trying not to retch.

"You see –" The old man set the spoon down and took a sip of Chardonnay from his goblet. He gave Blake a quiet smile, nearly indiscernible. "I realized I was wrong trying to fight them. Hopeless really. There's just too many of them now." He reached out a weathered hand and latched onto the bottle, pouring a dollop into his glass. The bottle rose, its neck canted. "Are you sure?"

Nodding reluctantly, Blake wrapped trembling fingers around his empty goblet and held it out as the old man filled it. He took a gulp and panted, barely tasting the dry tang.

The old man set the bottle down and went on with the morbid explanation of his dinner, "I was almost killed several times you know. I think they may be getting smarter." The ruby lips pursed out. "Do you think that's at all possible?"

When Blake didn't answer the low voice continued, "In any case I see no point in chasing them down anymore. It's so much simpler to go after their food source." The spoon moved again, scraping. A drop of horror splashed on the black shirt as the old man slurped. Unable to control himself, Blake shoved his chair back over the concrete floor and shut his eyes. Sweat rimmed the line of close cropped blonde hair and he smeared it away with a hand. The clicking spoon echoed like thunder. Blake was sure he was going to be sick.

"There's a colony south of here. Us, I mean, human."

Blake rubbed a sweaty hand over his eyes. He looked at it. The pale thin fingers were shaking.

"When the Catastrophe began this whole community simply folded itself up. There are more than a thousand people there and they are entrenched like a feudal castle. I'm sure that they are the main food source for the greater Los Angeles area." A low chuckle drifted through the dark basement. "I've been stalking them."

Finally unable to keep silent, Blake stared at the low unfinished ceiling and accused, "You're insane."

"You don't know what your talking about." The growl turned into a howl, "they were insane! The scientists who did this. They were trying to do what? Create a better Man. What they did was destroy Mankind for all time."

"It was a mistake." Angry now, Blake felt a rush of heat. "Genetics research has helped mankind in many ways." The paucity of his argument struck him and he pled now, terrified of the cost of one mistake, "they- went too far."

"That is the insanity not me!" A palm slammed on the wooden table. "But they were right." the old man's eyes gleamed with hate. "They did create a stronger human, one that can survive fire and bullets. Yes, this new race of Man is very hard to kill. It is too bad that their altered metabolism requires a high protein source, best supplied by the flesh of human brains. A slight drawback that those very sane scientists somehow missed. Now, tell me!" The hand slammed on the table again and the old man's glass fell and crashed on the floor. "Am I insane?"

"I'm sorry." Blake sagged, suddenly exhausted. "But what you're doing –" His blue eyes flicked to the dregs of the old man's dinner for a moment, far too long. His voice squeezed into a rasp, "you can't do this."

"Look you, you have no way of knowing how hard they are to kill. And what's left afterward? A dead zombie." A finger dipped into the grotesque slime on the plate and swirled. "This way I don't have to work so hard and I get a free supper to boot." The old man sucked his finger. "It's a simple logistical solution that I think is inspired really."

An uncontrollable sob of horror rattled in Blake's chest. "I came here because you promised sanctuary. Is that a lie?"

Dark eyes studied the long table against the wall, the silver casing of the ham radio gleamed in the dim light. The old man seemed almost apologetic. "It's fifty miles down there you know. Quite a ride in a city full of zombies. That thing with the radio started as sort of a joke." A dark chuckle. "Until people like you started showing up of course. Now it saves me a trip more or less. Nobody likes to go out for dinner every night, you know." The thin wrinkled face poised in place, waiting for a reaction. Dark eyes watched as the paleness of Blake's cheeks increased. The old man puffed out a breath of air in a disgusted way. "I guess that's a bad joke. In either case, I am very glad you showed up." A wicked smile flickered over the old man's face. "The larder's bare you see. He was the last." A hand patted the old man's belly and he sighed with contentment. "But thanks to you, I won't have to go out for breakfast in the morning, will I?"

"I traveled over two hundred miles and I fought them." Blake's voice was cold as ice. "I was almost killed! And for what? So you can eat my brain for breakfast?" Suddenly he lunged across the table and snatched up the machete. "I'll kill you first!"

The old man laughed so hard spittle splashed over his unshaven chin. "You idiot." A hand came up from beneath the table, holding a black gun. "I suggest you put that back down. I don't want to kill you yet but I'll do what I have to and you know I will."

His heart pounded with fear as Blake made his decision to risk death. It was dark; maybe the bullet would miss. He would be dead in the morning anyway. Legs shaking, he stood up, locking eyes with the old man. A terse voice ordered him to sit back down. Pure terror sliced down Blake's spine as he lurched around the table, swinging the sharp blade.

The gun roared. A grunt exploded from Blake and he staggered back a step. Shock numbed his body and he could feel no pain. In horror, he stared at the crimson hole in his tee shirt.

Seconds ticked by. The old man held the gun out like a shield. Blake watched him and he looked at the hole in his belly that didn't seem to be bleeding very much. He caught a glimpse of fear in the old man's eyes. And Blake knew. He took a step forward and the gun roared again.

The force of the bullet that smashed into his chest stopped him. But like the first wound this hole was bereft of blood. The gun fired again and again. Each tear in the shirt produced more damage to the cloth than to the dead flesh beneath. And there was no pain. Zombies never feel pain.

Blake blinked, looking at the gray pool of gravy on the plate. No longer disgusted by the exotic fare, he was instead outraged by the old man's gluttony. He smiled and moved forward again, raising the machete with a hungry leer.

The old man's voice was a horrified croak, "you – you were bitten?"

Blake displayed the bruised wrist. "Yesterday. I didn't know that this would happen." He barked a laugh. "I thought they almost killed me. I guess I was wrong."

"Please!" The gun clattered over the floor as the old man raised his trembling arms. "You don't have to do this. I don't even hunt your kind anymore. We don't have to be enemies."

"Only one problem with that." The machete began its deadly arc. "I seemed to have gotten my appetite back after all." The blade sliced through a flopping wrist and thunked into bone and brain. Blake caught the body and lay it gently on the floor. Taking the machete, he chopped a bit and widened the hole he'd made in the old man's skull, careful to avoid creating bone splinters. There was a tremendous amount of blood, enough for two brains, he thought. Blake's shirt and pants were sopping by the time he had his dinner cut free. He'd have to remember to avoid that.

He shoveled the old man's brain on the plate and sat at the table, eyes darting about for the spoon.

THEATRE OF PAIN
By Lee Pletzers

It was a short line in a grungy part of town, but it was the only theatre without lines going around the block. This line ended at the bottom of the steps. It was an old theatre, one screen, and had fake pillars at the entrance. Tim looked up at the movie poster stuck in a glass cabinet surrounded by small flashing lights. *This Halloween, gear up for the Theatre of Pain.* With a title like that how could he not see it on opening night?And judging by the lines of people through town, every man and his dog was standing in line. The hype had built over the last few weeks. Everyone was talking about it. Hollywood had produced a blockbuster, but for the life of him, Tim couldn't remember seeing a trailer or commercial for this film.

Bonnie pushed up against him, wrapping her arms tight across his midsection. He rubbed her hands and felt a tremor in them. He didn't blame her, this wasn't the part of town they usually ventured through, especially at night.

There were dubious characters lining the streets, with wandering eyes and snide comments. Tim felt their eyes on him and mostly on Bonnie. He refused to follow suit, refused to acknowledge their presence. Building rapidly, a flicker of worry coursed through him as the sky darkened, and the line inched closer.

At least they were moving into the realm of the theatre. They could relax, enjoy the horror movie and hopefully those guys would be elsewhere by the end credits. He would take Bonnie home and they'd have amazing 'after movie' sex, she'd stay the night and this area would be avoided forever. A lesson learned.

Shouts came from the street. A scuffle ensued. Bonnie tightened her grip around Tim. He wedged her arms apart and guided her to stand in front of him. His worry was at a standstill and a gentle calm settled over him. He turned to watch the scuffle and saw nothing. The street was empty. He walked down the steps. Looked left, looked right. Nothing. No one. No cars booming rap, no pedestrians. Nothing.

A flash of light caught his attention. In the dark sky amongst the clouds, multi-colored bands of light swept the sky. The yellows and greens

173

were captivating. He never knew Auroras appeared here.

"Tim."

Bonnie looked at him from the top of the stairs. He gave her a smile. He pointed to the sky. "Check that out."

Looking up, Bonnie shrugged her shoulders. "What?"

It was over. Gone. "Nothing," he said. "Thought I saw something." Bounding up the steps, Tim tried to wipe the image from his mind. Behind him, he heard the scuffle start up again and the streets were filled with loud exhausts, booming rap, the homeless, substance abuse and prostitution.

Looking over his shoulder he saw an old man watching him. He had a bushy beard and filth matted hair. His clothes were near rags but there was a presence about him that clicked with Tim. If he wasn't in this part of town, Tim would think it just another Halloween costume.

The man staggered up two of the steps, then faulted. He was breathing heavily and kept his eyes locked on Tim. Before he knew what he was doing, Tim was down the steps and close enough to see that the man wasn't as old as he thought. His skin was smooth and laughter lines creased his eyes.

Pulling out his wallet, Tim said, "I only have a few bucks. Don't usually carry cash."

"Run," the man said, his voice a fraction louder than a whisper. "Before the lights take you."

"What?"

Two men came from nowhere and grabbed him by the arms. They wore white starched shirts and white starched pants. "Sorry sir," one said. "Please enjoy your movie." They dragged the man around the side of the theatre and out of sight.

Tim moved to follow.

"Babe, we're up."

He glanced up at her and then back to the street. Tim had to check. He didn't know why but something nagged at him. On the side-walk, he pushed past a couple of guys dressed in gang colors and went to the side of the building.

Empty.

What the hell? Was he seeing things or was this some elaborate pre-show entertainment, he wondered. If that were the case, then where had they gone? He took a few steps down the alley, and then had second thoughts. Plus he had left Bonnie alone, that wasn't good. She was nervous in this area, and truth be told, so was he.

174

He turned back to the theatre. The gang guys watched him. Their expressions lacked emotion. Tim did his best to ignore them and kept his eyes on the stairs, though the need to turn was strong.

At the counter he bought two tickets. Bonnie snuggled into the crook of his arm as they strolled to their allocated seats. They were third row from the front. He hated being this close, but what could he do? They were last in line.

The curtains opened. *Advert time*, he thought, but instead a sunset played. Stars twinkled in the darkening sky. Beautiful bands of Aurora lights bled across the screen. Transfixed by shades of blue, green, red and purple, Tim thought he saw something move amongst the swirling colors. It stepped across the screen and through the screen.

Tim screamed, but heard no sound escape his lips. He kicked at the floor trying to stand up, but couldn't move.

The thing moved closer.

Movie goers in front stood and faced him. Their expressions blank, their faces blank. No features. Wax mannequins, arms reaching to him. Grabbing him.

Heart racing.

Bonnie laughing.

Skin tearing.

Hands reaching.

Pain.

Bonnie standing.

Creature, tentacles swaying.

Theatre of Pain.

The hype was real.

175

SUFFERING BEGINS IN THE MOUTH AND ENDS IN THE BELLY

By Alan Spencer

Laura Baxter had just become a floating spirit when she heard these words spoken to her, "Praise Satan, rise from the dead! Hear me and what I say. Human suffering beings in the mouth and ends in the belly. Once you understand this credo and make it your own, you will understand the work committed by the undead in these walls. Laura Baxter, the minions of hell have brought you back from death to ensure Halloween is as it should be once again."

Confused and watching the deathly looking woman addressing her, the corpse whose skin was literally sloughing off her bones, Laura opened her mouth to speak, but she was abruptly interrupted by the zombie woman, "And before you ask any questions, Mrs. Baxter, let me fill you in on the details. You're deceased. I had the pair of deadheads in the stockroom on the sub-sublevel dig you up last night from the local cemetery."

The dead woman pointed at a gurney across the room, which was loaded with Laura's naked corpse, her pallid flesh reflecting the over-bright ceiling lights. More shocking, her face was pulped, as if someone peeled back both her lips, literally breaking her jaw bones and destroying her nasal cavity and eyes. "The damage you see to your face didn't happen while you were alive. You see, once your corpse was placed in this room, your soul crawled out of your face as a ghost. And boy, let me tell you, it's a messy process!

"And before you ask me why you're a ghost, know this: many of the dead who are stolen from their graves change. They mutate. They deviate from humanity and become ghouls, beasts, werewolves, vampires, zombies, or in your case, ghosts. And we have reason for working in these chambers deep under the earth, but you have to think real hard and look into yourself to understand what I'm saying. Once you do, you'll feel it boil inside of you. The need, the visions, the beauty—do you feel it yet, Mrs. Baxter?"

176

Laura paused, still invisible to herself, a substance-less form. But then the temperature of the room increased, and it wasn't long before she was burning like an ember deep down in a roaring pit of fire, and experiencing this change, images consumed her, and she could see them as clear as if they were happening all around her:

Drowning bodies thrashing in boiling rivers of crimson.

Hooks raking across naked backs, and the victims' ensuing peals of terror—they sounded so beautiful to Laura, something to cherish!

Starving emaciated bodies laying out on their sides eating from a fellow human's torso, stuffing guts and raw meat into their desperate blood-caked maws.

The dead woman chimed in, unleashing her words with gusto, "You see them, don't you? You crave more. I love it so much, and I can tell you love it too. It's the gift the undead carry in their minds. Constant motivation to do the work we do. We're minions of hell. Satan's warriors. Lucifer's Undead. Forever live Halloween! Hail Satan!"

The sudden rap on the door was followed up an irate bellow from the other side, "Christ, Mindy, you done giving your spiel yet? We're behind schedule. I thought you said we had another ghost to keep the machine rollin'."

"Keep your pants on before they fall off again, Arnie," Mindy bit back, a flap of her cheek coming undone to show off a row of peanut butter colored teeth. "As I was saying, we're behind, it being so close to Halloween, so let me show you around. Call this orientation."

Without willing it, Laura was moving, sailing onwards, though she cast no shadow on the tiles. Mindy opened the door, but she flew through the wall instead, and entered the clotted hallway of shambling rotting corpses who were pushing carts stocked with bags of sugar, sucker sticks, razor blades, blocks of chocolate, and various brown bottles marked with skull and crossbones. On the ceiling, vampires crawled on all fours, hauling bags of caramel solids, food coloring, and assortments of candy packaging. A werewolf lugged two plastic tubs of boiling chocolate on a stick across his back, in a hurry to get to the opposite end of the building, and the lumbering creature nearly took down Mindy as they passed each other.

"Hey, watch it, you mindless beast!" Mindy then talked over the bustle of workers to Laura, saying, "You're a ghost, and that's why you're so important. you'll be a quality inspector. Nobody can see you, because you're incorporeal matter. Soul air, in other words. Perfect for a supervising job. You'd be like an invisible foreman, and whoever's not doing their job,

177

becomes a guinea pig in our experiments. So as I show you around, keep in mind, you'd be checking in on these creepies and making sure things get done right the first time. Halloween only comes once a year, after all."

Laura managed to ask the corpse, "So you're offering me a job then?"

New visions stole her attention, as real as if they were happening in the hallway right this moment:

The walls oozed dark crimson as the air emanated harsh screams.

The tiles were liquid, shimmering with bobbing bodies that were water-decayed, bloated and covered in slithering river snakes.

Eyeballs exploded out of severed heads stuck on pikes in the farther distance, the facial features active and alive, as the pink matter crept down their faces in gooey, clotted strands.

"You see more, don't you? Yes, yes, yes! It's why we live; it's why we thrive. Hell gives us these offerings in exchange for our work year round. We're perfecting ways to create mischief and agonies for the living during Halloween. It's why we were brought back from the dead."

Wrapping her bark-colored arms in a self-hug, Mindy shuttered,

"Oh, I love the sensations crawling through my body just thinking about the suffering to be inflicted. It's better than sex. It's better than chocolate *fucking* cake! Halloween must be as terrifying as ever, Laura. This is what Satan wishes. The holiday's been losing its edge, as of late. Nobody celebrates the holiday, and its dying. People trick-r-treat in malls and schools now, and since the living won't raise hell anymore, so shall the dead! The razor in the apple was only scratching the surface!" They manoeuvred a left at the next turn, and now the walls had many glass panes that showed off busy laboratories. The first window displayed a dead man with rotting gray flesh sitting alone on a chair in a room. The zombie was bored, reading a book, and out of nowhere, the man's mandible fell off, clacking against the floor and then shattering.

Mindy gave the zombie a thumb's up, and the jawless zombie returned it vigorously. A set of white lab-coated assistants, both with sunken eyes and ivory pale skin, led the zombie out of the room. Then another ghoul, this one with a hunched back and moving boils and tumors scattered about his neck and ears, scooped up the jaw into a dust pan and casually moved on.

"Our guinea pig, Mr. Jake Finley, has waited three weeks in that room, bored out of his mind, after eating a butterscotch hard candy. It was engineered to cause the jaw to fall off after 20 to 32 days after ingestion. I

178

can't wait until the living suck these down."

More questions flooded her mind, and Laura managed to spit one out, "So you're testing the effects of poisonous candy in all of these rooms, right?"

"On Halloween, children and adults alike stuff candy down their throats, like the pitiful fools they are, and we're here to see them in agony for it. Suffering begins in the mouth and ends in the belly. This is Satan's work, and it's this work we must do! It keeps us safe from hell, you see, Laura. If we preserve Halloween, making it a scarier, more gut-wrenching holiday, we get to roam the earth, but if we fail, Satan's sees to it that we're incorporated into the many visions he sends to our minds. They're very real —in hell, that is. We become the sufferers, not the spectators, and you don't want that, Laura, you best mark me."

Dark hideous visions corrupted her mind, and she lived the thrill of viewing them, though in the back of her mind, she took Mindy's warnings to heart:

Whips made of spinal columns split the backs of sun-burned backs. Victims were forced to reach down their own throats up to the elbow as they choked and vomited. Boiling flesh rivers carried off thousands of corpses towards a burning red horizon.

The visions ended, and down the hall they kept going, bypassing a wide-spanning room stocked with hundred gallon steel vats. Hulking werewolves stirred steel oars into boiling concoctions. Another work area not too far away, chocolate bars and hard candies of all kinds were spit out of steel factory machines as zombie children wrapped them meticulously by hand.

""This candy will go out with the rest of the Halloween candy sold in stores," Mindy revealed, suppressing a wormy grim by covering her lips with her gangly hand. "We have other ghosts who can sneak about undetected and place our candy into stores, and you should see what we've created this year to cause them great suffering."

She guided Laura further on, giddy in her step, and the demonstrations began one after the other in staggering shows behind the glass windows:

Guinea pigs, mostly consisting of rotting corpses and deformed mutants, were eating the special candy. Some ate *Fun-Dip*, the putrid subjects wetting the hardened sugar sticks with their blackened tongues, and then finally tasting the sugar powder. Within thirty seconds, their skull caps opened up like a lid and out came their brains in a burst of steamy confetti.

179

A rather large female vampire devoured a box of bat-shaped marshmallow filled chocolates, and out exploded its heart from its sternum like a live grenade. A werewolf chewed off the tops of twenty *Blow-Pops*, and then instantly, both rows of its teeth suddenly expanded so long and pointy, like enamel spears, that they sliced through its brains and out its chin. *Pop-Rocks* burst out of cheeks. *Dots* created polyps and tumors within seconds of ingestion. *Sweet Tarts* disintegrated tongues. *Charleston Chews* inspired the consumer to gouge out their eyes and eat the finger-skewered orbs. Peanut butter cups grew organs on the outside of the body: a heart, and lungs, and kidneys, and liver, and so on, until the person appeared to be inside-out. *Snickers* incited the test subjects to chew through their wrists and commit suicide. Rock candy changed into jagged shards of glass. *Life-Savers* dissolved into strychnine. Cotton candy into fiber-glass. Jaw breakers did as promised. Nougat rolls evacuated vital fluids out the bowels, the eater dying of instant dehydration.

Laura watched these spectacles, and she wanted to play her hand in the process, ensure quality, raise expectations, boost worker morale, create innovative candy killing treats, and with these thoughts came Satan's reward:

Severed hands boiled in pots of innards stew. Beer battered muscle tissue were eaten by trogs, trolls, and pig-faced cannibals. Bare feet were singed of flesh as they writhed and struggled through valleys of hot coals.

"Oh thank you, Satan!" Laura cheered, shuttering from the orgasmic concussions rattling up and down her body, the sensations easily granted by the dark master. "I shall make Halloween more terrifying than anyone has ever seen! Thank you! Thank you, Dark Master!"

Mindy beheld the new ghost, the freshly minted servant, with rheumy dead eyes. The zombie woman's enthusiasm was evident by how she clapped her hands and then marched down to the end of the hallway to a door marked by a bronze nameplate: "Quality Inspector."

"This is going to be your new office, Mrs. Baxter, so get acclimated to the filing system and the write-up forms, and in about a half hour, we're going to need you to double check on the vampires in testing unit 29B who are experimenting with chewing gum that glues both rows of teeth together." Imagining victims unable to open their mouths after chewing the special gum, Laura couldn't help but declare, "This Halloween will be the most gut-wrenching of them all." Entering her office, she added one more thing before getting to work, "Like you said, Mindy, human suffering begins in the mouth and ends in the belly!"

BLOODY CUP

By Kim Talafuse

If you offered me your bloody cup-
I would accept-
If you offered me your bloody hand-
I would not shy away-
After all, blood is the color red-
The color of passion-

Our bodies are soaked with the sweat of passion
I want you more with each heated touch-
I wish I could learn my lesson-

Your touch leaves me breathless-
Your kiss drives me wild-
I wish I was fearless-
I wish I was an innocent child-
So sweet and mild-

But I am not-
I have waged a war in my soul-
Something I wish I had never fought-
Love was the only prisoner-
The only one forgot-

I would drink from your bloody cup-
I would suckle the vein in your neck-
I would fall into blood covered sheets-
And shiver in ecstasy with your touch-

Passion-
Blood-
Your touch-
How evil is your touch?-
Is it vile?-

Is it?-
Your lips are smiling with red blood-
Your hands burn me when we touch-
Yes, I want you still and oh, so much-

No matter what your sin-
I will want you again and again-
I would take the punishment for your sin-
My lover-
My devil to attend-

Touch me again-
Kiss me-
Enter my soul-
Cover me with blood-
Please don't go-
Please don't go-

Offer me your bloody cup-
I'll drink and smile-
Shiver with your touch-
The blood on your soul does not make me want you less-

Our bodies are covered with sweat-
Our passion so great-
Falling into you without a safety net-
The passion-
I want more-

A new lesson-
Breathless when we make love-
Careless-
When we make love-
A beautiful puzzle we will never solve-

You leave me at night-
I have blood on my sheets-
Careless blood of my ungodly heat-
I can see the blood-You only walk out the door-

182

You have nothing to gain-

I have the everlasting stain-
You walk out the door-
I expect it-
It has happened before-
Blood soaked sheets-

I want you more and more-
The echoes down the hall-
The ring in your voice-
My heart slows to a lull-
My passion is something you could never fill-

The slamming of the door-
The blood on my sheets-
Another passion down for the kill-

ELSIE'S FRIEND

By Sharon M. White

Hear that tune and its beautiful melody?
Do you hear the lovely song he sings to me?

No, Elsie, I hear no tune. I hear your fanciful closet monster. Go to sleep
now, leave it be.

He's no monster. More likely a beautiful fallen creature--
fallen from the stars above, no doubt.

No, Elsie. Mom says all night-time monsters are from hell--
from hell or somewhere thereabout.

I bet he's beautiful like his song and lonely, too.
Would you turn on a light so I can see?

It's dark, Elsie, and we're in bed for the night.

If there's something there, don't you worry it will get me?

The crippled twin lays here all day, bored and alone and
you'd deny me a bit of a game because it's night?

Not tonight. I'm tired, your guilt trip is mean, and
won't work. Have your fantasy during the daylight.

It's boring during the daytime, Celia. The sun
makes it feel childish and mundane.

If I get up and turn on the light,
you'll see that night or day it looks the same.

Mom would play my game, if she were alive
and Daddy would too, but he's at work tonight.

Elsie, give it a rest. I'll play your silly game,
I'm up, see? I'll turn on the light.

* * *

Celia screams as the thing grabs a handful of hair
and pulls her into its lair…

Soon, Elsie hears the satisfied gurgle of her fallen pet--
the beauty from the stars

DIES IRAE

By Sharla Anderson

In Twilight's wake
embers stream silently
across a Utopian sky,
reigning its mordant fire
upon fated shoulders
the silver thorn slips from bleeding hand

as she rests her head against cold stone
listening to the chambers of his heart
echo her name once more
lips of granite pressed
with crimson prayers
let dust be her destiny
beneath the legacy of his feet
among sable petals languished there
epithets bemoan its dying requiem
from shadow of black wings
until Wrath becomes flesh
and death shall he bring

MY FINAL MASTERPIECE

By Richard H. Fay

Naked,
bound together
by rusty razor wire,
our bloodied bodies cry passion
and death.

(Originally published in the December 2008 issue of Niteblade.)

SERIAL

By Stephen D. Nadaud II

My fingers wrap around her throat,
a rush engulfs my brain.
It feels like an orgasmic burst,
a hard drug in my veins.

I found her on a darkened street,
I clubbed her with a stone.
She looked like sex in skintight jeans.
I jumped her teenage bones,
and dragged her to an alleyway,
the place where she will die,
in filth and scum and cockroach shit,
just food for hungry flies.

RAGGEDY HAG

By William A. Sanders

I beat you,
compulsively;
till battered black
and stained blue.
You piss your panties,
and rub your eyes;
moaning--
and crying,
like a mentally unnerved
Oxycontin addict,
who sits
trembling--
detoxifying--
on a cold metal chair
in the Rehab waiting room.

Stay down,
quit whining--
brush your fingers
through your hair;
unveil the panoptic purple tint
of eyes on the verge of shut.
Expose lips, severely ripped;
bleeding
while your voice quivers,
leaking murmurs,
whisperingly.
Best pray,
and repent
for cause of violence
you've summoned
from anguish churning
wildly in the depth of me.
When I'm done making
tough love to you,
you'll hear nothing--
more of me;
you'll see nothing--
more of me,
and I'll bury you
in a way symbolizing
what you truly are.
I'll leave you
in excess of invalid value,
in an abandoned dumpster--
with legs spread
for rats to come nibble
the sourly tainted ecstasy,
soliciting a malodorous STD.
Filthly little mouths
will salivate, hungrily--
in a morbid orgy;
extensively slow-paced
in dispersion of decay.

THE FIRST CUT
By Doree Weller

At first, euphoria
And relief
As a deep slice
Sets me free.
Then pain
And some disbelief
That it ends here
Quickly and completely.
One decision,
A moment only
Cannot ever
Be unmade.
The scar remains to
Remind me
That some acts
Never fade.

BLOOD BOUND
By Graylin Fox

Silence envelops her as she passes
through steel gates
her dress billowing lightly in the breeze.

Moving without thought
she floats toward his home,
the doors are open,
candlelight dancing on the walls.

Gliding across the graveyard,
Her gown flowing in the breeze,
Soon it will be time for him to rise.
Even in sleep he controls her.

She passes through carved doors
Carved with life like images
satyr, nymph and centaur
leaning out to greet you
with only slight leers
to warn of dangers within.

Tonight he does not stir,
her sharp intake of breath breaks the air
and his body begins to crumble into ash.

Gasping she hunts for the dagger,
Following instructions given her long ago
she slits her wrists
dripping blood onto the ashes.

Using wax from the candles
she molds his body from memory
chanting in guttural sounds.
Slowly his body reforms
as the clarity comes to his now open eyes
he sees his wife wiping blood from her arms
getting ready to join him
a love destined, cursed
and nourished by blood.

RATTLE THEM BONES

By Roxanne Hoffman

Make the most out of being a ghost!
Learn to spook the most sceptical host!
Newly dead wraiths,
Rise from your graves!
Get what you crave.
So what it's depraved!
Stop eating your shrouds,
For crying out loud!

Get those coffins unhinged!
Start a brain-eating binge!
Learn to drink blood,
Till they drop with a thud!
Scare the living daylights out of living people!

Rattle them bones!
Whimper and moan!
Chant Tantric tomes,
As you haunt their homes!
Carry your head,
While you fill theirs with dread!
Scare the living daylights out of living people!

Learn how to thump!
Go bump in the night!
Flicker the lights,
Give them a fright!
See how they run!
Isn't Death fun?
Scare the living daylights out of living people!

Float through the air
With hardly a care!
Suspend them still perched
on their dining room chairs,
Laugh as they stare,
Raising their hair!
Send them to church
saying their prayers!
Scare the living daylights out of living people!

Let's give them a hand!
Ain't disembodiment grand?
Then wriggle the stumps,
To give them goose bumps!
Quiver and quake,
While they shiver and shake!
Scare the living daylights out of living people

For comic relief,
Make them chatter their teeth.
Howl like the wind,
Get them guzzling gin!
Speaking in tongues,
At the top of your lungs,
Disappear into mist
With a flick of your wrist!
Visit them in
The Looney Bin!
Scare the living daylights out of living people!

Never again will they call you "Has Been"!
Never again will they say "Old Fogey"!

Once you were shy, now you are feared,
Just because you died and re-appeared!

Isn't the Afterlife wondrous and weird?

NIGHT OF THE DEMONS
By Stephanie Smith

Filthy demons creep
in the midnight hours
upon lonely lovers
weeping for the
death of the world

For their souls are next

The demons tear
at the couple's flesh
in a symphony of sorrow
Tomorrow fades
in a foggy haze
as the demons feast
on the meat of days

ARTWORK
By Darren James

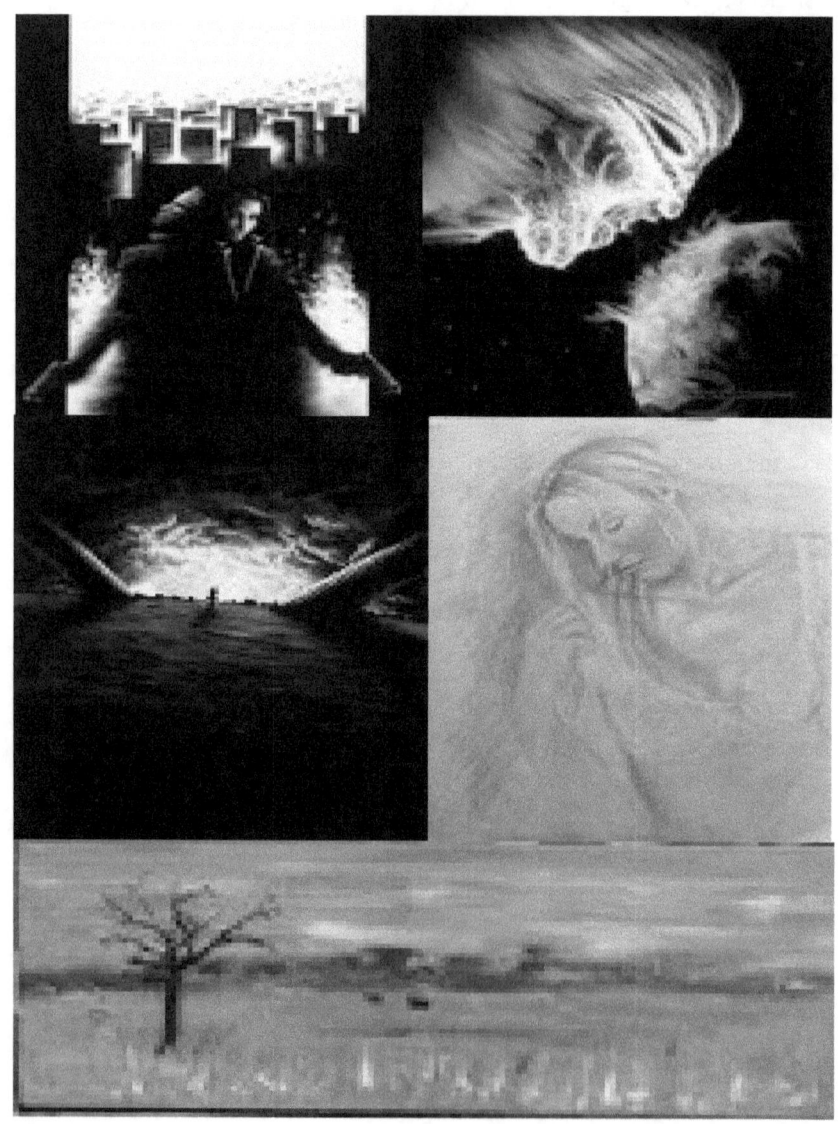

193

Darren is an aspiring illustrator who has many years of aspiring under his belt. He writes short stories and a few unpublished novels. He studied graphic design and creative writing at Stafford college, and now puts these skills to good use in a warehouse, where he puts boxes onto wooden pallets. Commisions for work are greatfully accepted, and Darren can be contacted at Dycebastion@yahoo.co.uk. A selection of the artwork can be seen at http://dyce-bastion.deviantart.com/gallery/

Prints can be purchased at http://dyce-bastion.deviantart.com/store/

PAINTINGS
By Nick Rose

Nick Rose is a traditional illustrator who is renowned for his of pictorial storytelling, and influence he acquired by studying the work and teachings of Howard Pyle, the father of American illustrations as taught to him by Master Daniel Horne. Not only has he trained under a Master, he also trained under Todd Lockwood, one of the all time greats in the fantasy field. Though the years Mr. Rose has done 100's of book and magazine covers as well as interior illustrations. He mainly works in the Horror and Dark Fantasy Genre. He is expanding his career into working in the movie industry, doing everything from concept sketches to movie posters.

PHOTOGRAPHY
By Sandy Swagger

Sandy Swagger is an artist based in the United States and is currently residing in her home-town of Richmond, Virginia. She is currently a Photography student at Virginia Commonwealth University and is expected to graduate in December of 2011. Swagger has been working with photography as her main medium for 6 years. She has worked with a diverse series over the past few years but has kept her work to narrative pieces that resemble movie stills. The series "The Undesirables" was completed in 2009. Like most of Swagger's work, it contains a loose narrative that requires the viewer to create a back-story for the subjects. The goal of this work was to create an alternate identity for her subjects through the use of stage make-up, dramatic lighting, and hand built sets. Swagger was hoping to make the viewer feel uncomfortable, as if they were invading the subject's space during a very vulnerable and hurtful time.

ARTWORK
By Bret Jordan

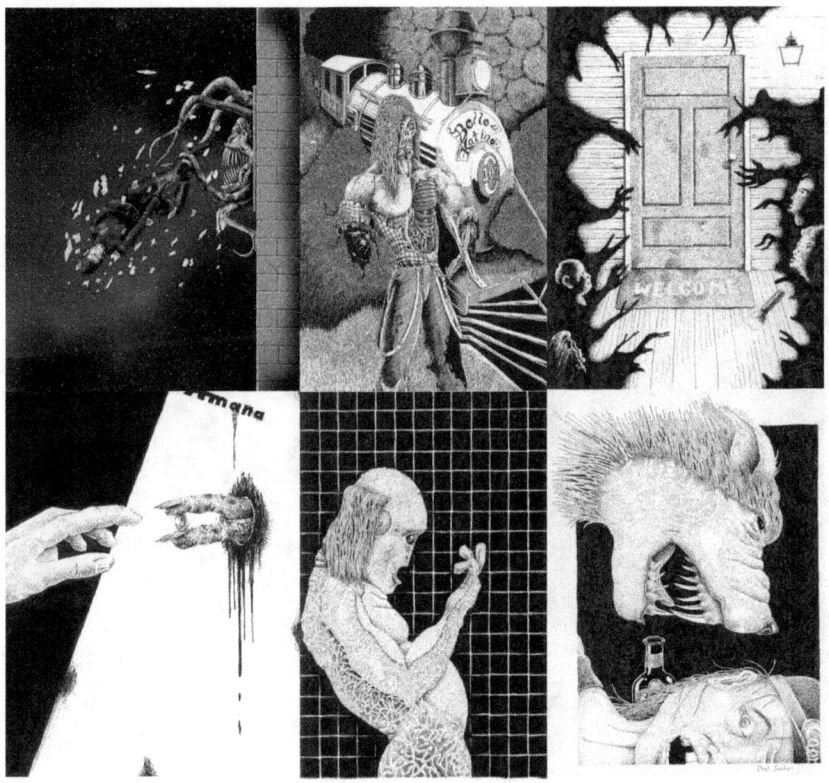

Bret Jordan is a resident of South-east Texas. He is avid reader who devours books in almost every genre and tries to bring a little of that variety into his writing. It's all about people, adventure, escape from the humdrum of reality and the ever-present question, 'what if?' When not writing or spending time with his wife and children Bret puts pen to paper as an illustrator and sometimes-digital artist. To get away from it all he can often be found riding the roads of Southeast Texas on the back of his motorcycle. To find out more visit his website at www.bretjordan.com.

PHOTOGRAPHY

By A.W. Gifford

On occasion A. W. Gifford is known to take a few photographs. He can be found at www.awgifford.webs.com He is a founding member and former president of the Great Lakes Association of Horror Writers and his work (writing mostly) has appeared in numerous magazines, webzines and anthologies.

ARTWORK

By Gary McClusky

Gary McCluskey has worked as a professional artist for the past 20 years. He worked his way through small press comics until finally launching his own comic book Rayne which ran for four issues and several short stories in the late 1990s. Since then, Gary has worked illustrating for sci-fi and fantasy magazines, gaming companies and the greeting card industry. His recent works seem to mostly involve zombies.

WRITING FOR YOURSELF

By Shells Walter

Remember when you started writing, the ideas, the passion and just the overall thrill of it? You wanted to write what you wanted to write. Now of course I'm not referring to freelance writing jobs, those you get paid for doing what the client asked for. I'm referring to the creative writing aspect; the short story, the novella – whatever. The fiction arena where our imagination runs wild and we discover new things.

If you have just started writing you feel that urge to get your words on paper. The awesomeness of getting a project done is enlightening and worth wild. You keep writing and get into a rhythm; a good rhythm that keeps your words flowing. You are excited that you have finally found your niche, your way of doing things. Then, yes then, you make the choice, I want to get published.

Getting published is not a bad thing and most authors after a time put that as one of their main goals. Many start with what is called an 'anthology' which is a collection of short stories normally but a list of different writers. There are several themes, word counts, guidelines that one may need to follow when submitting. In this case, you say fine I will do that and you follow the guidelines and submit a story; that feels good and so you do another story based on whatever the anthology wishes. You keep this pattern up for several months.

An anthology is not a bad place to submit stories, I myself have submitted tons. What an author needs to be aware of is that although you are writing for a particular anthology, not to loose yourself in that anthology. What do I mean by that? Simply to not forget why you started writing, how your own words became something important. When writing for a certain theme ect., don't loose that part of you that goes, wow, I like what I wrote, instead of wow, that does not even sound like my story. When saying this I'm not saying anthologies are bad, there are several out there that are great; just remember not to loose who you are in the process.

Besides anthologies, there are other things an author should be careful of. One of which is author's burnout. There has been a guideline that has been around for ages; write everyday no matter what. I say throw this to the wind. There are a lot of people who can write only when a feeling comes about, an inspirational moment if you will; I'm one of those. If I try to write everyday, some of the words just go on paper and don't make sense. I get bored and loose interest in writing period. This is of course not to say this guideline doesn't work, for some it has. What I'm saying is not to force yourself with the writing, take time to get into the characters, places and events. Of course with certain things you may have the dreaded deadline. These can make not having to write everyday difficult, but just plan ahead for this type of situation. It will work out.

Burnout can just be a simple; I need a break from writing. Yes, at times as s we all do. Take that break if you can. The 'I need to write everyday' situation won't allow you to. You don't wish to be sitting there one day and realize that you hate writing and you're bored with it. Well, maybe one day regardless you will find that out, but let's hope it's not from burnout.

Another thing authors wish to do is get their novel and novellas published. This is a great thing to do if you want to. There is something else to watch out for, contracts and editing. Why are those so important? Well, the contract says what your rights are with your work, read it over carefully. It is an important part of the publishing business. If you have questions ask the publisher or if you have an agent ask them. They should be willing to answer them. If not, go to someone that does and get rid of the load that does that wish to help you. Yes, there is this contract binding aspect, however, as said before read it over. There might be a way to get released from it or talk to the agent or publisher and see if you can work things out or work to release you from the contract.

Editing. Yes, your work will need to be edited as everyone finds out eventually. You want to work with an editor that will improve your story, not take it away. What do I mean by taking it away? I mean changing it to the point you don't recognize it anymore as your own. Oh yes, grammar, spelling the whole package needs to be done, but the content suddenly does not seem like your writing. You need to find an editor that works with you, that asks your permission before changing vital content of your story or one that suggests this is what works or what the publisher has asked. Then you can of course disagree or not. The choice should be yours. If you feel uncomfortable with any edits, you should be able to talk with the editor as to why, and speak up about it in a tactful way, don't hide what deep down inside is bothering you about your story.

What's one of the worse things authors can face? It is the dreaded rejection. Yes, in any form the rejection plain out can be devastating and cause an author to suddenly change what they wish to write just to get accepted. I mean there are times where the backbone of a story needs work for continuity, grammar ect., but there is also the fact that a lot of things being viewed are being viewed by a subjective opinion. Simply put, your work maybe good, maybe even great, but that particular publication may not like it. Here is where a trap maybe for an author, changing to fit the market.

Facing the markets out there can be challenging and sometimes out right brutal. One thing as an author you need to be careful of is writing just for that market. In writing just for a market, something can be lost of your own writing. What do I mean by this? Even though it is your own writing per say, you have written the words ect., you may loose what you wanted to actually write because you are more concerned about what that particular market wants for whatever reason it is. If you can seriously feel comfortable with doing this, then by all means do so, just be careful. It may cause you later on to doubt your own ability to write.

The one thing that I've seen and earlier on experienced myself is self-doubt. Another big reason some authors stop writing all together, and to be honest I did as well, for a time. When you are concerned with writing for others instead of yourself, at times you may doubt that you can even write. The dark point in my life is when I gave up writing for a time, said forget it, no one wants it anyways. It took some kicking in the rear by family and friends to get out of the mode and move forward, that was many years ago. Now I just take breaks at times to regroup. That of course is just my story.

However, self-doubt can cause you to stop writing, make you feel that if you don't write the way others want you to that no one will pay attention. In order to think about this, think about the many mainstream authors who did get published after several attempts and several years. If they would've stopped we may not have some of these books that we love so much. So with self-doubt take a break, talk to someone, and just relax. It may take some time but you will get the confidence back and move ahead. If you feel it's not working out for you change it, but only if you make the choice.

If you want to submit your work, find a place that will work for your writing not the other way around. Then you will know your writing has found a home you can be happy with. And always be confident, not egotistic, but confident about your writing, make improvements, learn some more things and take it out there, take that jump.

Writing for yourself can be difficult and exhausting as you see other things being accepted but not your own. There are risks involved with doing this, but in the long run you will feel that the risks are worth it as you

205

are still writing your own work. There is a quote in which inspires me everyday to keep writing:

"Better to write for yourself and have no public, than to write for the public and have no self." -Cyril Connoll.

LEARNING FROM THE BEST

By A.E. Churchyard

I'm currently reading "Sometimes the Magic Works: Lessons from a Writing Life." by Terry Brooks. I've read it before of course - about three times!

Each time I read it I discover something new, or it kickstarts my brain into writing something new. At the moment, TB has got me thinking about the NaNoWriMo Novel I did last year. I haven't finished the story line, but that was because I got lost in the middle - I was trying too hard to push it through, mostly because I wanted to get over 50k by the end of the month.

I'm going to break off about my current work and dive into the way TB and other seriously successful authors write...

TB follows these rules -

1) Write what you know.
2) Your Characters must behave in a believable fashion.
3) A protagonist must be challenged by a conflict that requires resolution.
4) Movement = Growth; Growth = Change; Without change nothing happens.
5) The strength of the protagonist is measured by the threat of the antagonist.
6) Show, don't tell.
7) Avoid the Grocery List approach to describing characters.
8) Characters must always be in a story for a reason.
9) Names are important
10) Don't bore the reader.

I have another fantasy writing hero - well actually, it wasn't one writer, but a duo – David and Leigh Eddings, neither of whom are still with us (RIP). In their book "The Rivan Codex" they also set out the rules that they used. They called it "a tacitly agreed upon list of elements that make for a good fantasy" –

1) Religion - when writing for fun, paganism is more fun than Christianity -

even Papa Tolkien agreed with that!

2) The Quest - No quest, no story.

3) The Magic Thingamajig - usually, but not always the object of the quest.

4) Our Hero - Galahad, Gawaine, Lancelot or Perceval; Galahad is saintly, Gawaine is loyal, Lancelot is heavyweight champion of the world and Perceval is dumb / innocent.

5) Resident Wizard - Merlin, Gandalf or Belgarath / Polgara... take your pick!

6) Our Heroine - Wispy blonde girl mooning around or little tiger who knows how to get what she wants?

7) Our Villain - Someone with diabolical intentions...

8) Companions - obvious I think!

9) The Companion's Lady Friends - again, obvious.

10) The World - Maps, Governments, Currencies etc etc. - too obvious to explain...

I suppose this is more of an outlining list than a set of rules, but by the time you finish working through it, you have a detailed world to work with. My first attempt at writing a novel (before I got a PC of my own) used the list from "The Rivan Codex". It created a lever arch file of world details and a slimmer folder of maps...

I'm sorry, but I got hooked on the map thing - I create a map of the area that the story is going to be taking place in, before I even think about the story.

The maps get amended as I go through the story as well - it gives me something to look at and seems to help with writers block at the same time! I do this for every book I start. The ones I didn't do it for don't go anywhere - I don't have a frame of reference.

Anyway. My third writing hero - and I've had a few people disagree with me on this one - is Piers Anthony. I've picked up bits and pieces from him as well, just nothing as well laid out as Terry Brooks or D & L Eddings.

I realised as I was reading TB's book that all three (four) of my writing heroes have one thing in common. They were all picked up by Ballantine Books when they first started out and they were all edited by Lester and Judy Del Rey (sadly, also deceased, RIP). So is what I have read their way of writing or the way that they were gently guided into by the Del Rey's?

TB has a mantra that he tells everyone who asks how to get

published / become a good writer -

Read, read, read.
Outline, outline, outline.
Edit, edit, edit,
Repeat!
I completely agree with him. By combining what I have learned from Terry Brooks and D & L Eddings, I can cover all of this mantra without breaking a sweat! I get three quarters of the work done before I even start on the story...

Anyway, back to "The Secret of Arking Down." I looked back through what I had written in those 30 hectic days and decided that it was worth keeping the idea and most of the first part of the story. But the rest of it didn't seem to work right.

That was when I realised I had contravened rules 3, 4, 5 and 8... *blushes – i*magine my embarrassment!

Of course that had only happened because I had ignored line two of the mantra - Outline, outline, outline.

So now I have to go back over what I have written and start again... right from the beginning!

Groan

Of course I'll get the Bog Boy done first - it forms a background story for Book two of the series, so I need it to work properly...

And as well as finishing TB's book, I'm going to read "On Writing" by Stephen King. TB recommends it, so I'm getting it out of the library as soon as I can. I'll probably add to my list of rules etc once I'm done...

You never stop learning in this job!

IMAGINATION

By Simon Marshall-Jones

Last night, my wife and I walked miles around the environs of this fair city of Milton Keynes, just to find somewhere dark enough for us to catch a glimpse or two of the annual Perseid meteor shower (in the event, we only spotted two… but hey, there's always next year). Along the way, Liz and I started talking about children's imaginations, a topic specifically prompted by both of us wanting to know how we saw things when we were younger, and the way we imagined we would be when we were grown up. You know the kind of thing: working in a chocolate factory so that you can make a creme egg as large as a house so you can dive in and swim about in it, or growing up to be a princess so you have pretty clothes and a bejewelled tiara and ride about on a pony all day. Or, as one other example that Liz told me about, filling the downstairs with water so you can swim up the stairs rather than using your legs. And when you're that young, it all makes perfect sense, doesn't it?

The conversation got me thinking. I had just finished reviewing Cate Gardner's superb Strange Men in Pinstripe Suits and Other Curious Things (published by Strange Publications on October 14th this year) and one of the enchanting aspects of Cate's writing is its childlike quality. That's not to say it is in any way childish, because it's definitely nothing of the sort. Rather, a kind of flawless logic pertains within the confines of the stories she writes that, were it to happen in the real world, only a child would feel un-threatened by the lack of sense.

And, I guess, that's the reason why these stories work so well: as adults, their very nonsensicality appears to be slightly threatening, because of their very unpredictability. Although we are aware when we read them that something weird is about to happen and we think that we are prepared for it, when it does happen it's still something of a jolt. Simply because it doesn't happen like that. That's where Gardner's stories derive their power.

It's also another reason why we should treasure the imaginative powers of children's minds. Because they have less knowledge of the world and the way it works, leaps of logic are a matter of course. We may think of the sky being blue because that's how photons are scattered by the atmosphere, but the child, not being privy to this, might think that because the sea is blue then the sky is the upstairs water and is where all the rain is stored. Makes absolutely perfect sense.

That wonder slowly evaporates as we grow up and we learn that the world isn't as plastic and fluid as they once comfortably thought. However, that doesn't mean that we should fetter our imaginations as we enter the adult world. While we may have to act sensibly in our everyday lives and be 'grown-up', giving up our sense of wonder blunts our relationship with the world around us, which, to me, is tantamount to handing over your soul. Even without the wizards and elves, or without the vast space-ports we read about as young children or created in our minds, there is still plenty out there to inspire us – natural beauty, art, science, books, the universe itself.

That's why, as writers, we should open our eyes (and ears) to the whole of life, as there is potential inspiration everywhere around us. The chance overheard out-of-context remark, the colour or shape of a flower, an abandoned vehicle somewhere, a derelict house, a piece of incongruous clothing left on a wall or a discarded toy, a line in a story, a newspaper article – these are all sources of inspiration, setting off creative sparks that grow brighter and brighter as more ideas bifurcate from the original line of thought. Try to see everything around you from a different angle, or in a different light. Why is that child's glove sat where it is? Was it accidentally dropped, or does it signify something else? Something strange and mysterious, or maybe something dark and sinister?

This is how all great fiction starts – I've often read about how a writer was doing a mundane activity, or went for a walk somewhere familiar and saw something unusual, which ignited a whole series of creative mini-explosions in his/her head. They metaphorically turned the image/idea over to see what it looked like from underneath, or looked at it sideways. Or even took off in a completely random direction, generating a totally unexpected line of thinking and surprising even the writer him/herself.

That's how plots for the best stories and novels often start, and it's why some writers rise to the top and others just kind of float. It's because they've taken things that everyone tales for granted and twisted them in some way, or just looked at it from a new perspective. As writers, we all need to develop this facility if we can – not all are able to, but we should at least give it a damn good try. If nothing else, it's a hell of a fun exercise in itself. And, who knows, YOU just may hit upon that magically imaginative idea that elevates you to the big-time.

If you liked this and want to read more, please visit http://simonmarshalljones.wordpress.com/

AN INTERVIEW WITH:
Alan Spencer
Author of 'The Body Cartel 'and 'Inside the Perimeter'

When he's not eating zombie cakes prepared by his lovely wife, Alan Spencer is promoting his first novel, "The Body Cartel," published by "Damnation Books." He is also marketing other novel projects such as "The Reels," "The Bloodthirsty," and "Inside the Perimeter." He welcomes e-mails at <u>alanspencer26@hotmail.com</u>.

House of Horror fans, please welcome Alan Spencer to The Lounge! Good evening to you sir, how are you?

I'm very excited to be talking to you again, thanks Sam.

So, Alan, you are the proud author of The Body Cartel, which won House of Horror's Most Horrific read 2009. Tell us a little about it.

I won't give to much away; I'll put it in a nutshell. Imagine drug cartels combined with cannibals versus a happy couple just moving into their dream home, and you've got "The Body Cartel." Lots of smoking barrels and flesh-eating.

What gave you the idea to write about such a gruesome situation and has it been received well with readers?

I've always loved zombies, but I didn't want to do another run-of-the-mill story featuring people shacked up in a house surrounded by the dead. And plus I've had a long running fascination with Italian and French zombie movies, especially from the late 70's and early 80's. Combine that with my love of authors such as Brian Lumley, Edward Lee, Jack Ketchum, and T.M. Wright, among others, and that's a lot of my inspiration for creating a gruesome situation and really pushing the envelope with the novel. Lee and Ketchum especially gave me the idea that gory details are okay as long as you find the right readership.

212

As far as reactions go, most horror magazine reviewers seemed to enjoy it, but most of the mainstream magazines were overwhelmed by the over-the-top and gory nature of the novel. And that's okay because I know "The Body Cartel" isn't for everyone. It gets morbid. I tried to make it as fun as possible, though some might not like to stretch their disbelief too far. But overall, I can't really complain. It's been a wonderful experience putting out my first novel.

So when you begin a novel, do you have any prerequisites before starting such as a drink or a smoke, or listen to a particular piece of music?

I've been trying to quit drinking soda while writing, though the battle goes up and down. I'll usually drink black tea and listen to anything from "Cannibal Corpse" to "Lizzy Borden." Anything metal, really.

What is your usual writing style? Do you go by the old traditional style of pen and paper and type it up afterwards, or do you go straight to your computer and begin typing?

As far as actually putting a story down on something, it has to be on my computer. I would've smashed a typewriter before chapter one was finished, and I write way too slow for pen and paper.

If you could invite anyone to a fantasy dinner party, who would it/they be and why?

It would have to be Jack Ketchum and Edward Lee, just because I love their fiction so much, and they both came up out of the small press and gained entry into the mainstream. These people make a living at writing, and I want to know their secrets. Food and booze would go a long way to get those secrets out, I might add. A close second would be Gord Rollo because I really enjoyed reading "The Jigsaw Man."

I hear you have now completed your next novel and are pitching it to publishers right now. How is all that going?

The newest one, "The Bloodthirsty," I've decided to re-tool a bit, and I expect to be actively sending it out in early February. I've got my eye on a

213

few publishers, so we'll see. Just imagine vampires hiding out in a cider mill in Kansas, and those vampires using the apple presses to press blood out of humans. It'll definitely be a mix of comedy and horror, though I try and keep the two separate from each other in the novel. Once the shit hits the fan, nobody's laughing anymore.

Can you tell us anything new and up-coming just to keep our appetites whet?

There's another novel that could potentially be accepted, though I haven't signed any contracts, but I've got somebody seriously interested in publishing it. Maybe in Spring, if they decided to accept it, but I don't want to jinx myself. The novel's called "Inside the Perimeter." Imagine zombies who would rather cut off your limbs and replace their old, decayed parts with your fresher ones instead of eating you.

What advice would you give to any new writers just starting out and taking that next step to getting their work seen by professionals?

Don't send your story off too soon. Write your draft. Sit on it for a while until you can read your work with fresh eyes. If you're just starting out, try sending to the small presses. Even if they don't accept your work, they might throw a tip or two in the rejection letter that may help you figure it all out. Usually in the mainstream presses, you'll get a form letter without any tips.

Thank you so much for being here and I'm sure all House of Horror fans wish you great success in your writing career. Do you have any last words for those reading this interview?

Thanks again for having me here. And if you like zombie short stories, check out the anthology "Love Is Dead" by Living Dead Press. It just came out to buy on amazon.com. I have a story in it under my real name called "Food for a Valentine." The anthology's all about Valentine's Day and zombies. Enjoy!

You can read House of Horror's review of The Body Cartel in Issue #7 and it also appears in the House of Horror Best of 2009 Anthology. The Body Cartel also won House of Horror's Horrific Read Award 2009. If you would like to purchase a copy of The Body Cartel, then please visit Damnation Books at www.damnationbooks.com

AN INTERVIEW WITH:
Shane McKenzie
Former Editor of House of Horror, new Editor at Pill Hill Press

Shane McKenzie has been a horror fanatic since he was a kid. He still watches any horror movie he can get a hold of, the gorier the better. He has only been writing horror for about 8 months, but knows a good horror story when he sees one. He has stories published at Flashes in the Dark and House of Horror (before becoming the co-editor), as well as stories in the anthologies Mausoleum Memoirs and Creature Features. He lives in Austin, TX with his fiancée and three dogs where he works for the police department.

Shane, I know you wanted to leave the terrors of the House of Horror behind you when you dragged yourself through the gates of hell, but you cannot escape that easily. Since leaving House of Horror as Co-Editor of Long Fiction, how has life been treating you?

Life has been good. I am about to get married in August, and we are very excited about it. It has been stressful as hell, but we're making it. Work has been crazy, I'm sure you have all heard about the plane that hit the building in Austin, well, I work for the police department, and it has been nuts. Things are calming down, though. I have been writing furiously every day, and am FINALLY about to start writing my first novel.

Has working with me and the ezine helped you in anyway?

Working for House of Horror has helped me dramatically. It taught me how to look for common mistakes in writing, as well as how to make my writing stronger. It's just so much easier to edit others work than your own, and it has taught me to look at my own work like someone else wrote it. It's taught me what its like to have deadlines and how difficult it can be to make them. The best thing about it has been Ruthless, by far. I have really enjoyed the experience, from making the cover, to reading the stories, to the editing

216

process. I learned to aim for the top and not be scared to do it. Bentley Little has been very cool about everything.

Tell us what are your plans now regarding your writing?

My plans are to write every single day. What I have been doing is writing a short story, just blazing through the first draft, then putting it away and not looking at it for at least 3 weeks. While it sits there, I write something else, then something else, and so on. That way, by the time I get to editing that first story, it truly feels like someone else wrote it. I find things in there that I can't believe I wrote, and it's easier to use that delete button. Besides shorts, I am about to start my novel, which I won't get into just yet. I have started about three books, and never finished any of them, but I have finally found an idea that I love, and I'm gonna pump all of my energy into it. I hope to have the first draft done in a few months, then I'll set it aside and not look at for probably two months.

You have taken full control of the RUTHLESS anthology, how do you plan on marketing this anthology and do you think this will be the first of many projects for you in the future?

I am exploring many different avenues for Ruthless, but don't want to say too much about that right now. I'll get back to you on that. As far as other projects, I would love to, but my own writing has to come first right now. I just don't feel like I'm anywhere near the writer that I want to be, which is why I left House of Horror in the first place. I really need to fine tune my craft, and I can't have any distractions. I'm aiming for the fences.

Tell us Shane, how long have you been writing and where do you see yourself in say, well you're still quite young, so in ten years?

I have been writing for just about a year now, and the amount that I have learned since I started is pretty amazing. Thanks to my friends at Zoetrope, I have improved much quicker than I thought I could. That being said, I have a long, long road ahead of me. I want to be able to write for a living, and I know that's ambitious, but I don't care. I will make it happen if it kills me. So to answer your question, in ten years, I'll either be a published author or dead.

Who/what has inspired you to write over the last few years alive/dead/real/fictional?

First and foremost, what inspires me is to make a great life for myself and my family doing what I love most. I love horror, I have always loved horror. I used to think I wanted to make video games, horror ones of course, so I graduated from the Art Institute in Dallas with a degree in Environmental Modeling for 3D games/movies. That sounds cool and fun, but I realized that I had no passion for it. It sucks, cuz I'm still paying for it. But, live and learn. So then, I thought I wanted to do special effects for horror movies. I spent a lot of money on materials and self learning books and videos, and got pretty good at it. The problem is that I'm way too messy and unorganized for that. It was really fun, and I still do it for fun sometimes, have made lots of friends and family into zombies. I'm actually possibly about to do a film, but not sure yet. Anyway, I started reading horror novels. Clive Barker, Bentley Little, Jack Ketchum, Brian Keene, and of course, Stephen King. I still read horror books constantly for inspiration. Once I actually started writing, I realized how much I loved it. I was able to get my horror fix in a whole new way, and I haven't stopped since.

When you sit down to write, do you have any pre-requisites i.e a drink, a smoke?

Well, I do most of my writing at work, so a drink would probably not be good. Although sometimes I wish I had a keg with the nozzle hanging from my lips. It can get pretty damn stressful, especially when I'm writing and getting interrupted every other minute or so. My only pre-requisite is to sit my ass down and do it.

What do you think the future holds for Shane McKenzie?

My immediate future holds becoming a husband, then getting a house, then impregnating my wife. I am very excited to start a family, and we are taking the first step this year. For the distant future, I hope to have multiple novels published, along with countless shorts stories. I am also in the process of building a robot that will destroy the world.

Will you continue to do the odd pro-bono work as in guest edit, illustrate for House of Horror?

218

I really want to concentrate on my writing right now, so I won't be doing any illustrating. I don't feel its strong enough to get me anywhere. The same goes for editing, at least right now. I am very determined to become a very good horror author, and if I have other things distracting me, it will just prolong that process. I love House of Horror, and I wish Sam and everyone else involved the best.

Do you have any last words for the readers of House of Horror, before we set you free?

Keep reading. House of Horror is a great ezine, and their anthologies are fantastic as well. I have no doubt that it will keep growing and becoming more recognized, Sam Cox won't allow anything else. Look for any and all books put out by House of Horror, and maybe, MAYBE, some day, you can find one of mine in a bargain bin somewhere. Now, I have some writing to do.

AN INTERVIEW WITH:
Lori Titus
Editor of Flashes in the Dark ezine and author of thw
Maradith Ryder series

Lori Titus started writing at ten years of age, spurred on by nightmares and a steady diet of The Twilight Zone, Bewitched, and Edgar Allan Poe. Over the past three years, Lori became serious about her secret writing hobby and started submitting short stories to horror sites. Since then she has been published by ShadeWorks, MicroHorror, DemonMinds, Crimson Highway, The New Flesh, The Daily Tourniquet, and of course, Flashes in the Dark. She was also the short story editor for Sonar4 Ezine. Future plans include the publication of an anthology of her short stories, Green Water Lullaby, in 2010. When not busy with other pursuits, Lori continues to plot new formats, stategies,and cliffhangers for The Marradith Ryder Series.

Everyone, please welcome Lori Titus to The Lounge. Now now boys and girls, I know she is the competition, but isn't everyone? A little competition is good for the soul. (And don't worry, when we're done here, her soul will be trapped in the House of Horror for all eternity *Cue Evil Laugh* Cough cough. Anyway Lori, how are you?

I am doing very well! Thanks for offering me a chance to speak with you here at House of Horror.

Tell the House of Horror fans a little about yourself.

I am from California. By day I work in human resources, which has given me a yen for interviewing people! I started writing when I was nine years old. In college I studied journalism, but was quickly told by my professor that I was too creative for that type of writing. I continued to write stories, but didn't start trying to get my work published until two years ago.

So, haven't you been a busy little bee. You're on part 72 now of the

220

Marradith Ryder series? Just how do you come up with all these twists and turns and when are you going to round it up and finish?

The first online book of The Marradith Ryder Series is complete, and the last episode will run on Flashes in the Dark in early June.

I am about fourteen episodes into the second book, which is called The Art of Shadows. How do I come up with the twists in this story? I honestly don't know. The characters lead me by the nose and I am happy to follow. I do have some specific benchmarks planned out for it, but as I write the story has expanded on itself. So far, my plan is to turn this story into a three book series.

Have you any plans to publish Marradith Ryder as series of books any time soon?

Yes, I would very much like to have the book published in a traditional manner. I do have plans to do an ebook version, and possibly a comic book as well.

You have also just released your collection of short stories, Green Water Lullaby through Sonar4 Publications. Tell us a little about that.

Green Water Lullaby was a project that seemed to come out of nowhere. As an exercise, I decided one day to start writing some short stories outside of Marradith Ryder's universe, just to have a change and keep my creative juices flowing. The first story was called Brotherhood, about twin brothers who run into some very unfortunate (and supernatural) goings on. I set the story in a make believe southern town called Chrysalis. Over the next few months, I wrote more short stories. I soon realized that all of them were taking place in Chrysalis. It was a great theme for a collection

How are you finding the promotion and sales of this book?

Green Water Lullaby just came out, so I won't know what the sales figures are for a few more months. As far as promotion, I have been quite fortunate. I am a host for the Sonar4 Magazine Talk show. I promote my work on Flashes in the Dark, on my blog, and Facebook, so I have a lot of resources for promotion that other new writers might not have.

Now talk to us about your eZine - Flashes in the Dark. Yours truly Ahem was published there back in August I think. How long have you been around and where do you see it going in the next few years?

Flashes in the Dark has been around for little over a year, and I have been at the ezine about eight months. Over that time we have seen a steady increase in our readership. There are two new serials poised to join Marradith Ryder on the website. Tales of a Reluctant Fangpire by Liza Larregui has already made its debut, and now runs every Friday. I have another author that is working on a serial as well, and we plan to release her story this summer.

When you sit down to write, do you have any pre-requisites i.e. a drink, smoke, some music etc?

I like to have some music on when I write. It helps the mood. If it's either late or very early (which is often when I write) I like to have a cup of coffee or tea.

What is next for Lori Titus and Flashes in the Dark. Tell us of any up coming projects that you have in the works?

I have so many projects! I am writing on Marradith, but I am also working on other stories. I have about four short stories going, and couple of ideas for novels. I am also fleshing out some Marradith related novellas which I'd like to market separately from the stories that are being posted on Flashes in the Dark. Meanwhile I am looking for authors to interview for the Sonar4 show and on Flashes in the Dark. And I am doing promotion for Green Water Lullaby.

Thank you so much for joining us for this interview. Before the zombies take you on a tour of the house, do you have any wise words of wisdom for anyone wanting to submit to your magazine?

My best advice is – just submit! Write a story that you find fun, engaging, and scary. If you're moved by your piece, it's likely that others will be as well. Flashes in the Dark ranks in Duotrope's top twenty five most approachable markets. If you're unsure about tone or style, have a look at the stories currently on site. We look forward to seeing your submissions!

AN INTERVIEW WITH:

David Dunwoody

Author of Empire and Unbound and Other Tales

David Dunwoody is the author of the zombie novel Empire, as well as the collections Dark Entities and Unbound & Other Tales. An ardent fan of Lovecraft, Matheson and Barker, he writes horror with a bent toward the weird and the subversive. Dave currently resides in Utah. Published works include the zombie novel EMPIRE (Permuted Press) and the collections DARK ENTITIES (Dark Regions Press) and UNBOUND & OTHER TALES (Library of Horror Press).

Please welcome David Dunwoody to The Lounge. Woah, wait!! David, you of all people should know not to get too close to my zombie girls. That one in particular will have your arm off quicker than you can say "Eat Shit Zombie." Now back away slowly and sit, please. How are you this evening?

I'm well! And right at home, even if the zombie girls aren't crazy about me. I just hope you don't have a clown lurking around here somewhere. Though I suspect you do. Story of my life.

Now you are quite a prolific writer, how many projects do you have in the works at the minute?

I have a few things in various stages of development - I'm learning as I go how to set my hours, and not to load my plate with too much at once. Right now I'm writing a novella for Library of Science Fiction and Fantasy, while outlining a few stories and a novel that I will start on in the coming months.

You wrote and published the zombie novel Empire, put out by permuted press. Can you tell the zombie fans what this book is about?

EMPIRE is set 105 years after a global zombie outbreak. Death himself leaves his post to restore order by slaying the zombies wandering the American badlands. He ends up crossing paths with a lot off oddball

223

characters and some very unusual zombies.

You have been in more than ten horror anthologies, have you not? If you had to choose, which of them is your favorite and why?

I'd say THE UNDEAD: HEADSHOT QUARTET, which is actually a collection of zombie novellas by four authors. The other tales are great and my contribution, "Lost Souls," is one of my favorite works, and is actually an update of one of the first stories I wrote as a little kid.

Where will David Dunwoody be regarding success in ten years time? What are your goals as a writer?

I can't say I have a ten-year plan. I'd love to be making a living just off of my writing, but to be where I'm at now - writing and selling at a fairly steady clip, and having a blast doing it - is pretty cool in itself.

Who are your influences when writing, dead or alive?

H.P. Lovecraft, for the way he tapped into our most primal terrors, and built a mythos around them. The filmmaker David Cronenberg's exploration of what threatens from within continues to have a growing influence on my stories. Clive Barker creates beautiful and original monsters that make for fascinating characters.

Tell the fans something about David Dunwoody, they don't know.

In 2005, I co-wrote a short film with my buddy Gene Mazza II that appears on a DVD called DETOUR INTO MADNESS VOL. 1. The short is a fun little bit of T&A (torture and abuse) called "Snuff," of which a full-length version was written just this past winter. I love the lead characters and hope it'll be produced.

If you had to choose one greatest moment in your writing career so far, what would it be and why?

The easy answer is the acquisition of EMPIRE by Simon and Schuster last year, which has been an incredible and unexpected blessing. But I have to say that seeing the first edition in print for the first time was just as awesome. Having the two editions side-by-side now...that's just surreal.

Do you have any words of wisdom to any young aspiring horror writers who may be reading this?

Read. Read often, and mix in different genres. I think that's the best advice I can give. There's no surefire key to breaking out, but always exploring what's out there - including the works of other aspiring newcomers - is essential to one's own growth.

Finally, before I open the trap door and send you straight into the Dungeon, do you have any last words?
Trap door?? I sense a dungeon clown in my future. Dungeons and clowns - story of my life. Well, thanks for having me, and supporting small-press horror!

AN INTERVIEW WITH:
Eric S. Brown
Author of Big Foot War

Eric S. Brown is the author of numerous books including Bigfoot War, Season of Rot, How the West Went to Hell, Anti-Heroes (with David Dunwoody), and Kinberra Down to name only a few. His novel, War of the Worlds Plus Blood Guts and Zombies (with H.G. Wells), was recently picked up by Simon and Schuster and is slated for a December, 2010 release. Some of his upcoming books include ,The Human Experiment, The Weaponer, and Undead Down Under. Eric's short fiction has been published hundreds of times in the small press and beyond. He has also been featured as an expert on the zombie genre in books like Zombie CSU: The Forensics of the Living Dead and the upcoming Extreme Halloween: Behind the Scenes of America's Fright Night. His monthly comic book column in Abandoned Towers magazine won "Best Nonfiction 2009" in the Preditor and Editor awards this year and his book Season of Rot was nominated for a Dead Letter Award for "Best Zombie collection 2009" as well. Eric lives in North Carolina with his loving wife and son where he continues to write tales of adventure, rotting flesh, and blazing guns

Ladies and gentlemen of horror, please sit back and welcome once again the tamer of the un-dead, Mr Eric. S. Brown to the Lounge. How have you been man?

Busy, busy, busy. The writing never ends. So many books, so little time.
So Eric, tell   us what have you been up to since you last sat in that chair being fondled by my zombie girls?

I have out numerous new books this year including Bigfoot War, How the West Went to Hell, and Kinberra Down. Also The Human Experiment, The Weaponer, Anti-Heroes (with David Dunwoody), and Undead Down Under (my first hardcover) along with the Simon and Schuster release of War of the Worlds Plus Blood Guts and Zombies are all slated for the near future.

226

In early 2011, The Brethren of the Dead (a direct sequel to The Queen from Season of Rot) will be released as well.

So you have a new novel coming out with Sonar4publications this year – The Human experiment. Can you tell House of Horror fans anything about this?

The Human Experiment is my first full on venture into the superhero genre. It's a dark and fantastic novel about a smart ass, C.I.A. operative named Agent Robert Death. He's a character I have been thinking up for years who will also be featured in the book Anti-Heroes and the upcoming comic book "Agent Death and the Angels". I can't say much about the plot at this point but I will say this is a team book despite Death being the main character and it has a very Doom Patrol feel to it. I can assure you, it certainly has the level of action and weirdness I usually bring to all my projects.

Alongside The Human Experiment, you also have another zombie novella with Sonar4 slated for publication in 2011 – Brethren of the Dead. Tell us a little about this project.

The Brethren of the Dead is a zombie pirate book set in the post apocalyptic world of my novella The Queen (available in Season of Rot from Permuted Press). It's a book that is best described as Waterworld meets Dawn of the Dead. It's my current project so it's a still a work in progress but I think folks who enjoy my take on the zombie genre will certainly find it lives up to The Queen. I can tell you for folks who read Season of Rot that you will see the war between the remaining humans and the dead really pick up on the waves of the ocean in this book.

So, how have you been balancing success with your family life?

It's not easy, I'll tell you that. It's hard to find the time to keep up with my writing projects and my four year old son but I juggle it as best I can. I just kind of dive into everything headlong and hope for the best. It's worked so far.

You won "Best Non-Fiction 2009" in the Preditor and Editor awards for your monthly comic book column in Abandoned Towers Magazine.

How did you feel when you heard the news?

It was very flattering and I felt very honored. Being a comic book geek my whole life, it was pretty cool to win for writing about them.

Your book, Season of Rot was nominated for a Dead Letter Award for "Best Zombie Collection 2009." How on earth do you keep up with all these nominations and awards? I didn't even know when I was nominated "Best Fiction eZine Editor," until someone informed me that they had voted.

Well the Dead Letter Awards are given out by the Canadian horror/zombie show Mail Order Zombie. They sent emails to all the people chosen to be nominated by their panel of horror judges. It was really cool to hear I was on the list regardless of whether I won or lost.

What is it like knowing that you are adored by many many zombie fans and probably hated by unsuccessful authors? How does one cope with the attention such success brings?

Yeesh, I hope I am not hated! And I certainly don't feel that successful either. I think I have a long way left to go as a writer besides, I am really just a fan with a pen in my hand who can't stop writing. If by the grace of God my work can give a reader or fan something they always wanted to see done in the genre that no one else was crazy enough to try, then I am happy. Take my latest book, Bigfoot War, now available on www.amazon.com, etc. It's a book truly from the heart of my lifelong fandom of horror. I loved Bigfoot movies but always wanted there to be more than one monster. I longed to see a movie or book where there was like a whole pack of Sasquatches just tearing people to shreds so I made it happen. There isn't a lot of hardcore Bigfoot horror out there in book form and certainly not any that feature over five dozen of the creatures descending on one poor, little town to my knowledge. It's a deeply personal book to me on a lot of levels and I really hope that folks give it a shot.

Do you have any advice for those approaching the next rung on the ladder, keeping up-to-date with everything, while trying to balance their fiction life with their real life?

Pray, work hard, and hope for the best. It's what I do.

Thank you so much for coming back to visit us Eric, it is such an honor to have you here. Now, if you're staying the night, I do charge and if you're taking one of my zombie girls with you, I charge for that also. Either way, I hope you enjoy your stay.
Thanks, it was great to have a chance to chat again and if any one wants to check out the new release of War of the Worlds Plus Blood Guts and Zombies from Simon and Schuster's Gallery line, www.amazon.com already has it up as a pre-order so you can reserve your copy now.

AN INTERVIEW WITH:
Jerrod Brown
Horror Artist

O.K., this was uncomfortable! Definitely not the usual way I like to do my interviews. I already had a strange feeling when this Jerrod guy told me about the location to meet him, which was at the entrance to a graveyard outside one of our oldest suburbs. Then his paintings... bloody, dark, frightening and of course everything horror. Nevertheless I was here, stranded. The cab had long left, it was getting dark and it was a little foggy too. I checked the surroundings. No one was in the streets. No voices filled the air, the place was completely isolated. Perfect... I checked my watch. 9:00 pm already and Jerrod wanted to meet me here at 8:30. I decided to wait another 15 minutes before I would call a cab. I crossed the street. The old graveyard was not inviting at all... as if any graveyard at night is. But this one could have easily been used for any George Romero movie. A huge iron gate with some old rusty ornamental elements was the only entrance, and obviously the last caretaker for this place was probably buried here. It looked as if no one had been in there for years; the weeds had definitely taken over the place. I shivered.

The sudden noise of a big block engine filled the air, and an old car, badly in need of a paint job and a tune up approached me. Must be the undertaker, I thought, or a grave robber. The car stopped right next to me and the black tinted side window moved down.

"Sorry I'm late Sam", the silhouette in the car said, "jump in and we'll go to your House of Horror".

Please welcome Horror Artist Jerrod Brown to The Lounge.

Sorry bout' that, but I just had to meet you there. People kind of expect that from me...

Now, I see that you've brought with you the cover paintings you did for Sonar4 Publications - 'Bite This' and 'The Blooming'. So, tell me, how long have you been working with the fabulous Shells Walter?

It's been about two years now and I've done about 17 covers for her so far. I paint nearly every day... commissions, requests or whatever I'm inspired by at the moment. But, when a book cover request comes up, I push everything aside and get right on it.

When Sonar4 commissions you for a piece of artwork, do you get full reign on what you do or are you given specific instructions on what they want for a particular project?

Usually Shells will give me the tentative title and a synopsis. From that I'll spend several days, sometimes up to a week, thinking about the direction I want to take. The goal is to represent as close as possible what the author is thinking. Represent what the novel is truly about. After the final painting is finished, I send it over to Shells for final approval.

How long does it take you from start to the finished product (commission or otherwise)?

I'll work on a canvas (on and off) for a week average. I'm strictly a traditional (non-digital) artist, working with 'real' paint on 'real' canvas with 'real' brushes.

Please tell House of Horror fans a little about yourself.

I worked as an artist in the Theme Park industry for many, many years. In October of 2008 I was laid off. From that point forward, I decided to start painting what I love most... the Horror genre. In the scenic industry, everything I painted fell under the blanket of the corporations I worked for. Therefor you're basically a "ghost-artist". I took great pride in what I was doing there and truly loved my job, but now everything I paint has my name attached to it.

How would you rate your success at the moment, and what goals do you have for the future?

Actually... I feel like I'm just getting started. I keep a running list of requests and ideas, so the subject matter is endless. My goal is to have some of my work on the cover of any of the mainstream Horror magazines, such as 'Famous Monsters of Filmland', 'HorrorHound', 'Rue Morgue', 'Screem', etc. Maybe someday they'll accept my work...

Please tell us about any projects you have coming up.

Of course the upcoming book covers for Sonar4, 'Dead Practices' and 'Devil's Own' by Shells Walter, The anthologies 'Twisted Fairy Tales Vol.2' edited by Lori Titus, 'Throw Down Your Dead' edited by Rob Walter and 'Ladies & Gentlemen of Horror' edited by Chris Bartholomew. Also, a comic book cover for 'Vincent Price Presents' for Bluewater Publications, which will be in most comic shops and 'Books-a-Million' stores. I'm also scheduled for various Horror Conventions, Clubs and Gallery shows.

Which piece of art, old or new, are you most proud of? What is it about the piece that makes you step back and say 'Wow?'
Well actually I'm never really 100% satisfied with anything I've done. Even now, I'll look back at paintings and think to myself "that could've been so much better". I just keep looking ahead and listen to my obsession calling.

Thank you very much for your time here tonight and I wish you great success for the future. Before you leave us, do you have any words of wisdom for any young aspiring artists out there?

If you stop chasing your dream, you're already dead.

O.K. Jerrod, before you go, where can we see your work and how can we contact you?

Facebook: http://www.facebook.com/HorrorArtist
Myspace: http://www.myspace.com/JerrodBrown
E-Mail: SouthpawCreation@bellsouth.net

AN INTERVIEW WITH:
Kevin Wallis
Author of 'Beneath the Surface of Things'

Kevin, welcome to my House of Horror, how are you? Here have a glass of red wine. . . or at least, I think it's wine. . .

Hmm, I'm more of a beer drinker . . . Less bodily fluids to confuse beer with. Well, I guess that's not true.

So, you have a book out now, Beneath the Surface of Things. Please tell us a little about it.

It comes out September 1st through Bards and Sages Publishing. It's 25 stories of horror, sci-fi, and fantasy, woth a humor piece thrown in for grins. It's gotten some good, positive reviews so far: Gary Braunbeck said, "An impressive, often unnerving, and always gutsy collection . . . showcases Wallis' determination to break through the so-called boundaries of dark fiction . . ." Bailey Hunter from Dark Recesses Press said, ". . . a vivid tapestry of horrific prose.   While the stories seem to have an underlying theme of human condition, they are anything but common.   This collection runs the gamut of the classic cool creep to the more visceral and gut-wrenching."

It's been a long time in the making, from the writing to editing to finding a publisher, so I'm very excited about it, and I hope it's a springboard to bigger and better things. I've always wanted to be a major league catcher, so maybe this will help.

You also work as an editor for Liquid Imagination Publishing, I see. I can imagine that takes its toll on your spare time. How do you manage your own writing with that of being an editor and also your personal time?

I usually let the submissions from Liquid Imagination build up until I can't ignore them any longer, then I spend a few days ignoring my own writing and strictly going through the LI stories. It works good for now, but when Liquid Imagination blows up and takes over the online literary world, I'll probably need to hire some help.

You're a family man with a wife and three children. What do they think about what you're doing?

Ha. They're extremely supportive and proud of me, but my wife does not understand, appreciate, or have any need for anything horror-related. I think the Amityville Horror traumatized her as a kid, and I'm paying for it now. But, her dislike for scary stuff just makes her support of what I do that much more special to me.

As for my kids, they understand that they won't be able to read most of my stories for another decade or so. I write stories specifically for them, though, so it evens out. (One of the stories I wrote for them, and starring them too, is being published in Yarns For Our Youths by Static Movement soon.)

What other genres do you write?

I still write mostly horror, but I like the more subtle scares. I don't write blood and guts stuff. That's boring to me. I still try to keep it about the characters rather than the scare.

I write sci-fi occasionally if the plot calls for a setting like this, but I'm not smart or tech-savvy enough to pull it off usually. And there are several stories in my book that aren't horror or sci-fi at all, but more mainstream and personal stories that don't fit nicely into a specific genre.

Tell us about any other projects you have coming up or in the works.

I finally started my first novel, after saying I'm gonna do it for ten years now. Hopefully it'll help attract an agent, which is the next step in my writing goal flowsheet.

What were your inspirations for writing this collection?

Every story was inspired by something different. I actually include a short explanation after each story stating what inspired me to write that particular story.

I grew up reading King, Barker, Lovecraft, Poe and the like, so I guess much of my writing is directly inspired by the masters, especially Lovecraft.

When did you first begin writing and at what moment did you realise that it was what you wanted to do most in life?

I've been writing since I was a kid, although not many people knew I was doing it. After getting a couple stories in my high school fiction magazine (man, those stories were bad), I didn't write much until after college. Maintaining my stellar B and C average just didn't allow for the time.

I finally got serious about it about 3 years ago. I never thought I'd even get one story published, but after having a modicum of success these past few years, I want more and more - score an agent, publish a novel, become the starting catcher for my Houston Astros . . .

Do you have any words of wisdom for those seeking advice from a pro?

This sounds cliche, but just don't quit. Take every rejection and turn it into a lesson to improve your writing. Study the craft, don't ever take rejection personally, and put in the hours. Too many aspiring writers want success but aren't willing to put in the hard work to achieve it.

Thank you so much for being here Kevin, I was beginning to wonder what I could feed to the zombie girls. Do you have any last words before I let them loose on you?

I have 23. Thanks for the time. I hope people enjoy my book. And next time feed me some O+. O- goes straight to my thighs.

Run Kevin, run for your life! It makes your meat taste better mwah ha ha ha ha!

AN INTERVIEW WITH:
Suza Kates
Author of 'Whispers of a Witch.'

Suza Kates was born in Jacksonville, Alabama, the youngest of five children. Growing up surrounded by siblings and parents who were bookworms, she naturally developed a love for the written word. She attended Jacksonville State University, majoring in English and biology.

After receiving her degree, Suza pursued a lifelong dream to live abroad, teaching English to students from various countries. A long, cold, German winter caused her to pick up the pen and begin writing. Then she was hooked.

Upon her return home to the States, she taught at a local community college while going back to school herself for a degree in nursing. During the few hours that remained between classes, clinicals, and studying, she worked on her novel, She Who Is Hidden. This book opened the door to a world of romance fueled by history, adventure, and peril that developed into the She Trilogy.

Shortly after graduating, Suza moved to Savannah, Georgia. It is there among the moss-covered oaks and whispered secrets that she continues to find inspiration for The Savannah Coven Series and the various kinds of trouble her witches seem to conjure.

Welcome Suza to my House of Horror, probably a little different to your other interview locations huh?

Different, yes, but I feel right at home. I was a horror fan long before I discovered romance. The first movie I ever saw was "Bambi." The second was "Jaws." I've been warped ever since. Halloween is THE holiday, so... thanks for the change in venue!

Now, this book was very forthcoming with details of the craft. Are you in fact a fellow Wiccan?

I don't practice Wicca but have a great deal of respect for the basis of the craft. I embrace many of the same ideals in my life and find some

236

similarities between Wicca and Native American customs. Having said that, I am fascinated by the idea of potions and spells and would love to find a little power in myself someday. Who wouldn't?

Tell us a little about the book Whispers of a Witch

"Whisper of a Witch" is the first of book of the series, so it introduces us to the coven as well as telling Shauni's story. The nine women that make up the coven find themselves pulled to an island off the coast in Savannah, Georgia. There they discover something about themselves and a prophecy they are meant to fulfill. Oh, and there are a few "hot points" (as my mother calls them) between the hero and heroine, just to spice things up a bit.

What were your inspirations behind writing "Whisper of a Witch"?

I've always wanted to write a book about witches, and the opportunity presented itself after I moved to Savannah. The scenery here is gorgeous and mysterious, the perfect setting for my witches! The idea of a group of women banding together to fight evil surrounded by a rich, southern background seemed delicious, and I can hardly wait to start plotting each witch's story!

I hear that there will be a sequel out next year. Can you tell us anything about this one and will it follow the trait of being centred on one member of the coven.

Yes, it will be another witch's time to play her part, though I can't tell you who it will be! I've gotten a great reaction to the coven, and some readers have written in asking for a certain woman to be next. I love these witches, and I'm so glad others do, too.

How long have you been writing for?

Technically for about nine years, but seriously writing for three. Something clicked inside me, and I realized I wanted to write full time. I'm not there, yet, but the response to "Whisper of a Witch" is very encouraging. My dream life is waking up every day to make coffee, fire up the computer, and have a cat in my lap as I write the next book.

Tell us about any other projects you have coming up or in the works.

"Conviction of a Witch" will be out in February of 2011, but a couple of other projects are slated for this fall. My first romantic suspense titled "She Who is Hidden" involves some history, adventure, riddles, and, of course, hot romance! I just found out another of my books will be released in e-book format in September. "Hallowed Eve" is also a romantic suspense and will be out just in time for Halloween. It definitely satisfies my horror addiction. Mua ha ha!

If you were to have a fantasy dinner party, who would be your guests - living or dead - and why?

Ooh. Fun question. Of the dead, I would pick River Phoenix, because he was just gone too soon. I would also love to have Joan of Arc, because c'mon, how cool was she? Mary Queen of Scots and Sir Isaac Newton because they are both supposed to be ancestors of mine. I'd like to know if that's true or not. :)
In the world of the living, I would have M. Night Shyamalan. I love his twisted mind! Nora Roberts, to ask her how she writes so fast. And if I can play a little with this fantasy, I'd like to have Eric Northman from True Blood, because...well, isn't it obvious?

Do you have any inspirational words of wisdom for those seeking to become a better writer to trying to get published?

Absolutely. Go to writer's conferences and join a critique group, but try to stay in your genre. I have found that a sci-fi writer does not always understand romance, just as a romance writer might want to soften up a horror novel. Other writers in your genre will know the market you're writing for and give more valuable feedback. A new author might also want to submit shorter works to e-book publishers. Be open, and don't hoard your works for that "big break." Small presses are a great way to get started, and any editorial advice is worth its weight in gold. (Oops. That was a cliché.) Plus, it will get an author's name out there and the sooner the better. Words of wisdom? I tend to be a little bit of a rule breaker, so I would tell authors to write to please their readers, not agents and editors. If the story is there, the readers will be, too.

238

Thank you so much for being here today, Suza. Just because I like you, I am going to give you a free pass out of here. Just take this bag of past guests brains and throw it at the zombies as you near the door. If they get you, it ain't my fault! Any final words?

If I don't make it out of here, make sure someone feeds my cats!

AN INTERVIEW WITH:
Tonia Brown
Author of 'The Blooming' and 'Lucky Stiff – Memoirs of an Undead Lover'

Welcome Tonia, how are you this evening. It's not often we get such beautiful women in here. The zombie girls aren't best pleased about not being fed tonight. (They only like hot male meat.)

Now you are the author of the highly acclaimed "Lucky Stiff" Published by The Library of Horror. How does it feel knowing that everyone wants a piece of Peter?

I am super sexcited about it! I highly encourage folks to get their hands on my Peter! Put him into the hands of your friends and family. Take him out at the office and show him off. Spread the love for Peter!

What gave you the idea to write this book? Especially from a male perspective?

I was finishing up another erotic zombie novel, which was careful to keep the zombies and sex away from one another, when I wondered how it would work to mix the two. I was careful to ask about, questioning a few folks as to what boundaries such a thing would require. Peter's zombieism arose from these discussions. As for a male perspective, I have always felt more comfortable writing from a male POV.

It talks a lot about voodoo and tantric sex, did you do a lot of research or have much help writing the book?

I am Wiccan in faith, so my background in occultism gave me a hand up for writing this puppy. I did have to read a bit on voodoo and tantric sex, but only as a refresher. I also included a forward from the Madam explaining that the magic is all home brewed, and not to write me complaining that I got stuff wrong about it!

240

How long did it take you to write it?

97k words in 56 days. It was exhausting, but he told his life story from beginning to end with little need for adjusting. It was like a good, long bedroom romp that ended with the birth of a novel instead of a baby.

What made you decide to become a writer?

Does one ever? When I wasn't paying attention, the urge to write leapt on my back, like a squealing monkey that refuses to let me go, no matter how many support groups I go to begging them to get rid of the damned thing.

How does writing horrotica differ from writing regular erotica apart from the obvious?

Very little, actually. The key to any good horrotica or erotica is weaving the sex into the story, rather than tacking it on. It is hard to do right, but hopefully I manage from time to time.

Who or what are your inspirations for your writing?

My husband is a constant source of inspiration. He gives me ideas, helps me sort out plot lines and even names almost every novel I have ever written.

Tell us of any upcoming projects you have in the works.

In March 2010 The Library of The Living Dead will release my novel, "The Cold Beneath." It is a steampunk zombie story set in the late 1800's and featuring the Victorian race for the North Pole.
I am also working on editing several anthologies, and a new novel that will read like the old 'Road to...' movies from back in the day, only with a zombie.

Do you have any words of wisdom to anyone writing in this particular genre?

Read! If you don't have time to read, you don't have time to write. Read the genre before you attempt it. It will show if you don't!

Lucky Stiff along with other titles by Tonia Brown can be found at Amazon.com and most good online retailers.

HOUSE OF HORROR REVIEWS:

Inside the Perimeter

By Alan Spencer

When the world of horror seems to have been dumbed down somewhat to make way for the young adult versions they still like to call horror, out crawls a relatively unknown horror writer to make those films and books look like a walk in the land of fairies. Alan Spencer has once again brought the word 'Horror' to its knees. He has stripped away all the overdone and over used tiresome plot-lines and themes and given life to something new and never before seen.

Inside the Perimeter on first look would seem like your average run of the mill zombie novel, where the dead come to life and attack the living blah blah blah. Oh no my friends! THIS book puts other zombie books to shame.

What I love most about this book is the way that Spencer gives us both good guy and bad guy perspectives by having each alternate chapter in the other's point of view. He is able to give us what is going on in each of the character's heads giving you reasons to pity or hate them and identifying with their plight.

Inside the Perimeter begins with Detective Boyd Broman being taken out of prison where he is being held for accidental murder. Boyd is

243

taken to a facility that is surrounded by high walls and barbed wire and literally thrown inside. On first look, the facility looks like an abandoned town, with a post office, a school, hospital and houses, but something eerie floats about the place and something doesn't sit right with Boyd. On answering a strange phone call, Boyd is given his orders; to capture cannibal serial killer, Hayden Grubaugh and bring him to the Perimeter walls to be taken into custody. Then Boyd would be free. Or so he assumes. Easy right? Not so much.

It soon becomes apparent to Boyd that the abandoned town isn't so 'abandoned.' Creatures that appear to be some sort of zombies begin attacking him and when he gets away and hides he watches exactly what they are and what they do. But even blown apart by his gun, the severed pieces keep moving, pulling themselves back together or go in search of new parts. And the new parts come in the form of other prisoners that have been thrown into the facility.

But Boyd is not alone. Through the many of the dead humans feeding the crazed undead, he comes across a young woman, Cindy who attaches herself to him as they move through the facility in search of Hayden.

But Hayden is also looking for them also. He is sick of feasting on the dead and wants fresh meat again. But for now he will make do with feasting off the undead until he can clasp his hands around Cindy who becomes overly desirable to him.

In a frantic mad mess of cat and mouse, Inside the Perimeter is certainly not one for the squeamish. Spencer's ability to make words on a page become real, it so great that you can almost smell the rotting corpses as he is describing in great detail everything that the characters come across whilst in the facility.

And this definitely shakes all the cobwebs off any other zombie novel out there. It's very different, gruesome and gory and has the ability to put you right there next to the characters.

Another great read for hardcore horror fan's, a book you just won't want to put down with almost every chapter leaving you on a cliff-hanger.

Just be warned, those with weak stomachs shouldn't eat before reading this book. You may never want to eat anything again!

HOUSE OF HORROR REVIEWS:

Unbound and Other Tales

By David Dunwoody

When I found that I would get the privilege of reading a book by David Dunwoody, I felt truly honored. I had heard a lot about this author around the web and in our writing community. His book, Unbound and Other Tales, did not disappoint me.

In this book of one novella and eight short stories, we explore the depths of Dunwoody's psyche and some may be afraid of what they find on the pages of this book. Some of the collection are stories previously published on and off the web in anthologies and magazines, while the others are new stories. Though I haven't completely finished reading the short stories in detail yet, I have a clear idea of the type of writer Dunwoody is and I like what I see. He has no boundaries – or not many, and will let the story speak to him rather than the other way around. You can most definitely see it in this book. The novella Unbound, held my interest right the way through. I was really intrigued by the story of horror writer, Matthew Rudd, whose evil character in his book comes to life to continue writing the series of brutal murder books, Rudd so desperately wants to bring to an end. The character Sharpe is an evil man, who drives up and down the 1-15 highway in his truck, delivering goods and murdering innocent people for kicks. On his travels he comes across victims from all walks of life. No one is too

245

young or old or innocent for their life to end at the hands of him.

The main character 'Josh Talbot' believes along with Agent Logan that Sharpe in the Sharp books is actually the alter ego of Matthew Rudd. But upon find him after being missing for some time, Rudd pleads his innocence claiming that Sharpe has literally stepped out of his books and is on a real life killing spree.

Confused yet? Well you should be! This book will have you believing one thing, then having to second guess yourself. It is filled with numerous plot twists and exciting explanations. I for one, could not put it down.

If you're one for enjoying the psychoanalysis of an author when reading a book, then Unbound is most definitely one for you.

You can purchase a copy of Unbound and Other Tales from the Library of Horror Press. If you would like to learn more about this author, you can catch an interview with him in Issue #12 and also a more in-depth interview when Dunwoody sits down with The House Madame in The Lounge, House of Horror's Blog Talk Radio Show.

HOUSE OF HORROR REVIEWS:
Ruthless
By Shane McKenzie and Pill Hill Press

When editor of Ruthless, Shane McKenzie first approached me with the idea for this Shock Horror anthology, he was actually working as an editor for House of Horror. I was a little unsure at first, I thought it too way 'out there' for our audience even though we are a magazine of horror. These days a lot of the so called horror that is put out to the public is so diluted that I don't know why it even as the word 'horror' associated with it. And that goes for films as well as books. You have to be very careful and very aware of political correctness when you are addressing the public in such a way that we are. But you know what? Why the hell should we? Its a simple case of if you don't like what we put out then don't read it!

Shane's idea of bringing together the most gruesome, vulgar, horrific pieces of writing, was ingenious and it works. Being one of the most popular anthologies on the web at the moment, sadly I wish I was apart of it.

Unfortunately House of Horror was under so much pressure at that time and could not continue with the project. But stories had been chosen and contracts signed. Boy am I glad that Shane decided to take the project and go solo. He did everything so professional – from hiring a model and using special make-up effects and a professional photographer, to hunting down the famous Bentley Little of all people to write an introduction to the book.

Mr McKenzie worked so damn hard on seeing this project to the end and it most certainly paid off. I am holding a print copy now in my hands.

Regarding the stories themselves, well they are some of the sickest stories I have ever had the pleasure to read. The premise behind this book was to seriously make the reader question the sanity of the authors. And they did just that. My favorite stories have to be 'Crankin' by John Arthur Miller and 'To Boil' by Lucas Pederson. They have most certainly made me question whether I want to be associating with gruesomely awesome talented writers.

Ruthless was eventually picked up and published by Pill Hill Press and was brought out just recently. If you haven't gotten a copy already, I highly recommend that you do. Stop reading the boring teen claptrap horror and come read some real deep and terrifying horror for a change. With 19 stories and an introduction by Horror author Bentley Little, this anthology is not for the faint hearted. The morbid and macabre words on these pages will surely cause night terrors. Do not read near children. Do not read aloud. And one final warning; do not read alone after dark...

HOUSE OF HORROR REVIEWS:
Whispers of a Witch
By Suza Kates

Whispers of a Witch is an enchanting tale of mystery, adventure and sexual awakening. The tale of Shauni, a young woman with the ability to talk to animals, takes us on a path of enlightenment where Shauni's life will change forever.

The story begins with nine young women suddenly sensing the need to pack up everything and move to the beautiful Savannah, but why, they do not know. It is a calling and they all must answer it. Shauni is one of them and takes her cat – who she can communicate with – along for the ride. It turns out that when all of the women come together, they all own cats and their names are unusually meaningful. The nine women are confronted with another young woman named Anna and are taken to a large secluded house where they are told why they have come together and what they must do.

Amongst the madness and the magic, Shauni manages to find love. The delicious Michael. And we know that he is delicious because Kates describes him in so much detail, you can feel your eyes glazing over and your heart pumping faster when he enters the scene. Even with all of her secrets, Michael wants her and will do anything to have her. But he too has his own secret and will eventually use it in a bid to save Shauni's life and inadvertently put his own in danger.

Kates has a remarkable way of expressing every little detail throughout the book. She concentrates on painting a picture so vivid, that the reader can almost smell th fresh air and feel the wind on their face. Her ability to make the readers read the words like they are playing out like a movie in front of their eyes.

I really enjoyed living Shauni's adventure with her and sharing her thoughts and feelings about her new life. And when things get hot and heavy with her new found love, well, lets just say I could not put the book down. I enjoyed the underlying tone of this book too. The fact that despite everything that is tossed in front of you, love and understanding can conquer all in the end. Even if there are bumps a long the way, fate will find a way for two people to come together.

I look forward to reading the next instalment of this enchanting tale and more from this wonderfully talented writer. If you are going to pick up a book this week, then let it be, Whispers of a Witch. This is one book that you can snuggle up with by the fire.

Exciting, enthralling and at times erotic, you will surely not want to put down Whispers of a Witch. Suza Kates is an upcoming name to look out for.

HOUSE OF HORROR REVIEWS:

Lucky Stiff: Memoirs of an Undead Lover

By Tonia Brown

Well, what can I say about Lucky Stiff! This book had me roaring with laughter, biting my lip in tears and almost all the way through it trying to force myself NOT to read the book with one hand! Tonia Brown is an amazing writer of horrotica. Her ability to make each and every scene something new and unique is amazing, after-all there is only so many words you can use for the male and female genitalia!

The story begins with young Peter Lyles visiting New Orleans with his friends for spring break. But of course he isn't into the partying his scene much to his friends despair. After studying hard, all Peter wants to do is rest, relax and enjoy the scenery. But for some reason he cannot seem to switch off and rest. Stupidly, he accepts what he thinks are sleeping pills off one of his friends and winds up dead. Of course you would think that was where the story ends. But you are so mistaken. This is where the story begins.

Peter's friends drag his body to the house of a mystery voodoo witch where she is able to bring his body back. But there is a catch. He an only come back as a zombie. But no ordinary zombie. He is still looks and acts relatively human.

After saying goodbye to his friends and telling his mom and dad he won't be going back to school or coming home for a while, Peter lives with the voodoo witch, Madame Sangrail where she teaches him how to stop himself from eating human flesh like the M.O of a zombie. The only way for him to do this is to feed off the light given off when a woman orgasms. Madam Sangrail teaches him all kinds of things until it is time for him to leave the nest and go out into the world, and even make a visit back home to see his mom and dad. This he does, but things don't go so well.

Peter travels the world, shagging his way through the female population to feed his hunger, and meets a whole load of people. He even works for an escort agency and his new Madam, Niki, advertises his services as a vampire escort. He uses a range of medical conditions to explain his features, one of which is a constant erection and the inability to come.

I loved this book. At times, I wondered whether the sex was over-done as there was a sex act on almost every page, but the rest of the story balanced it out well and Tonia's ability to take it from the boring x goes into y, made it a much more interesting read.

I have never really been into zombie stories, but this mix match of zombies, love, hate, sex and rivalry and betrayal was exciting and I thoroughly enjoyed joining Peter on his journey to sexual enlightenment.

There really is only one word to describe this book and that is H.O.T. Trust me, once you start this story, you better cancel all dates, unhook the phone and turn off the TV. You are in for one hell of a ride and you will not want to put this book down until you have ridden Peter all the way. Let him take you to the brink, let him dangle you there while you scream his name and let him FUCK the living daylight out of you!

HOUSE OF HORROR REVIEWS:

Desiree

By Ken Goldman

Don't kiss Desiree Chappelle!

Desiree is a weird and wonderful tale by author Ken Goldman, of a young woman who literally possess the kiss of death. Anyone who gets close enough to touch her lips becomes madly obsessed with Desiree up until the point she is practically controlling their every thought and move.

On the outside Desiree looks and acts like a normal beautiful young woman, but even at the age of thirteen, she was desired by almost every adolescent boy. They all strangely wanted to be near her.

The story begins at Tommy and Tamara (twins) thirteenth birthday party. The young teens decide to play a game of spin the bottle. Tommy finally gets his wish to kiss Desiree Chappelle but at what cost? As Goldman puts it, it was Tommy's best birthday ever, but it would also be his last.

Goldman then takes us through various point in the characters life, winding strange little side tales within each section. There really are no chapters, just broken up sections. One thing that did annoy me about this layout, was that I occasionally got lost within the story because each section did not always follow suit. But it did make me go back to sections and made sure that I did not skip any parts. I did however like the twist that Goldman set up towards the end.

Desiree was published by Damnation Books in 2010, was edited and copy edited by Heather Williams and Penny Lockwood Ehrenkranz. The cover art was created by Julie D'arcy and the book layout by Ally Robertson.

HOUSE OF HORROR REVIEWS:

The Occult Files of Albert Taylor

By Derek Muk

Meet Albert Taylor, an anthropology professor who investigates cases of the paranormal on the side.

The Occult Files of Albert Taylor written by Derek Muk, is a collection of stories told from the point of view of anthropology professor, Albert Taylor. Each story is sectioned into cases from a haunted asylum, a vampire on the University Campus to Jack the Ripper coming back from the Dead.

Personally, this book wasn't my cup of tea – I can only tell the truth, but that is not to say that it isn't an enjoyable book. I thought the stories that I read were interesting and the plots very well thought out and I am sure anyone who enjoys paranormal investigative collections, would love to get their hands on this book. There are eleven stories in this collection, though I am sure that after reading all about Albert Taylor, you will want to learn more about him.

One thing that I personally think this book could have benefited from was some sort of introduction to Albert Taylor, as I felt that his character was repeatedly described in every story and wasn't needed. If we had learned something about his character in an introduction then I think I personally wouldn't have rolled my eyes every time his character was described. Other than that, I thought the stories were very interesting and executed excellently and the other characters making an appearance in each one stood out as likeable.

The Occult Files of Albert Taylor was published by Impact Books in 2010 and printed in the USA. A handful of the stories can also be found in various other publication on and off the web including Sonar4 Magazine, Switchblade Magazine and Night to Dawn, to name just a couple.

The Occult Files of Albert Taylor can be found at Amazon.com Amazon.co.uk, derekmuk@jps.net and all other good retailers.